LOVE AND DEATH
AMONG THE CHEETAHS

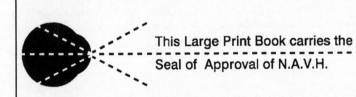

This Large Print Book carries the
Seal of Approval of N.A.V.H.

LOVE AND DEATH AMONG THE CHEETAHS

RHYS BOWEN

THORNDIKE PRESS
A part of Gale, a Cengage Company

Farmington Hills, Mich • San Francisco • New York • Waterville, Maine
Meriden, Conn • Mason, Ohio • Chicago

Copyright © 2019 by Janet Quin-Harkin.
A Royal Spyness Mystery.
Thorndike Press, a part of Gale, a Cengage Company.

Thorndike Press® Large Print Core.
The text of this Large Print edition is unabridged.
Other aspects of the book may vary from the original edition.
Set in 16 pt. Plantin.

LIBRARY OF CONGRESS CIP DATA ON FILE.
CATALOGUING IN PUBLICATION FOR THIS BOOK
IS AVAILABLE FROM THE LIBRARY OF CONGRESS

ISBN-13: 978-1-4328-6710-2 (hardcover alk. paper)

Published in 2019 by arrangement with Berkley, an imprint of Penguin Publishing Group, a division of Penguin Random House, LLC

Printed in Mexico
1 2 3 4 5 6 7 23 22 21 20 19

*Dedicated to two mystery-loving women
who won the right to name a character
at the Malice charity auction:
the real Diddy Ruocco and Angel Trapp.
I hope they enjoy who they have become!*

ACKNOWLEDGMENTS

As always, thank you to my brilliant team: editor Michelle Vega, agents Meg Ruley and Christina Hogrebe, and my first reader and most picky editor, husband John.

AUTHOR'S NOTE

This has been a difficult subject to tackle, because so much about it is repugnant to us, with modern sensibilities. I realize that some of you might be offended at the way my characters speak of the native Kenyans. I'm afraid I am trying to be realistic. I am portraying a time when Britain essentially ruled about a third of the world. There was a feeling of superiority, of the right to rule because Britain was bringing peace, hospitals, railways and Western culture to societies they considered primitive. The white settlers definitely treated the local tribesmen as if they were lesser beings, in many ways as if they were children. They took grown men to work in their houses, calling them "boys." In Kikuyu and Maasai society the males did not do housework so this was an ultimate insult, but money, rather than cultivation and barter, was now necessary to survive in the colony. However, it's no

9

wonder that there was finally the Mau Mau uprising in the 1950s, when the Kikuyu engaged in brutal guerrilla warfare, attacked many farms and killed colonists, finally bringing an end to the colonial era in Kenya.

CHAPTER 1

July 31, 1935
On a houseboat, outside Marlow, Bucks

This is my first diary entry as Mrs. Darcy O'Mara. I can hardly believe it. We've been married three whole days now and frankly I haven't found much time for writing in my diary. We seem to have been awfully busy. . . .

"You know what I really fancy right now?" I sat up, almost banging my head on the roof of the small cabin of our houseboat.

I looked down at Darcy, who was lying beside me. Lying naked beside me, actually, but with a sheet draped discreetly over the important bits. It was a hot and muggy afternoon and we had been taking a rest from more strenuous activities (it was, after all, the fourth day of our honeymoon).

Darcy opened his eyes slowly and they

11

flashed with that naughty and sexy look I had always found so irresistible. "Really? Again? Already?"

I slapped his naked shoulder. "No, silly. Not that. What I really fancy right now is a cucumber sandwich."

"But we don't have any cucumber. Or any fresh bread."

"Precisely." I sighed. We had been lent this houseboat on a deserted stretch of the Thames outside Marlow in Buckingham-shire and had escaped here right after the wedding. Darcy's pal who had offered his boat had also stocked it with all kinds of good things — oysters, smoked salmon, runny cheeses, chocolate, peaches and lots of champagne. In short, everything anyone would want after the stress of a wedding that included the king and queen, not to mention the two little princesses as brides-maids. Amazingly the ceremony had gone off without a hitch. I had not caught my foot in my train and pitched onto my face halfway up the aisle. I had not dropped cake down my front. It had been wonderful, magical, the perfect start to a life of bliss ahead. And the houseboat had been a brilliant idea too. Nobody around for miles. No servants to intrude at awkward moments. Only a couple of cows behind a fence to spy on us. We had eaten, drunk, made love and repeated the aforementioned over and over. We had lain out on the top deck with a glass of champagne in hand and watched the stars. We had even seen shooting stars, which was remarkable so close to London. It had been absolutely perfect.

But now reality was creeping in. We had eaten all the good food. The ice had melted in the icebox. The bread was stale. The chocolate had turned into a brown puddle. And we had no cucumber. This meant a long hike along the canal path to the nearest shop. Which was not particularly inviting, given that we were experiencing a heat wave, or that my maid, Queenie, had packed only my elegant shoes and not my summer sandals. The other alternative meant admitting the first stage of our honeymoon was over and we should return to civilization where cucumber sandwiches, a long soak in a real bathtub and changes of clothes awaited and I could wash my hair. The joys of living in primitive conditions are glorious, but one does miss basic comforts after a while. Also the height of the cabin ceiling and the doorway from the galley had meant several bruises on our heads. Neither of us had wanted to admit it, but we were ready to go home.

Well, not home exactly. I wasn't ready to go back to Eynsleigh — the country house I had sort of inherited — back to life with my mother, my grandfather and Sir Hubert, much as I loved them all. I wasn't too keen to go over to Darcy's castle in Ireland, although it was certainly remote enough. I was not ready to stay with my brother and sister-in-law at Rannoch House in London. Golly — can you imagine Darcy and me trying to have interesting sexual encounters knowing that my sister-in-law, Fig, was listening? Probably trying to peek through the keyhole? It would inhibit my sexual freedom for life! The same would be true for our friend Zou Zou, the Princess Zamanska, in whose elegant London home we were always welcome. She wouldn't mind what we got up to in bed. She'd probably even offer suggestions. But none of the above seemed right at the moment. It was our honeymoon. We were supposed to be alone, getting to know each other without outside interference.

Before we married, Darcy had actually promised that he would take care of the honeymoon. "Don't worry. I have it in hand," he had said. Somewhere wonderful and exotic, he had said. I didn't like to say anything, because I knew he didn't have

14

oodles of money to fly me around the world. But at this moment I was wondering whether these four days on a boat outside London were it — my entire honeymoon. All I had to look forward to. I hadn't even had a chance to wear my new silk knickers!

Darcy was still looking up at me. "So what do you think?" he asked. "Have we had enough of seafaring life?"

I laughed. "You can hardly call a houseboat moored to the bank of the Thames 'seafaring.' But yes, I am finding it a little confining. I'd love a proper bath and not in the river and I really would love a cucumber sandwich."

"So you want to go home?"

"I suppose so. What about you?"

He sighed. "I admit, I have banged my head on that bloody doorway one time too many."

"Are you allowed to swear in my presence now that we're married?" I asked with mock primness.

"Oh absolutely. Abso-bloody-lutely." He laughed and wrestled me down to the bed again. "I have to make sure you don't start turning into your great-grandmother now that you are married."

"But she adored Prince Albert. They had the happiest marriage in creation."

"But she was also not amused by a risqué joke," he pointed out. "Although some do say she had a fling with her Scottish chappie, Mr. Brown."

"It was hardly a fling. She was seventy-something, wasn't she?" I started to laugh.

"Anyway." Darcy turned me toward him and stroked back my hair. "You're going to have to put up with me as I am, including my faults, of which occasional swearing is one. And we'll be as happy as Victoria and Albert and have at least nine children."

"Nine?"

"You like children, don't you?"

"Yes . . . but nine?"

He laughed and ruffled my hair. "We're going to have a lot of fun, Georgie. Life is going to be an adventure."

"I hope so." I nestled up against his naked chest, feeling safe and secure for the first time in my life. I hadn't really thought about it before but my mother bolted when I was two. My father spent his time in Monte Carlo and eventually killed himself. I was never allowed to see my nonroyal grandfather. I had a kind nanny and then a strict governess but nobody who clearly loved me and cherished me. And now I did. I was wife of the Honorable Darcy O'Mara, heir to Lord Kilhenny of Ireland. I would still retain my own title and be addressed as Lady Georgiana because I was the daughter of a duke. It was all very satisfactory.

I sat up again. "So, talking of adventure, do we have something planned after this? And you'd better not tell me that you've been called away on some kind of hush-hush assignment." (I should mention that my husband doesn't have a proper job but he does seem to be whisked away to strange parts of the globe doing something for the British government. He won't exactly tell me what he does.)

"There won't be any more hush-hush assignments now, Georgie," he said gently. "I told you that they offered me a desk job at the Foreign Office."

"But you don't really want it, do you?" I gave him a worried look.

"It's more fitting for a married man, isn't it? We'll start having children. It's important that their father is at home. It's important for you that I'm there."

"Let's not talk about it now," I said. "Let's not worry about the future, except perhaps where we are going to go when we leave this boat."

"We could go back to Eynsleigh," he said. "It's got lovely grounds. We could maybe persuade your godfather to put in a swim-

17

ming pool."

"I agree it is lovely, but it also has my mother and grandfather in residence as well as Sir Hubert and the servants. Mummy will surely be barging in on us and we'll have no privacy. Besides, Eynsleigh is where we'll live from now on. It will be going back to real life and I'm not ready for that yet."

"Then what are the alternatives?" he asked. "We could always pop over to Kilhenny Castle. I know my father would like that. Zou Zou might be there too."

"Precisely," I said. "And your crazy aunt and uncle . . . too much family too soon."

"I presume that also means your brother and sister-in-law."

"Certainly not Rannoch House with my darling brother and sister-in-law," I replied, more sharply than I had intended. "I mean, they were jolly nice to host our wedding reception, but I can only take Fig in very small doses."

"We haven't looked at our wedding presents yet," Darcy reminded me. "We should at least put in an appearance and arrange to have them shipped down to Eynsleigh."

"Yes, I suppose we'd better do that. Actually that will be rather fun, won't it? I'm dying to see what we have been given, aren't you?"

"I'd say Eynsleigh is quite well furnished right now," he said. "I can't think what we still need."

"It would be nice to start life with one's own china and silver, wouldn't it?"

He made a face. "I suppose women do think that way. For me, as long as I have a plate to put my food on I don't care if it's Royal Doulton or tin."

"You're awful," I said as he grinned at me.

"Less than four days married and you are calling me awful," he sighed. "I guess the honeymoon really is over."

"Oh golly, I hope not," I said. "I thought we might be going somewhere special."

"You don't consider this special?"

"It was absolutely lovely," I agreed. "Perfect, in fact, but I had hoped for a little longer time on our own. I'm not ready to face Fig and my mother and the world."

"We'll go somewhere else, I promise," he said. "But at this moment . . ."

"You don't have anything else planned, do you?" He could hear the disappointment in my voice. I was about to remind him that he had proclaimed, in front of witnesses, that he had a wonderful honeymoon surprise for me. Was this it? I wondered. I knew I should be grateful. There were plenty of people in this world who worked in factories

19

or were out of work, standing in soup lines with no hope of the sort of life we took for granted. Time to grow up, Georgie, I thought.

"I have a few things that need sorting out first," Darcy said. "You just need to be patient."

I managed a bright smile. "All right," I said. "We'll go and look at our wedding presents at Rannoch House. If we hurry we'll be in time for tea and I know Mrs. McPherson will make cucumber sand-wiches."

CHAPTER 2

July 31
Rannoch House, Belgrave Square,
   London W.1.

Back to the real world. Sigh. I wish our
delicious bubble could have lasted longer. I mustn't show myself to be disap-
pointed that Darcy hasn't managed to
wangle a long, exotic honeymoon for us.
I'm sure he tried. And I do have the rest
of my life to be with him!

"Welcome home, my lady." My brother's
elderly butler, Hamilton, beamed at me as I
stood at the front door of Rannoch House
on Belgrave Square. "I was not informed
that you were returning so soon or I'd have
had the maids air out your room."

"Hello, Hamilton." I smiled back at him.
"You weren't to know. It was an impulsive
decision on our part, due to a sudden desire

for cucumber sandwiches."

"Indeed? Then let me go and inform Mrs. McPherson immediately that sandwiches are requested and I'll have them brought out to the terrace, where Her Grace is currently awaiting her tea. Would you like me to go through and announce you?"

"I think we can find our own way, thank you. Please go and arrange the sandwiches."

Hamilton nodded to Darcy, who had just joined me after paying the taxicab driver. "Welcome, Mr. O'Mara," he said. "If you leave the bags there, I'll have them taken up for you in a jiffy."

"Thank you, Hamilton," Darcy said. "Good to see you looking so fit."

"It's the fine weather, sir. It works wonders for my rheumatics after Castle Rannoch, which does tend to be just a tad damp and cold." He gave a little nod of a bow before retreating belowstairs. Darcy slipped an arm around my shoulder as we went through the front hallway. "If only we manage to find a butler like Hamilton," he muttered.

"They are in short supply, I'm sure," I whispered back. "They don't make them like that anymore."

We opened the door to the ballroom at the back of the house. The room itself was not often used but it had French doors that opened onto a lovely terrace beyond. That was rarely used too, given the normal English summer weather. But we had held our wedding reception out there and jolly nice it had been too. The French doors were now open to the terrace and someone was sitting in a deck chair. Darcy gave me a little push. "You should probably be the one to let your sister-in-law know we are here."

"Coward," I hissed.

He grinned. "Just following protocol. It wouldn't be right for a mere son of a baron to precede the daughter of a duke onto a terrace."

I stuck my tongue out at him and stepped from the darkness of the ballroom into the blinding sunlight. Fig was reclining in a deck chair, wearing shorts and a halter top of a rather lurid shade of pink, which matched the color of her skin and made her look like a large cooked prawn.

"Hello, Fig," I called cheerily.

She sat up, startled, blinking at me. "Good God, Georgiana. We weren't expecting you so soon. Ah well, don't say I didn't warn you."

"What on earth do you mean?"

"Well, the marriage is obviously over. You've discovered the truth about your husband and his depraved habits. I knew you would. One has heard rumors, you know."

I was about to say that my husband was a perfect gentleman and I couldn't be happier, when Darcy himself stepped out onto the terrace. "You've found out the truth, have you, Fig?" he said. "She's left me for an Italian trapeze artist. My life is shattered."

Fig gave us both her "we are not amused" frown. "So what are you doing back so soon?"

"My wife had a sudden craving for cucumber sandwiches," Darcy said, pulling up a lawn chair for me, then one for himself.

"Don't tell me you are pregnant already, Georgiana?" Fig's eyebrows rose.

"Hardly, after four days," I replied. "We were on a houseboat, Fig. We had all kinds of yummy foods and champagne and for three days it was heaven. Then the food spoiled or ran out, the ice melted, we bumped our heads on the ceiling too many times and there was no cucumber to be had for miles. So we beat a reluctant retreat."

"And where shall you be heading now? Back to that place you seem to have inherited in the country?"

"We're not quite sure yet." I glanced at Darcy, waiting for him to say something.

"We thought we should come here first and arrange to have our wedding presents shipped down to Eynsleigh."

"That's certainly a good idea," Fig said. "They have completely taken over our drawing room. Mummy called the other day and I had to entertain her in the morning room . . . in the middle of the afternoon!"

"I'm so sorry," I said. "Where's Binky?"

"He took Podge sailing."

"Sailing? I didn't know Binky could sail!"

"It was a model boat on the Round Pond in Kensington Gardens," she said. "Such a stupid occupation, if you ask me." She paused, listening. "Ah, it sounds as if they are back now."

The sound of running feet could be heard. My nephew, Podge, came rushing out through the French doors. "Mummy, we had a race with another boat and we won," he said.

"They are only toy boats, Podge," Fig said. "And completely at the mercy of the wind, or lack thereof, therefore don't think any particular skill is needed to sail one."

My brother, Binky, followed his son out onto the terrace. He was wearing an open-necked white shirt and his face was quite red. "We jolly well did use skill to win, didn't we, Podge," he said. "You're such an

25

awful killjoy, Fig."

"I am not. I am merely a realist. I want the child to take pride in the important matters of life, not playing with toy boats."

"More than a realist, I'm afraid. You're an utter dismal Desmond, old thing," he said. "If you can find the one fly in the ointment, you find it."

Fig frowned and went to say something but Podge had already spotted Darcy and me. "Auntie Georgie!" He flung himself into my arms.

"There you are, Binky. One afternoon alone with you and the child is quite out of control," Fig admonished.

"He's pleased to see Georgie and Darcy, as I am," Binky said. "Lovely to see you, old beans. Had a good honeymoon so far?"

"Brilliant, thank you. It's just that the houseboat wasn't near any shops and we ran out of things to eat."

"So you're going to stay here for a while, I hope? Jolly good." He sank into another deck chair and hauled Podge onto his knee.

"I believe they said they'd be taking their wedding presents down to the country house as soon as possible," Fig said quickly.

"That's right," I agreed, having no more desire to spend time at Rannoch House than my sister-in-law had the wish to have me around. "We'll take a look at the presents and arrange to have them packed up and shipped."

"Quite a good haul you've got in there," Binky said. "I had a little peek. Better than we got, eh, Fig?"

"Oh, I don't know. My aunt Esmerelda did give us that lovely aspidistra. Such a pity it died so soon."

Binky suppressed a grin. "We haven't given you a present yet, I'm afraid."

"A present is absolutely not necessary," I said. "Seeing that you gave us such a lovely wedding reception, and you walked me down the aisle so beautifully, Binky."

Binky went a little pinker than his already sunburned face. "Proud and happy to do it, old thing. I have to tell you I was a bundle of nerves, wasn't I, Fig? Terrified I'd put my foot through your train or stumble into one of Their Majesties or trip up the steps."

"But you didn't. And neither did I." I smiled at him. "We must both have inherited a tendency for clumsiness from some past relative. It must have been a Scottish one. I'm sure Victoria and Albert never stumbled."

"She wasn't allowed to," Fig interjected. "She always had someone holding her hand when she came down the stairs."

"Anyway, coming back to wedding presents," Binky said. "We wanted to give you something apt, but we couldn't quite agree on what to give you."

"Seeing that you had inherited a very well-appointed stately home," Fig said bitterly.

"Fig was all for giving you one of the stags' heads from Castle Rannoch," he said. "A lovely gesture, I know, but I didn't think it would look quite right in Sussex."

I just nodded.

"I did think of naming our new calves after you," Binky went on. "We are trying to up the quality of the herd of Highland cattle and bought a new bull. And we've got the first splendid calves. I thought we'd call them Georgie and Darcy."

"And then slaughter them," Darcy commented dryly.

Binky gave an embarrassed chuckle. "Crikey. I hadn't thought of that. Bit insensitive of me, what?"

"It was a lovely thought, Binky," I said.

Fig was still frowning. "What is that child still doing down here? Ring for Nanny."

"It's almost teatime, Fig. I promised him he could join us for tea."

"Mrs. McPherson's making cucumber sandwiches for me," I said, smiling across at my nephew. "You like those, don't you,

Podge?"

"I like cakes better," he replied.

As if on cue footsteps could be heard and a footman carried out the first tea tray, with one of the maids following with the sandwiches and cakes. Tea was poured and for a while conversation lapsed as we worked our way through cucumber sandwiches, tiny meringues, Mrs. McPherson's specialty shortbreads and slices of plum cake. As soon as Fig had finished eating she put down her plate. "Tea's over, Podge. Time to go back to the nursery. Will you take him, Rose?" (This to the maid who had remained to pour tea.)

"Oh, come on, Fig," Binky said. "Give the little chap a chance to enjoy his aunt and uncle, for heaven's sake. I had to spend my life alone in a blasted nursery. I don't see why he should."

"You are becoming very argumentative lately, Binky. I don't know what has got into you," Fig said. "Very well, Podge. You can stay a little longer if you are on your best behavior."

"Where is Adelaide?" I asked. "Is she not brought down at teatime these days?"

Adelaide was Podge's younger sister, now a rather naughty two-year-old.

"We don't think the sun is very good for

Addy, with her fair skin," Fig replied.

Binky shot me a quick glance. I tried not to smile.

"So are you staying in London for a while?" I asked, changing the subject tactfully. "I thought you usually liked to be in Scotland at this time of year. You never miss the Highland Games at Braemar, do you?"

"We were going to go home, but as it happened we have to attend a royal garden party," Fig said, relishing every word. "The king and queen had such a lovely time at your wedding reception here that they insisted we attend a garden party at Buckingham Palace before they go up to Balmoral. They also invited us to stay at Balmoral, but Binky pointed out that we are practically neighbors anyway."

"Between you and me, I can't stand the place," Binky said. "All that tartan. Enough to drive a fellow mad."

"Be that as it may," Fig went on, annoyed at his interruption, "I believe Their Majesties have finally realized that we are close relatives and should be included in family gatherings, which has not happened until now." She was looking incredibly smug. Her face said "We've been invited and you haven't." "But after all, Binky is in the line of succession, isn't he? Something you have renounced and thus you will probably no longer be part of their inner circle."

"He's thirty-second if I've counted right," I reminded her. "He's hardly likely to become king unless there is a repeat of the Black Death and Castle Rannoch is the only place spared because it's on such a ghastly moor."

"Stranger things can happen," Fig said. "An anarchist bomb thrown into Buckingham Palace when they are all assembled."

"Or at a garden party?" Darcy suggested, giving me a wink.

"Anyway, the British public would never accept a King Hamish, would they?" I chuckled.

"Golly no. I'd change it to something suitable like George if called upon," Binky replied. He was deadly serious. "George VI, I suppose."

"It's only a garden party, Binky. Not a coronation," I said. "Although I rather think you'd make a better king than the current heir to the throne."

"Old David is a good chap," Binky retorted.

"He would be if he were not under the thumb of a certain American woman," Darcy commented.

"He'll put her aside when the time

comes," Binky said staunchly. "He'll do the right thing. You'll see."

"I hope you are right," I replied. He had not seen Mrs. Simpson in action nearly as frequently as I had.

"So I shall require your assistance, Georgiana," Fig said.

This was something unexpected. "In what way?"

"You've been to these royal events. You know what people wear better than I do. You can help me decide on an outfit. I may even have to buy a new hat."

"I'll certainly help you choose something suitable, Fig. Is it formal or informal?"

"I've no idea. The actual invitations haven't arrived yet. The queen just expressed a desire that we should attend but didn't give us a date. Before Balmoral she said. That must be in the next two weeks."

Hamilton appeared at the French doors. "A letter for you in the afternoon post, Your Grace," he said, handing a large envelope to Binky. "And one for you too, my lady." And a similar envelope was handed to me.

Binky opened his. "There you are, old thing," he said, looking pleased as he handed it to Fig. "Exactly what we've been talking about. Garden party at Buckingham Palace on August third. Formal dress."

I had also opened mine.

Their Majesties King George V and Queen Mary invite Lady Georgiana and the Hon. Darcy O'Mara to a garden party at Buckingham Palace on August 3rd.

Underneath the queen had written, in her own hand:

If you're not still away on your honeymoon we do hope you can attend.

I waved my invitation at Fig. "Surprise! We have one too," I said.

CHAPTER 3

July 31
Rannoch House

Spending the night at Rannoch House so that we can look at our wedding presents and arrange for their shipment to Eynsleigh. I'm so glad it's only one night. Fig is positively furious that we've also been invited to the garden party.

"Your sister's face," Darcy said to me when we were safely alone in our bedroom. "If looks could kill you'd be lying in a pine box by now."

"I must say I really enjoyed that," I said.

"And I thought I married a sweet and gentle little thing," he teased.

"No, you didn't. You knew exactly what I was like," I said. "You know that I've hit a couple of murderers over the head before now."

"That I knew," he agreed. "But this malicious joy at baiting your sister-in-law?"

"She deserves every second of it, Darcy," I said. "She has made my life miserable from the moment she married Binky and moved into Castle Rannoch. She told me I was not welcome in my family's ancestral home, persuaded Binky there was no money to be spent on me and even suggested if I stayed on in Scotland I should become Podge's governess to earn my keep."

"Damned cheek," Darcy said. "Especially since you outrank her by birth."

"That's not what really irks her," I said. "It's that I've become quite pally with the queen — well, one doesn't actually become pally with a queen, but she has come to rely on me to do small tasks for her."

"To do some spying for her, you mean?"

"And to retrieve a stolen antique once." I smiled. "The queen is not above subterfuge on occasion."

"So I presume you'd like to stick around London until the garden party?"

"Oh gosh, not here," I said, louder than I intended, and glanced at the door, fearful that Fig might be listening at the keyhole. "We could take the presents down to Eynsleigh and then come up to town and spend the night before the garden party with

Zou Zou, if she's in town."

Darcy nodded. "That sounds like a good plan. And what do you want to do now — given that you've had your fill of cucumber sandwiches."

"I want to look at our presents, but first I'd love a long hot bath," I said. "How about you?"

"Sounds like a good idea. I might do the same."

"In the same bath?" I teased.

"Why not?"

"Don't be silly, Darcy. Water would slop over onto the floor and it would come through the ceiling and Fig would make a fuss."

Darcy sighed. "All right. You take the bathroom on this floor and I'll use the one above."

"Only don't lock the door." I grabbed his arm as he went to get his towel. "Binky got himself locked in that bathroom and almost missed my wedding."

"You never told me that."

"There are probably a lot of things I've never told you, or you've never told me either." I slipped my arms around his neck.

"Then we shall never run short of stories to tell each other as we get old." He pulled me close to him. "When I'm too old for

36

other things."

"You'll never be too old." I smiled up at him and he kissed me.

A little later, refreshed, with clean hair and in clean clothes, we went down to the drawing room to examine the presents.

"Golly!" I said, looking at the motley array of packages on all the surfaces. I frowned, annoyed with myself. I had sworn, when I became a married woman, that I would stop using girlish words like "golly." "I mean, good gracious. There are rather a lot of them. I didn't realize we knew that many people."

"I have plenty of relatives and friends," Darcy said. "And you have a large extended family too."

Darcy had already started to tear the paper from one of the objects. "This is extra heavy," he said. Then he paused. "Oh, how interesting. It's a stag."

"A stag?" I hadn't forgotten that Fig had wanted to give us a stag's head from Castle Rannoch, where the walls are lined with an abundance of the things. I went over to him. "What kind of stag?"

Darcy held it up. "It's silver," he said. "It's quite nice but absolutely useless."

I took it from him. It was incredibly heavy. "Oh, I've seen stags like this before," I said.

"They are displayed in the middle of dining tables, usually at hunting lodges. I think we have several at home."

"Do they have any function? You don't keep the salt inside, do you?" He turned the stag upside down.

"No." I laughed. "Their only function is to say 'Look at me, I'm so rich I can afford to put these silver animals in my hunting lodge.' "

"That won't ever apply to us, I fear, but I expect we can find somewhere to display it — even if it is a bit out of place in Sussex."

"At least it's better than the other stag we were offered," I said in a low voice. "Can you imagine wanting to give us a stag's head? It's about the worst present I could imagine."

"No, it's not." Darcy looked up from the next gift he was unwrapping. "This one takes the cake, I believe."

He held up an oil painting. It was of a house and gardens, daubed in bright primaries as if painted by a six-year-old child or a clever chimpanzee. A woman with a parasol was strolling among roses on one side — at least I think that's what it was. As oil paintings go it was absolutely hideous.

"Who is it from, do you think?" I asked and went to see if there was a card attached to the paper.

"I don't need to look. I already know," he said. "It's my great-aunt Ermintrude. She believes she is a gifted painter and sends the family paintings for special occasions."

"Oh heavens, we won't actually have to display it on a wall, will we?"

"Only if she comes to stay, which she probably won't, given that she lives in Yorkshire and no longer likes to travel."

"Phew. That's a relief. Wait a second. Don't open any more until I've written this down. We have a lot of thank-you letters to write."

"And also a lot of presents to hide in an attic until the giver comes to stay — then we'll have a desperate rummage for them and display them in the appropriate setting," Darcy said, holding up a rather awful purple vase with green vines curling up the sides of it and a giant red hibiscus on one side.

"What makes people think that a young couple would want to start out life with things like these?" I asked. "It would be so much more sensible to give us things we'd actually use like bed linens and teapots."

Darcy grinned. "I rather suspect that they are objects stashed away in their own attics, maybe former wedding presents that they never liked. We'll wait until someone else gets married and we'll pass them along to continue the everlasting cycle."

"Darcy, I'd have to hate someone an awful lot to give them that vase," I said. "Perhaps it can accidentally get broken during shipment?"

Darcy laughed. We opened more packages. Some were quite baffling. One aged relative had sent one silver spoon. One.

"Perhaps she means it to be a christening spoon in advance," Darcy suggested.

But some were actually nice, and useful. Silver fish knives and forks, pastry forks, a Royal Worcester coffee set, crystal brandy glasses, an Irish linen tablecloth big enough for the table at Eynsleigh. I was touched that the king and queen had given us a beautiful ormolu clock. *This was a gift to your great-grandmother at her wedding,* the queen had written. I stood looking at it in awe. I knew, in theory, that Queen Victoria was my great-grandmother, but having an object that had actually been given to her on her wedding day somehow meant that the connection was real.

It took us until we had to change for dinner to work our way through them all.

"I'll telephone Carter Patterson in the morning and have them come and pack them up and ship them to Eynsleigh," Darcy said. "We'll have to see what Sir Hubert actually wants to use and display."

I went to say something but he added, "I know it's officially your house now but as long as he's around I think we should tread carefully, don't you?"

"I quite agree. But I think he might welcome some of these. A lot of his good silver was stolen by that awful gang and probably won't be recovered."

"Good. Then we can put the stag on the dining table." Darcy gave my shoulder a squeeze as we went up the stairs.

Next morning the moving company arrived to pack and ship right after breakfast.

"So we'll be off, then, Fig," I said. "I'd like to be back at Eynsleigh before the presents are delivered."

She looked distraught. "But you can't leave now, Georgiana. You absolutely can't."

Fig, actually wanting me to stay? This was something new. Then she added, "You promised to help me select my ensemble for the palace garden party. You are there so often. You know what is worn. I, on the other hand, hardly ever have a chance to mingle with the royals, except when they are up in Scotland and it's always Highland dress anyway."

I took pity on her. I had known that feeling so often — worrying about what to wear, knowing that I didn't possess the right sort of dress, that other women would be in Paris creations while I wore something run up by the gamekeeper's wife. Now, thanks to my mother and Zou Zou I did own some smart frocks.

"Silk or lace, I think," I said. "And probably long."

She shot me a despairing look. "Silk or lace? I own a couple of calf-length summer dresses but that's about it. It's never warm enough for summer clothes at Castle Rannoch."

"You could wear what you wore to my wedding, Fig," I said. "That looked very nice."

"Did you really think so?" She went rather pink.

"Oh absolutely," I lied. She had chosen a cerise-colored two-piece that had not actually enhanced her pasty white skin or gingery hair.

"Not a little too formal, do you think?"

"I don't think one can be too formal for Buckingham Palace," I said. "Maybe not such a big hat. It might get in the way at a garden party — poke someone in the eye."

This was extremely tactful of me. Fig's hat had bright pink feathers that stuck out in all directions and made her look as if a large bird had landed on her head and proceeded to make a nest there.

"Oh, maybe you're right," she agreed. "But I don't have much in the way of hats. Except summer straws and felt hats for church."

"We could go and see Zou Zou," I said. "She has hatboxes full of them. I'm sure she'd lend you one."

"I couldn't borrow a hat from a foreigner," she said, scathingly.

"She is a princess," I reminded her.

"A Polish princess. I gather the place is full of them."

"Then you'll just have to make do with what you have," I said. "How about taking one of your plain straw hats and attaching some of these feathers on one side."

"That might work." She looked quite hopeful. "Would you help me?"

"All right," I agreed. So we spent the rest of the morning playing with hats and feathers and silk rosebuds and the end result was actually quite satisfying.

"Gosh, thanks awfully, Georgie," she said as she put on the hat and examined herself in the mirror. "You are a brick. And so talented. I could not have done this without you."

I didn't know what to say. These were probably the first kind words she had ever uttered.

CHAPTER 4

Saturday, August 3
Buckingham Palace

Off to Buck House, as Darcy calls it. I still feel a tad in limbo about what happens next. Will it really be back to normal life at Eynsleigh, and Darcy accepting that desk job at the Foreign Office or wherever it is, going up to work on the eight forty-five? Still, I should be jolly happy and jolly grateful. I am married to the most wonderful man in the world. What more could a girl want?

The big day dawned fine and sunny. We had enjoyed such a long spell of fine weather that I was quite nervous it would finally break and the garden party would be conducted under umbrellas. But it was already warm by nine o'clock when Darcy and I joined Zou Zou for breakfast at her lovely home on Eaton Square.

"What time is this bean feast to start?" Zou Zou asked, helping herself liberally to scrambled eggs and smoked haddock.

"Two o'clock," I said.

"It will be absolutely roasting by then if you're not in the shade," she said. "I hope you're wearing something cool."

"I was going to wear my new powder blue silk," I said.

"Oh, darling, don't do that," she said. "It has sleeves. You'll sweat under the arms. Yes, I know a lady never sweats, but you will. And it will show. Something sleeveless and light, I suggest."

"The only sleeveless dresses I have are cocktail," I said.

She wagged a finger at me. "I know. You should wear that delightful new Chanel number I brought back from Paris the other day."

"Zou Zou, I can't wear your new dress," I said.

"Why not? I think it will fit you."

"I meant because it's your new Chanel. It wouldn't seem right."

"Oh, fiddle-faddle. You know it's my mission in life to make people happy," she said. "Speaking of which, I'm off to Ireland on Monday. I promised your father-in-law. Big race coming up, you know."

I knew very well she wasn't going to Ireland to see her horses, but to be with Darcy's father, but I just nodded. We had hoped that something would come of this romance but they still seemed to be skirting around each other cautiously. And frankly I couldn't see Zou Zou ever settling down in a remote Irish castle.

So I allowed Zou Zou to kit me out for the garden party. Not only her beige silk dress with the navy trim but her jaunty little navy hat and gloves that gave it a nautical air. I looked *très, très chic,* as Darcy put it. He, poor fellow, was going to suffer in the heat as gentlemen never took off their morning suits and hats.

"I'm going to find a big tree and stay under it all afternoon," he muttered to me as our taxi drove toward the palace.

"You can't. You have to be sociable and chat."

He made a face. "Between ourselves, I'm dreading this," he said.

I looked at him with surprise. I had never known Darcy to be afraid of anything.

"Are you apprehensive about meeting royals en masse?" I asked.

"Absolutely," he said. "You forget. I don't mingle the way you do."

"But you're now related by marriage," I said. "And most of them are awfully nice. You know the Prince of Wales, don't you?"

"Yes, but I gather he's not here."

"No?"

"Sent abroad on a mission to visit the Commonwealth, to keep him away from a certain lady." Darcy muttered this, in case the taxicab driver was listening.

We drew up at the side entrance that led straight to the gardens and joined a line of other suitably dressed visitors waiting to enter. Binky and Fig were in line ahead of us and Binky turned back and waved. One by one our invitations were scrutinized and we were allowed onto the grounds. A band was playing. Small tables had been set out on the lawns. Binky and Fig came up to join us.

"Spiffing, absolutely spiffing, wouldn't you say?" Binky looked as delighted as a small child.

"It's jolly nice," I agreed.

Champagne and lemonade were handed round. Then came the trays of canapés. I took a vol-au-vent and was about to pop it into my mouth when I realized it was too large to eat in one bite. I bit into it and puff pastry flakes promptly flew all over my navy front trim. What's more there was a lot of dry pastry and very little filling.

"I don't think much of these, do you?" Fig commented.

"There's too much pastry and not enough . . ." I began, when a dry pastry crumb went down the wrong way. I realized, to my embarrassment, that at any minute I was going to cough. I put my hand up to my mouth, half choking as more pastry flakes came flying out.

At this moment there was a roll of drums, "God Save the King" was played, the doors leading to the terrace at the top of the steps opened and Their Majesties came out, followed by their children and spouses. I tried to stop coughing, swallow the remains of the vol-au-vent, brush off the crumbs and look respectable as we were lined up to be presented. If only the trim hadn't been navy blue. . . .

"Are you all right?" Darcy whispered.

"Went down the wrong way," I tried to whisper back, which only made me start coughing again. I was brushing furiously, while holding my breath, as the royal couple came closer. Queen Mary, as usual, looked calm and elegant in gray silk. The king, I thought, looked tired and frail. He had never really recovered from that bout of pneumonia.

I had been feeling rather proud of myself when we arrived at the palace. I was no longer the shy awkward girl. I was a sophisticated married woman, here with my husband. And I looked jolly nice, even if it was Zou Zou's frock I was wearing. But now I had lingering pastry flakes down my front and I was terrified that if I opened my mouth to speak to the king and queen more pastry flakes might come flying out.

The royal couple had drawn level with us and stopped as they recognized me.

"Ah, young Georgie. Back from your honeymoon so soon?" the king asked as I curtsied to him. "I wasn't expecting to see you here."

"We're back from the first part of it, sir," Darcy said. I shot him an inquiring look.

"Oh, so you're off somewhere else now?"

"I've told them they should go up to Balmoral ahead of us," the queen chimed in. "They can have the estate to themselves. It is the perfect spot for a honeymoon. All alone with that glorious scenery and trout fishing . . . Should I have my secretary telephone and let them know that you will be coming?"

"It's very kind of you, ma'am," Darcy said, which was good as my brain had gone numb with panic. "But I'm afraid our

50

honeymoon trip is already planned."

"Really? And where shall you be going?"

"Kenya, ma'am."

I gave a little gasp, which was the wrong thing to do. I put my hand up to my mouth again as another cough threatened. I didn't dare breathe. I just stood there, holding my breath.

"Kenya? You're going to Africa for your honeymoon?" The queen looked surprised.

"That's right," Darcy said, giving me rather a smug grin.

I shot him a quick glance, still speechless, still holding my breath.

"My goodness. How ambitious," the queen said.

"You'll be going on safari, I expect," the king chimed in, giving a nod of approval. "Going to try and bag an elephant or a lion?"

"I'm not sure of our plans yet, sir," Darcy went on. "Only that we'll be leaving in a day or so."

"How terribly exciting. Shall you be traveling by ship?" the queen asked, turning to me.

I took a cautious breath. "I've no idea, ma'am. Darcy has kept me in the dark about our plans."

"I wanted it to be a surprise for her,"

51

Darcy said. "So I said nothing until everything was in place. We are going by aeroplane. It only takes five days instead of a long steamship voyage."

"We shall certainly miss you at Balmoral this year," the queen said, "but I'm sure it will be a great adventure."

Equerries stepped in to chivvy them along the waiting line. As soon as they had passed I turned to Darcy. "Did you just make that up or is it true?"

"Now, why would I make it up?" he asked. "Of course it's true. I didn't say anything because I wasn't sure of all the details and whether we could secure a passage by air. But now it's all set. I managed to snag the last two seats on the next flight out and we leave on Tuesday."

I had sworn never to say "golly" again now that I was a married woman but it just slipped out. "Golly," I said.

The band struck up a lively tune, the crowd broke apart as the presentation had finished and more drinks and eats were handed around. I avoided any further food embarrassments and sipped a lemonade as we chatted with other guests. The Duke and Duchess of Kent came over to us. I hadn't noticed before that Princess Marina was expecting a child. That was jolly good news.

I offered congratulations.

"Maybe you'll have your own good news before too long," Prince George said, giving me a knowing wink. "I don't imagine that husband of yours wastes any time."

They had just moved on to converse with other guests when one of the footmen sidled up to me. "Her Majesty would like a word, my lady," he said. He addressed Darcy then. "If you could spare your wife for a few moments, sir?"

I was led away to where the queen was sitting in the shade of an enormous beech tree.

"Ah, Georgiana, my dear," she said. "Do sit. Do you have a cool drink? It's rather warm, isn't it?"

I noticed that in spite of her long sleeves, she didn't appear to be sweating at all. I don't know how the royals do it. They never seem to exhibit any of the bodily functions of us mere mortals. I think they can go all day without visiting a loo!

A footman handed me another lemonade. I sat, beside her, praying that this wasn't to persuade me to go to Balmoral instead of Kenya. She did like to get her own way.

"So you're off to Kenya," she said. "Such a long way for a honeymoon. What made your husband decide on that country?"

"I have no idea, ma'am. Darcy had promised me somewhere special," I said. "But this came as a complete surprise."

"I'm sure you'll have a wonderful time," she said. She hesitated, toying with her glass. "Did you know that my son will be arriving in Kenya any day now?"

"The Prince of Wales?" I said, careful not to call him David in public.

"Indeed. The king dispatched him on a long Commonwealth tour, hoping, of course, that a certain lady might find someone else during his absence, or, failing that, might blot her copybook in a way that even my son found unforgivable." She leaned closer to me. "One does understand that she has not exactly been faithful to my son during their relationship. A secondhand car dealer?" She raised her eyebrows. "The German ambassador? So many rumors but I'm assured that most are true. The question is how much my son is prepared to forgive."

"You are giving her enough rope to hang herself," I said and she chuckled.

"Precisely. On the other hand . . . the latest cable from David says that he plans to stay on in Kenya after his official engagements are concluded and spend a few days with a certain Lord Delamere." Again she leaned closer to me. "One wonders why. He

54

has never shown that much interest in safaris before; in fact he once made it known that he thought it was poor sportsmanship to kill a magnificent animal just for a trophy. So I'd like to know just what he plans to get up to there."

She patted my hand. "Which is why it's so fortuitous that you will be there at the same time. You will be my eyes and ears on the spot. I know I can rely on you, Georgiana."

"Of course, ma'am," I said. There was nothing else one could say.

CHAPTER 5

Sunday, August 4
Eynsleigh, Sussex

I swore I wouldn't say "golly" anymore but I just can't find another word. Oh golly. Too many surprises for one day! I had no idea Darcy was planning such an amazingly exotic honeymoon. This would be so wonderful but it seems my honeymoon is turning into another of Her Majesty's spy missions. I don't know how I'm supposed to keep an eye on my cousin David. Beg to go along if he goes out on safari?

Why are things always so complicated, and what made Darcy come up with Kenya in the first place?

The moment we were alone in the taxicab my shock and frustration came bursting out.

"You might have given me an inkling in advance that we were going to Kenya," I said. "I felt like a complete fool, having to tell Her Majesty that I had no idea you were planning something like this."

"I wasn't sure myself whether it would work or not until yesterday," Darcy said. "I didn't want to get your hopes up and then have to tell you we couldn't go after all." He gave me a nervous glance. "You do like the idea, don't you? I wanted it to be a once-in-a-lifetime trip."

"I'm sure I'll adore the idea once I get used to it," I said. "I confess I know very little about Kenya, except that it's in Africa and full of wild animals. What made you think of it? Have you always wanted to go on a safari?"

"An old pal of mine, Freddie Blanchford, wrote to me recently saying he was now living out there. He said what a glorious life it was and if we ever wanted to come and stay we'd be most welcome. . . . It seemed quite fortuitous, so I thought, why not. And I started looking into ways to get there. We'd have had to wait a while for a steamship and then a voyage of several weeks, so I tried to see if we could take an aeroplane. And guess what? There is now an air service all the way to Cape Town, with a stop in

Kenya."

"Gol— Amazing," I said.

"And we leave on Tuesday."

"You are talking about next Tuesday? That doesn't give us much time to choose what to wear and to pack, does it? Will we be sleeping in tents? Will it be terribly primitive?"

"Rather the opposite, I understand," he said. "We'll be staying in what they call the White Highlands, where the British aristocrats live pretty much as they lived at home."

"So no wild animals and things?"

"Oh yes, I think there are plenty of wild animals. And native peoples. The Maasai and Kikuyu. The servants will all be natives, which will make it jolly interesting."

"English country houses, native servants, wild animals. I have no idea what I should wear."

"Ask Zou Zou. She'll know what you should take."

I was still digesting this as the taxicab pulled up outside Zou Zou's house and an awful thought struck me. "They won't be expecting me to bring my maid, will they?" I was trying to picture Queenie in Kenya. She had been enough of a disaster in the British Isles. I could foresee far too many opportunities for someone as accident-prone and clueless as Queenie to wreak havoc in Africa. Queenie, being charged by a rhinoceros, flashed into my mind. Actually, if Queenie and the rhinoceros collided, I wasn't quite sure who would win. She was a formidable young woman in many ways . . . just useless as a maid.

"I expect they can lend you a maid," he said, "and now you have a husband to help you undress at night."

"That's true." I gave him a wicked little smile as we went up the steps to the front door.

"Kenya?" Zou Zou exclaimed. "My dears, you astonish me. How delightful. Young love among the lions . . . And the cheetahs," she added with a knowing wink. "Don't forget to take stout trousers."

"Trousers? Me?"

"Of course, my dear. The women live in trousers out there. And sensible walking shoes."

"But Darcy said to bring evening and cocktail dresses."

"Those too, if you're planning to be among the smart set in the Happy Valley."

"We are," Darcy said. "Staying with someone called Freddie Blanchford, do you know him?"

She shook her head. "I only know Lord Delamere, and who is the other chappie who has recently become a peer?" She paused, thinking. "Ross Hartley. That's right. Remember him? He's recently become Lord Cheriton. His cousin died. He was a live wire when he still lived in England. No woman was safe. I believe they used to call him Octopus because he seemed to have so many hands." And she gave a delighted laugh.

"Freddie Blanchford is the only one I know," Darcy said.

"Nonsense. You know Idina, don't you? Everyone in the universe knows Idina. Not sure what her married name is at the present. One loses count. . . . The Bolter, darlings. The infamous Bolter. Now I understand she's the doyenne of smart society over there."

"What is her last name?" I asked as "Idina" did not ring a bell with me.

"Who knows at this moment? It was Lady Idina Sackville. She must have worked her way through four or five husbands by now. And God knows how many lovers. But I understand she gives wonderful parties. You'll have such a fun time. You must tell me all about it. . . ." She paused again. "I'd offer to take you in my little plane but it's only a two-seater and one does need luggage. I might fly down to join you. How many days does it take?"

"At least five," Darcy said. "But it's a long and dangerous flight, Zou Zou. I think you had better stay put."

"You forget. I took part in the round-the-world race," Zou Zou said. "I had to crash-land in the Arabian Desert and nobody came for three days. In the end I fixed the struts on my plane by tying them up with my silk stockings and managed to fly on. A trip down to Kenya would be a piece of cake."

"Zou Zou, you are amazing," I said.

She smiled modestly. "Nonsense, darlings. I just do what I can to survive. I always have."

We arrived back at Eynsleigh to find Sir Hubert was still in residence, as were my mother and grandfather. I should explain for those of you who don't know that Eynsleigh was Sir Hubert's ancestral home. He had given it to me as a wedding gift, as I was his only heir and he was a mountaineer and explorer, rarely in England. He had said that it made no sense to leave the house empty, so he planned to keep a suite of rooms in one wing and wanted me to start married life as mistress of Eynsleigh. It was a miracle, also a perfect solution. You might wonder why I was his heir — he had once been married to my mother, had adored me and wanted to adopt me. The royal family said no. But he also knew that I might be left penniless by my own family, given my father's gambling habits, which proved to be the case.

And now he and my mother were in the same house again. I sensed that they were still fond of each other. She had just been dumped by her rich German industrialist, so who knew what the future might hold? My mother was not usually long without a man in tow. This made me think of the woman, Idina, whom Zou Zou had referred to as the Bolter. I mentioned her to Mummy after I'd given them the news that we were off to Kenya. Mummy looked absolutely furious.

"Don't speak of that woman to me," she said. "The Bolter indeed. I bolted before she did. I ran away from your father before she left her husband for a younger man. And yet she has gone down in history as the famous Bolter. I suppose because she was the daughter of an earl and I was only a humble ex-actress, daughter of a nobody."

"Oh, I think everyone is perfectly aware of

you and your bolts," Darcy said.

"How very kind of you to say that, dear boy." Mummy reached out to pat his hand, giving him her dazzling smile.

"I don't think Granddad likes being referred to as a nobody," I said.

Granddad gave me a wink. "That's all right, ducks. She's called me worse over the years. So you're off to Africa, are you?"

"We are," Darcy said.

"And how long do you plan to stay?"

"I'm not sure yet. At least a couple of weeks." Darcy gave me a quick glance.

"I was thinking about going back to my own little house myself," Granddad said, "but if you're going to be away I should probably stay on here to keep your mum company."

"That's kind of you, Daddy," my mother said. "Especially as one never knows when Hubert will be off again and poor little *moi* would be left all alone in the world with no one to protect me." She glanced across at Sir Hubert, who had just come into the room.

I stifled a grin but Darcy actually chuckled. "As if you ever needed anyone to protect you, Claire. You're as tough as old boots."

"What a horrid thing to say." Mummy

frowned. "If you wanted to describe me as strong you might use a different simile. As strong as a diamond would be fine. I wouldn't mind that at all."

"Anyway, Claire, you don't have to worry about my abandoning you at the moment," Sir Hubert said, perching on the arm of the sofa beside her. "I have promised to write a book on my travels in South America and I have to finish that before I can take off again."

Did he have to write a book, I wondered, or did he actually want to stay with Mummy? Frankly I would much rather that she went back to someone like him, than to Max von Strohheim. Max was clearly in cahoots with the Nazis and I got the impression that his factories were now making guns rather than motorcars and household appliances. Germany was not the sort of place I'd want to be, with those mass rallies and belligerent talk.

"Have you heard from Max?" I asked her when we women had retired after dinner that night, leaving the men to their brandy and cigars.

"Not a word, the rat," she said. "He's staying at the family home with his mother, one gathers. She never approved of me, you know. Horribly strict Lutheran. Divorce and adultery send one straight to hell. And since his father died Max is completely under her thumb."

"Then think of it as a lucky escape," I said. "If she'd been your mother-in-law she would have spent her life trying to make your life miserable."

"You're right." She gave a dramatic sigh worthy of a great actress. "I should be grateful that my kind daughter has taken me in and given me a place to stay. And Hubert has made me feel most welcome too. Such pals in my hour of need." She took my hands in hers. "So you don't need to worry about me when you go off and have a wonderful time in Kenya. Only be a little careful, won't you, darling? I gather they are frightfully naughty over there."

CHAPTER 6

Tuesday, August 6
On the way to Africa

In a few minutes we'll be leaving for Croydon Aerodrome. Ever since Darcy gave me the news that we were going to Kenya I've been in a state of shock. But now that it's about to happen I'm nervous but excited. What an incredible adventure.

I had finally finished my packing, most of which I had done myself, knowing Queenie's habit for leaving out one shoe at crucial moments.

"Are you taking your new silk knickers, miss?" Queenie asked, seeing them lying on the bed. "I wouldn't think they'd be much use if you're about to be charged by a rhinoceros."

"I don't think that cotton knickers would

be much use either, Queenie," I said, laughing. "I'll still be on my honeymoon and I want all my lovely trousseau to be with me."

"Then why are you taking these old brogue shoes?" She held them up, then promptly put them down on top of my white silk petticoat.

I retrieved them hastily. "Because the princess said that stout shoes and trousers were a necessity. And I use these for tramping through the heather at home in Scotland." I hadn't any stout trousers that were presentable enough to be worn in public but I had managed to find a pair at Swan & Edgar that I hoped would be suitable. They weren't exactly stout enough to keep out thorns or charging rhinos, but they would have to do. Other than that it was cotton frocks for sunny afternoons, my new evening pajamas and ensembles I hoped would be suitable for cocktails.

"Are you sure you don't want me to come along, miss?" Queenie asked. She still persisted in calling me this, even though I had never been a miss and was now a married woman. "I wouldn't mind facing the dangers of the bush if you needed someone to take care of you. And I don't want the other ladies to look down on you because you don't have no maid."

She never ceased to surprise me. She was undoubtedly the world's worst maid, but also one of the bravest, and having come from the East End of London, she was amazingly open to adventure.

"That's jolly sporting of you, Queenie. But I'm sure our hosts will be able to lend me a maid," I said. "And Mr. O'Mara has only managed to secure two seats on the aeroplane."

She nodded. "Then it's probably a good thing I ain't going. My stomach gets awful queasy on the swing boats at the fair. I hear them aeroplanes don't half bump around a lot."

With that she went back to wrapping my shoes. Oh crikey. I wish she hadn't mentioned that. I had flown in an aeroplane a couple of times but only short flights. And now all the way to Africa? What if I too became horribly sick?

Good-byes were said. Mrs. Holbrook, the housekeeper, forgot protocol and gave me a hug. "May you just return safely to us, my lady," she said. The look on her face made me realize that we really were undertaking a journey that was not without danger. I gave her a brave smile.

"We'll be home before you know it, Mrs.

Holbrook," I replied, with more confidence than I felt.

Sir Hubert insisted on driving us to Croydon Aerodrome, which luckily was not far away. He chatted in a relaxed manner as we drove. "Fine place, Kenya," he said. "Of course, the mountains aren't much of a challenge. I went up Mount Kenya once. Almost an afternoon stroll, or would have been if there hadn't been any damned elephants. Got charged a couple of times. But you'll have a great time. Give my regards to Delamere, won't you? Splendid chap. Salt of the earth."

I was now so nervous that I could hardly speak. Darcy chatted happily, but then, he had taken long flights before. We reached the aerodrome. Porters came for our luggage. We said farewell to Sir Hubert. For the first time I saw those aeroplanes lined up on the tarmac. They looked rather small and frail from this vantage point — not much bigger than Zou Zou's little biplane.

"Gol— Good heavens," I said. "Are we going to fly all the way to Africa in one of those?"

"Oh no," Darcy said. "From here we fly to Basel in Switzerland. Then we take a train overnight through Italy to Brindisi. From Brindisi it's a flying boat to Alexandria.

From there it's a Handley Page Hannibal to Cairo, Khartoum, Juba, and finally Kisumu."

"Go-sh," I said. "But why the train? Don't planes fly to Italy?"

"It's over the Alps," he said. "Yes, they fly, but the schedule is always precarious because of the weather and frankly the flight is horribly bumpy. I thought you'd rather have a smooth train ride and a good night's sleep on the train."

"Oh yes," I said. "That's a lovely idea."

"It's what most people do, I gather," he said. "At least those who have experienced flying over the Alps on a bad day." He smiled at me. Such a wonderful smile that reminded me why we were going to Africa in the first place. It was supposed to be a honeymoon I'd never forget.

We were summoned for our flight and led across the tarmac and up the steps to the aeroplane. A young steward in a white coat welcomed us on board. The propellers were spun, the engines revved; we sped down the runway and were miraculously airborne. Fields and farms were below us and then Beachy Head and the English Channel. It was so magical I forgot to be nervous. Darcy was taking snapshots out the window with his new camera. The steward served us a nice ham and salad lunch on fine china and a good white wine to accompany it. Luckily we had just finished eating as we approached the mountains of Alsace. Then it became distinctly bumpy, as well as horribly cold in the cabin, and I was so glad when we started coming in for our landing.

"I'm relieved we are not going to fly over the Alps," I said to Darcy as a taxicab whisked us to the train station. "That was quite enough bumping around for me."

"Then let's hope the legs across Africa are smooth flying for you," Darcy said.

We had a sleeping compartment to ourselves on the train and set off in late afternoon. The view was enchanting, as we skirted lakes with snowcapped peaks as backdrops. Butter-colored cows with bells round their necks watched us from alpine pastures and the chalets all sported balconies adorned with geraniums. I was almost tempted to tell Darcy to heck with Kenya — let's just stay in Switzerland! Dinner was eaten as the train climbed through the St. Gotthard Pass to Italy. Night fell while we were eating and we returned to find our beds made up.

"This is one night when I'll leave you in peace in your own bed," Darcy said. "The train does sway around, doesn't it?"

I found it hard to sleep in my bottom bunk, being jerked from side to side and then abruptly halting in one station after another. The next morning we arrived in Rome at first light, had to change trains and reached Brindisi by midday. Another taxi sped us to the docks where the flying boat was at anchor, looking like a large, lumbering bird with double wings. Seeing it bobbing there, so ungainly, it was hard to believe it could ever take off, let alone fly, and I felt renewed twinges of apprehension. Once again passports were checked. Darcy was eyeing the other passengers with interest. "I wonder how many of this lot are going on to Kenya after Alexandria," he said. "Perhaps the steward has a manifest."

"Does it matter?" I asked.

"Just curious," he said, turning away to look at the approaching launch that was to ferry us out to the flying boat.

I studied the other passengers waiting to board. Two middle-aged men, one definitely a man of military bearing, the other so tanned that he had to be going back to his life in Africa. The tanned one had his wife beside him, a rather ferocious-looking woman. Then there were a couple of businessmen in dark suits. As I scanned the line a voice right behind me said, "I know you, don't I? Georgiana Rannoch?"

I turned around and tried not to let the dismay show on my face.

"Rowena Hartley," she said. "We were at school together."

As if I could forget. Every school has its gaggle of mean girls, the wolf pack who pick on the weaker ones and make their lives hell. Rowena was the leader of that pack at my school. A year older than me, wordly-wise and rich, she took great delight in my lack of clothes, my naïveté, my general cluelessness about the ways of the world, and the fact that my mother was not only a serial bolter but had been a common, or garden, actress. In fact if Belinda hadn't been there to defend me my school life would have been utterly miserable. Luckily Belinda feared nothing or nobody and was quite the match for Rowena. Dear Belinda, I thought now.

But now I was a sophisticated married woman. "Why of course," I said, with a gracious smile. "Rowena. How lovely to meet you again. Are you going to Egypt?"

"No, we're going on to Kenya," she said. "We're going to stay with my father, who lives there these days. This is my twin brother, Rupert." She grabbed the arm of a rather chubby and self-satisfied-looking young man, dressed in blazer and boater as if he was about to play tennis or row on the Thames. "Rupert, this is an old school chum, Georgiana Rannoch."

"Well, hello there. Delighted to meet you," he said, his eyes looking me up and down appraisingly. Obviously acting like a wolf ran in the family. "Any friend of Ro's is a friend of mine." He held my hand a little too long. The hand was pudgy too, and somewhat clammy.

"And this is my husband, Darcy O'Mara," I said hastily before he could get any ideas. "We're going out to Kenya on our honeymoon."

"Are you really? Then we'll be seeing quite a lot of each other, I'm sure. I presume you are going to the highlands?"

"We are." Darcy was introduced and shook hands. "You're Lord Cheriton's children?"

"That's right. From his first marriage, of course. To Lady Portia Preston. You've obviously heard that our father has just inherited the earldom. That's why we're going out. He wants to get to know Ru better since he's now the heir."

"Good idea," Darcy said. "So you don't actually live out in Kenya with your father?"

"Good heavens no," Rupert said. "Hardly

seen the old man since we were four. Only on his occasional visits home."

"And what do you do, Mr. O'Mara?" Rowena asked. The question seemed innocent enough but I understood the cutting edge behind it. We're all aristocrats and you're just a mister.

"Oh, a little of this and a little of that," Darcy said.

I couldn't stay silent. "Darcy is the heir to Lord Kilhenny," I said. "He sometimes helps with the racing stud."

"Oh, an Irish peer. How fascinating," Rupert said. "Do they let you into an English colony these days?"

"Fortunately I chose to retain my British citizenship," Darcy replied with great civility. "And my mother was English. One of the Chatsworth lot."

That, of course, shut them up. Anyone connected to the Duke of Devonshire clearly outranked them, as did I. Conversation ceased. I glanced at the other passengers. All smartly dressed, all apparently relaxed and ready for this next stage of the journey. One would have thought they were lining up to go to Paris, not embarking on some great adventure to the wilds of Africa. The first passengers were being helped into the launch — a dark-haired woman whose clothes clearly came from Paris. This made me take a second look at Rowena's outfit. Not this year's model. Then Daddy didn't keep them in the lap of luxury while he was in Kenya.

It was our turn to be assisted into the launch and we set off across the calm water of the harbor. It was a busy place with everything from small skiffs to sleek luxury yachts moored nearby. Jaunty little fishing boats passed us. A ferry to Greece was setting out. We reached the steps to the flying boat and more hands helped us up. We were shown to our seats and handed a glass of lemonade as the air inside the cabin was warm. The last passenger came aboard. We waited for something to happen.

"I'm afraid we're waiting for the arrival of one more passenger," the captain announced on his intercom. "We should be underway very shortly."

Then through my window I saw a speedboat leave an impressive yacht. I watched without too much interest until I saw that it was heading for the flying boat. We heard the roar of a powerful engine, then it dropped to a gentle *putt-putt* as the boat came alongside.

"Here you go, ma'am," one of the stewards said.

"Thank you so much," said a voice I recognized instantly and Mrs. Simpson came into the cabin.

CHAPTER 7

Wednesday, August 7
Brindisi, Italy. On a flying boat.

We have accomplished the first half of our journey with no mishaps. Now comes the more difficult part, I suspect. We are about to leave Europe on a flying boat, heading for Egypt. And then all the way into Africa. At this moment I'm rather wishing that Darcy had decided on a honeymoon in Eastbourne or Torquay . . . a safe and solid seaside resort. And now I have Mrs. Simpson as well as Rowena Hartley to contend with. Oh gosh, a thought just occurred to me: she's going out to Kenya to join the Prince of Wales. Just what Their Majesties wanted to avoid!

Mrs. Simpson made her way down the cabin, nodding graciously as if she was royalty. When she drew level with Darcy and me she stopped, a look of astonishment on her face.

"Well, of all the people in the world you were the last one I expected to see," she said in that low American drawl. "How are you, Georgiana, honey?"

"Very well, thank you," I said. "You remember my husband, don't you? Mr. O'Mara."

"Oh, that's right. You're married. David commented that we didn't get an invitation to the wedding." She said this loud enough for the whole cabin to hear. I felt myself flushing red.

"We only wanted a very small wedding, I'm afraid," I said. "And the reception was at my brother's house. So just a handful of family and friends. The queen insisted that she and the king were invited and that the princesses were bridesmaids."

"Well, she would, wouldn't she?" Mrs. Simpson said. "She doesn't like to miss out on anything. And she does love to show off those little girls. Shirley Temple and the little horror."

"Shirley Temple?" I was confused.

"That's what David calls the older one, Elizabeth. Such a little Goody Two-Shoes. Perfect little lady. But he rather likes the younger one. Little firecracker. So naughty. I'm sure they looked adorable at the wedding."

"They did."

"And Cookie was there watching over them, of course."

"Cookie?"

"You know. The dowdy duchess, their mother. Looks like somebody's cook. And poor old B-B-B-Bertie. What a hopeless pair. An utter embarrassment to the royal family."

I was itching to say that a twice-married woman who had affairs with secondhand car salesmen was probably more of an embarrassment, but I knew that the newspapers were sworn to silence over this affair. Such was the power of Lord Beaverbrook that the general public had no idea Mrs. Simpson existed. She must have found that really irking.

"You're going out to Kenya, I suppose," Darcy said because he could see I was riled up at this attack on my relatives.

"I am. Not my idea of a good time, let me tell you. I was really enjoying the Duke of Westminster's yacht but I got a desperate cable from poor David, who has been stuck on a ghastly colonial tour. He's planning to take a few days off in Kenya and is frightfully lonely, so would I join him? You know I can't say no to that man, so I'm on my way. However uncomfortable it's going to be."

She looked around her with distaste. Frankly the cabin was well-appointed, with big comfy chairs, and rugs over our knees, so I didn't think she had much to complain about — except being stuck with our company for the next few days. The door was closed, the engines revved up; the large bird started across the water. Then the engine noise became deafening. The whole contraption shook and we lurched forward, faster and faster. It seemed impossible that such an ungainly giant could ever be airborne, but suddenly I saw fishing boats below us. There was that ferry, now clear of the harbor and on its way to Greece.

As soon as we had leveled out the steward took orders for cocktails. A late lunch was served — smoked salmon and then some sort of fish in a cream sauce, followed by strawberries and cream, biscuits and cheese, then coffee. This occupied a good deal of time while we glided over smooth blue water and the occasional island. After lunch I think I dozed off, having not slept much on the rocking train. I awoke when Darcy nudged me and pointed out that we were starting to descend. The coast of Egypt came into view. Water from the ribbons of the Nile delta glistened in the setting sun. Lower and lower we circled and then the sea came rushing toward us. We bumped, hopped and then were skimming the surface to a halt. We had landed safely in Alexandria.

From the flying boat we were taken to a hotel for the night, one of the tall modern buildings along the seafront in Alexandria, making it look like any European city by the sea. Not a bad hotel but it was very hot and muggy and the mosquito net had a large hole in it, which resulted in buzzing in my ears and quite a few bites by morning. The other passengers didn't look as if they had enjoyed their experience any more than we did as we met for breakfast. And the runny fried eggs did little to improve our mood. From the hotel we were taken to an airfield for the short hop to Cairo. On the way we got our first real glimpse of Egypt. Camels and donkeys laden with goods or firewood, funny little pigeon houses in the fields, men and women in long robes, donkeys working waterwheels . . . It was all very exotic.

Here a new type of aeroplane waited — a biplane with giant wings. This was the famous Hannibal, the newest in the Handley Page fleet that was now going to fly all the way to Cape Town. The cabins of the other aircraft had been pleasant enough but this one was really luxurious, rather like a Pullman coach on the Golden Arrow. We sat in little upholstered booths with tables, twenty-four of us altogether. And two stewards to take care of our every need, including a glass of champagne to welcome us on board. We took off and a half hour later we landed again at Cairo. After a short stay in a makeshift lounge, which was really little more than a glorified shed, horribly hot and stuffy, we were led out again to our plane and took off. This time we had a brilliant view of the pyramids and then the Nile as we followed it southward. It was amazing: on either side of the river there was a bright strip of green cultivation and beyond that absolute desert — just yellow sand as far as the eye could see.

"Make sure you get a good shot of the pyramids, won't you," I said to Darcy, who had his camera out again.

He smiled. "We'll be able to bore everyone with our holiday snaps."

"Not everyone will have the pyramids and the Nile," I said. "Isn't it amazing?"

"Here." Darcy handed the camera to me.

"You should take pictures too."

"I'm not much good with a camera," I said. "I usually cut off the top of people's heads. I'll leave you to document our adventure." And I handed it back to him.

Rowena and Rupert, as well as Mrs. Simpson, were farther down the cabin, which was divided into sections so that we didn't actually have to see them. I was glad of this. Clearly Rowena hadn't changed her stripes and it seemed her twin was equally obnoxious. And the farther away from Mrs. Simpson the better.

Most of the time I stared out at the view, absolutely fascinated by the Nile, the boats on it, the strings of camels walking along dusty roads and, on either side of the narrow strip of green, the burnt-sienna-colored desert with no life at all. Nothing moving, no trees. No roads. Just sand . . . sand swept into graceful dunes with patterns of light and deep shadow. It was fascinating but rather disturbing. If we came down there, who would ever find us?

I kept these thoughts to myself until we were finally descending into Khartoum. The city, from what we could see from the air, looked like an extension of the desert. Red-brown mud buildings blending into the sand beyond with hardly a glimpse of green anywhere. A camel train was just heading west as we came in to land. The air hit us like an oven as we stepped into harsh evening sunlight.

"Do we go into the city for the night?" I asked our steward.

"Oh no, my lady. Imperial Airways has built a rest house nearby. Khartoum is not the sort of place you'd want to spend the night. This way we can keep you safe."

Hardly reassuring. We were driven in an old American car over bumpy sand to a new-looking bungalow. The walls were white-washed and a tin roof extended to form a veranda. All the same no attempt had been made to beautify the surroundings. No plants, no trees. The rooms were equally spartan, but clean, and we were able to have a bath before dinner. Dinner was taken at long tables in a dining room where fans moved constantly across the ceiling, stirring the warm air. We were served a hearty stew. Mrs. Simpson poked at it with her fork.

"What kind of animal was this when it was alive?"

"I will ask the cook, madam," said the white-robed bearer who stood at attention behind the table. He disappeared into the kitchen then came back. "The cook he say it is goat, madam."

"Goat?"

"Yes, madam. Very fine goat."

Mrs. Simpson's expression was wonderful.

"At least it's not camel," the woman sitting beside me said. She was, like Mrs. Simpson, dressed in the height of Paris fashion but her face indicated she might have been out in the sun a lot, hence someone who lived in the colony.

"God forbid." Mrs. Simpson raised an eyebrow. "I didn't realize we'd be leaving civilization totally."

"Only for tonight," the woman said. "You'll find the colony itself is as civilized as London. With whom shall you be staying?"

"With Lord Delamere, I gather," Mrs. Simpson said.

"Lord Delamere. You really are starting at the top." The woman raised a perfectly plucked eyebrow.

I realized with a jolt of delight that nobody knew who Mrs. Simpson was. Thanks to the press staying silent she was traveling incognito. I wondered whether she would divulge her association with the Prince of Wales. She was obviously considering the same thing, for she hesitated, then said, "So we can look forward to something other than

86

goat, do you think?"

"Oh yes. Tom Delamere keeps a herd of beef cattle. And fish from the lake. And chickens, as well as all kinds of wild game. Yes, you will certainly eat well. And you will be invited to dine with all the neighbors — of which I am one." She held out a hand. "Pansy Ragg, formerly Pansy Babbington-Vyle. I don't believe we've met before."

"Wallis Simpson. How do you do." Mrs. Simpson extended a gracious hand.

"Oh goodness. I know who you are," Pansy said. "I'm sorry. I should have recognized you. You're a friend of the Prince of Wales, aren't you? And you must be going out to stay with him. How dense of me."

Mrs. Simpson nodded regally. "The prince is taking a break from an exhausting royal tour around the Commonwealth. He thought I might like to join him for a few days."

"A long way to come for a few days," Pansy Ragg said. "But you must definitely come to dinner if Lord D can spare you. My husband is Harry Ragg. We have a big spread quite close to Lord Delamere. My husband also runs cattle but we have a dairy ranch. And we grow wheat and corn. We tried coffee but we're a little too high for it." Having established herself as queen of the table she looked around at the rest of us. "So is everyone going to Kenya?"

"We are," Rowena said. "We're going out to stay with our father. I'm sure you know him. Lord Cheriton?"

An interesting expression crossed Pansy Ragg's face. Amusement? Astonishment? "Oh yes. Everyone knows Bwana Hartley. That's what he's always called. Bwana. He was one of the original white farmers, wasn't he? I seem to remember hearing that he had a family back in England, but you've never been out before, have you?"

"No," Rupert said. "Until recently our father chose to act as if we didn't exist. And our mother married again so we've really had little contact with him. But he's inherited the title and now that I will be his heir he felt we should reestablish relations. He sent us the air ticket so we thought, why not?"

"Why not indeed? Your father has done very well for himself, as I'm sure you know," Pansy said. "His current wife has poured buckets of money into the house and the farm. A veritable palace. You'll be amazed."

"His current wife — what's she like?" Rowena asked.

"Pleasant enough. Rich. A rich American. Angel Trapp, that was her name. . . . Isn't that perfect, don't you think? Although I'm not sure who trapped whom. She has the money, after all. Drinks like a fish, but then everyone does. I don't think she's particularly happy in Africa. It may not last."

Rowena and Rupert exchanged a glance.

"And you, you gorgeous man," Pansy said, turning the full force of her charm onto Darcy. "What brings you out to Africa?"

"They are on their honeymoon," Rowena said for us. "Isn't that absolutely sweet? Who ever thought that awkward, shy Georgie would snag herself such a yummy man?"

I felt my face going bright red as Pansy Ragg turned to examine me and Mrs. Simpson had a sarcastic grin.

"And who might you be?" Pansy Ragg asked. "Your face is vaguely familiar."

"This is Lady Georgiana Rannoch — you know, the cousin of the king — and her husband, the Honorable Darcy O'Mara." Rowena chimed in again before we could answer.

"Delighted to meet you," Pansy said. "You couldn't pick a better spot to honeymoon. God's kingdom. You like to hunt, do you? Elephant? Lion? Anything you choose. It's like living in a zoo."

I had come to the conclusion that I really did not want to hunt. I had joined in enough shoots on our Scottish estate. But shooting a grouse did not seem the same as bringing down an elephant or a lion. That seemed cruel and wicked to me. But I stayed quiet as Darcy said something innocuous.

"And who are you staying with?" Pansy went on, clearly determined to be the life of the party. "Also with Lord Delamere?"

"Freddie Blanchford is the one who invited us," Darcy said.

Pansy looked horrified. "Blanchford? The government chappie? The district officer? My dears, he lives in a poky little government bungalow with one servant, down in that hellhole called Gilgil. You can't possibly stay with him. Besides, settlers don't mix with government. It simply isn't done."

"He and I are old chums," Darcy said. "I expect he will have made arrangements."

"One hopes so." Pansy raised those perfectly plucked eyebrows. "You certainly wouldn't want to stay in that ghastly little town with the natives and Indian shopkeepers. If it's not to your liking come to us. We have oodles of space and Harry would welcome a good chin-wag."

"You are very kind," Darcy said gravely.

"An awfully long way to come for a honeymoon," Pansy went on. "Unless you are planning a really long one. Or scoping out the place to see if you might want to settle out here."

"We'll have to see how long we stay and how much we like it," Darcy said.

I glanced across at him. This was something that hadn't crossed my mind — that Darcy might be thinking of going out to one of the colonies and settling out there. I wasn't at all sure I wanted to live in a place full of wild animals — and wild people, it seemed, from what my mother and Zou Zou had told me — even if it was with Darcy. This train of thought was interrupted by a voice from the far end of the table.

"So tell me." The young man at the end of the table spoke up for the first time. He was fair and boyish-looking with hair that flopped across his forehead and a perpetually worried look. He had been relegated away from Mrs. Simpson and Pansy. "It sounds as if all the white settlers are neighbors, is that right?"

"A lot of us live in the Happy Valley, as it's now known," Pansy said. "Bwana Hartley, I mean Lord Cheriton, certainly does. Lady Idina, of course. And those people at the next table: Tusker Eggerton and Chops Rutherford with his wife, Camilla. All farmers. Then Harry and I . . . Lord D lives a little farther off."

"But what about Nairobi?" the young man went on. "Are there no English settlers closer to the capital? Because I was thinking that's where I should be heading."

"Of course there are. The whole of the highlands has been settled by Europeans, but you'll find that around Nairobi it's more small farmers who came out on the farmer-settlement scheme. Not exactly our type of people. And most of them don't approve of us. Who are you planning to stay with?"

"Golly, I've no idea yet," the young man said. I was delighted that he had been the one to say "golly"!

"Are you coming out to work then?" Pansy sounded as if this was something sinful.

"I jolly well hope so," the young man went on. "I'm a third son, you see. No chance of inheriting anything. The pater gave me some money and a plane ticket and told me to come out to Africa and make something of myself. I could hardly say no, especially as he drove me to the aerodrome and put me on the plane."

Rowena gave a snort of laughter.

"So what do you think you will do?" Pansy asked. "What are your skills?"

"Absolutely bloody useless, I'm afraid. I

failed my exams at Oxford. Can't add up properly. Hopeless at foreign languages. I'm not bad around horses. Animals seem to like me."

"Well then, you'll find yourself a job on one of the farms. We've people who breed polo ponies and racehorses. You're rather tall but incredibly thin so I don't suppose you weigh too much. You might be some use as a jockey in the point-to-point. What are you like as a rider?"

"I have a tendency to fall off over fences, I'm afraid," the man said amiably as if he didn't mind confessing all of these failures. "The pater said I was a disgrace to his hunt. Frightfully good huntsman my father is. Master of Hounds and all that."

"So I take it you aren't all that hot at polo either?" Pansy asked.

"Crikey, no. I've only played a couple of times and I hit my own pony on the rump when I swung the mallet and it bolted with me."

"What's your name, young man?" Mrs. Simpson asked, eyeing him with amusement.

"It's Jocelyn. Jocelyn Prettibone."

Rupert burst out laughing. "Jocelyn Prettyboy? Are you making this up? Is it some kind of stunt?"

Jocelyn flushed now. "It's Prettibone, not Prettyboy," he said huffily. "Norman French. The family came over with William the Conquerer in 1066." He gave Rupert a hard stare. "And I can't help my name, any more than you can help who your father is."

"What do you mean by that?" Rupert started to stand up. "My father is one of the leading men in the colony. Ask anyone."

"Yes, but he ran off and deserted your mother, didn't he? I heard people talking about it on the plane."

"I don't think my father is exactly the only person who left a spouse for greener pastures," Rupert said. "Lady Idina is the classic example. And . . ." He turned to look at Mrs. Simpson, then decided, wisely, to say nothing more on that subject. Instead he added, "Look here, if you want to get along with people in the colony, you don't question them about their past. Everyone here has a past they would rather forget."

Waiters collected our plates. Nobody had finished their stew.

"And what delight are you going to tempt us with for dessert?" Mrs. Simpson asked dryly.

"Marmarlade pudding, memsahib," the servant replied solemnly. "With custard."

Mrs. Simpson gave an audible sigh.

94

CHAPTER 8

Friday, August 9
Leaving Khartoum in the Sudan

Thank heavens. I can't wait to be off again. It was a ghastly night with lumpy beds, incredibly hot, and before it was light we were woken by the call to prayer from every minaret.

I'm not sure if I like our traveling companions. Rowena and her brother both seem to have that beastly streak that preys on others, and there is something about Pansy Ragg that I find disquieting. I hope some of the other inhabitants are easier. But as Darcy said, we don't have to stay long if we don't like it.

We took off from Khartoum at first light after a breakfast of more runny fried eggs but no bacon. When one of our party asked for it they were told, haughtily, that one did not serve parts of the pig in a Muslim country. Of course. I feel that I have a lot to learn so that I don't put my foot in anything (literally and figuratively). The steward mentioned to Darcy that this was the most difficult part of the journey, subject to dust storms and even violent thunderstorms as we approached the Rift Valley with its sudden up-currents of air. And if we had to set down in the desert, there was no civilization for hundreds of miles.

"We'll probably have to start eating each other," Darcy said, clearly enjoying the whole thing. "That Prettibone chap will last longest. No meat on him at all." He grinned to me. "I wonder what made his father choose Kenya for him. I should have thought he'd have had a better chance of surviving in Australia or New Zealand. I wonder how long he'll last. He'll probably be eaten by a lion or gored by a water buffalo on his first day out."

"That's probably why he's heading for the safety of Nairobi," I said. "At least it has a vestige of civilization. I feel rather sorry for him. I mean we both know what it's like to have no money or prospects and unsupportive parents, don't we?"

"Yes, I suppose we do," he agreed. "I

suspect Pansy Ragg will take him under her wing. She'll enjoy the challenge."

"I don't know what to make of her," I said, lowering my voice even though the noise of the engines meant that we couldn't be overheard. "She's so fashionably dressed and heading for a dairy farm. It must be frustrating to own Chanel and Worth so far from anyone who appreciates them."

"Oh, I think you'll find life among the farmers here has many elements of high society," Darcy said. "They are nearly all aristocrats, after all."

"I wonder why they left England if they have titles and money." I stared out the window at the rugged brown hills below us. Coming to a place as remote as Kenya seemed a rather rash decision to me.

"Some people relish a challenge. They don't want to be fenced in by ordinary life and you have to admit life for many aristocrats is pretty boring, unless there is hunting, shooting or fishing going on. And don't forget many families have lost their fortunes in the great crash of '29."

"You're right," I agreed. Darcy had just spoken the word "crash" when the aeroplane dropped suddenly with no warning. Like a stone. Items flew out of the racks overhead. My stomach went up to the ceiling with half our belongings. It was all over in a second and the airliner flew on as if nothing had happened. I stared out the window, but there was blue sky with no sign of clouds.

"What was that?" I asked shakily as one of the stewards rushed to pick up the items that had fallen. I noticed that he had spilled coffee down his white uniform.

"An air pocket," Darcy replied. "I told you the air becomes unstable as we approach the Great Rift Valley."

"Golly," I said, forgetting sophistication. "I hope that's not going to happen too frequently. My stomach is still somewhere near the ceiling."

Darcy smiled and took my hand. "All part of the adventure. Something to tell them when we get home."

"You like adventure, don't you?" I studied his face.

"I do. I like not knowing what's going to happen next." He stroked my cheek. "Whereas you like order and security. You take after your great-grandmother."

"I suppose I do," I agreed. I was thinking about that desk job he had promised to take when we got home. Would he ever be happy with routine and security? Would he come to resent being married to me and tied down? I turned to stare out the window again and noticed a great bank of clouds ahead of us. One minute we were in brilliant sunshine, the next we plunged into dark cloud. The plane started shuddering and bucking. I grabbed Darcy's hand.

"What this time?"

"Thunderstorm," he muttered. He didn't look quite so calm anymore.

The storm seemed to go on forever. It was time for our lunch but the stewards could not stand up to prepare or serve it. We jerked and bucked as if we were riding an unbroken horse.

"Don't worry, ladies and gentlemen," one of them announced. "We've got a good captain here. He's used to this sort of thing."

Just when I was about to tell Darcy that I had had enough and I wanted to go home right away the clouds parted and we were again in brilliant sunshine. Stewards leaped up to offer cocktails and snacks. Normally I wouldn't want to drink in the middle of the day but I willingly took Darcy's suggestion of a brandy and ginger ale. And thus fortified I managed to eat my lunch.

We came in for a landing in a harsh desert landscape at a small place called Juba, and endured a most unpleasant wait in a hut while the plane was being refueled. Then we took off on the last leg. A mountainous country was now below us. Brown rugged landscapes with only occasional trees and no sign of towns or villages. And then ahead what looked like an ocean. I frowned, trying to recall geography lessons of Africa. If we were approaching the east coast it would surely be on our left, not extending to our right. Before I could admit my ignorance Darcy leaned across me. "Lake Victoria," he said. "Largest lake in Africa. We're over Uganda now but part of Kenya also borders the lake. We'll be landing at Kisumu. They chose it because originally this route was going to be operated by flying boats." He paused, listening. "Ah, we're starting our descent. Jolly good."

There were signs of human occupation now — cultivated fields, palm trees, occasional bungalows and funny little round thatched huts cut into clearings in the thick green carpet of forest. The aeroplane circled lower and lower and then made contact with the ground, bumping to a halt. We had arrived safely. I said a silent prayer of thanks. We collected our hand luggage and waited for the steps to be rolled to the door of the plane. Mrs. Simpson positioned herself to disembark first, in a slight jostling match with Pansy Ragg. We followed, again hit immediately by a wave of hot air. Only this time it was not dry, like opening an oven. It was so humid that it felt hard to breathe. We were led to a shed where His Majesty's government officer, dressed impeccably in tropical uniform, greeted us and checked our travel documents.

"You'll all be catching the afternoon train to Nairobi, I take it," he said. "You'll find vehicles waiting to drive you to the station. Have a safe onward journey."

We came out of the airport and I realized with delight and amazement that we were actually in Kenya. We had made it! Kisumu wasn't much of a town. A few bungalows with corrugated iron roofs strung along a red dirt road, a ramshackle shop, shacks with bright creepers growing over their roofs and tall stalks of maize and banana trees growing in gardens. Not many people around in the heat of the day, except for a couple of little boys kicking a makeshift ball around and a gaggle of skinny dogs watching them. The taxi took us along the one macadamized road lined with spectacular trees, some of them with bright red flowers and others with bright purple. They almost looked too bright to be real.

"Flamboyants and jacarandas," Pansy Ragg said, as I pointed at them. "They are not native here, but we've come to love them in the colony." She had been assigned to the taxi with us although she had brought so much luggage that it had to be crammed around our feet and strapped to the roof.

"You've been away for some time, Mrs. Ragg?" I asked.

"A month," she said. "My mother is no longer in good health so I like to visit her once a year. And Harry is so understanding. He never minds what I do. He has his farm and his safaris that keep him nicely occupied." She gave a cat-with-the-cream smile as she said this.

"You've taken an awful lot of clothes for a month," I couldn't help saying, although as I said it I realized it sounded rude.

"No, darling." She patted my hand. "I'm *bringing* an awful lot of clothes. Shopping spree in Paris, you know, and a visit to Molyneux in London. One so tires of last year's fashions."

Darcy took out a handkerchief and dabbed at his face. "I had no idea it would be so hot and muggy," he said. "We were told a temperate climate."

"Ah, well, we're at lake level here, aren't we?" In spite of the heat in the taxi she looked remarkably fresh. "Once we're in the train we start climbing. If you're going to the Happy Valley we're close to eight thousand feet. Quite a different landscape altogether."

The railway station wasn't much more than a hut beside a platform. The train stood waiting for us, a great fire-breathing dragon of an engine puffing and ready to get going. It seemed rather too impressive for the four carriages behind it. We were escorted to a carriage while a stream of African porters swept up our bags and loaded it into the luggage van, chattering and laughing loudly the whole time. When we were aboard there was a whistle from down the platform and the train lurched forward. The compartment was unbearably hot. I hoped we didn't face too long a journey ahead of us. When we opened the carriage window smoke from the engine blew in so we closed it again hastily.

Shortly after leaving Kisumu the landscape changed. We could feel the engine laboring as we started to climb up a steady grade. The vegetation was no longer tropical. The forest thinned out into a wide grassland, dotted with occasional flat-topped trees. The tall grass was bleached yellow by the sun. Then I saw something strange. A group of misshapen leafless trees. As the train approached, those trees broke into an ungainly canter and I cried out loud.

It was a group of giraffes! After that I was glued to the window, spotting herds of antelope, zebras, buffalo, even a rhinoceros. It was like driving through a zoo. Darcy was smiling, enjoying my childish excitement.

"You'll have a chance to shoot some of them, if you like," he said.

"I don't know if I want to shoot things," I said. "It's not exactly fair, is it? I mean, it's their country. We've no right to shoot them."

"You'd better not let the settlers hear you talking like that," he said. "They live for their safaris. It's their major sport. We'll certainly have to go on one."

"Then I shall claim to have poor eyesight and be a rotten shot," I said.

We had reached the top of the grade. The train came into a small station to take on water and to give the engine a rest. We climbed out and stood in the shade of eucalyptus trees, enjoying the cool air. Then it was back on board and we were descending rapidly again.

"We're going down to the floor of the Rift Valley," Darcy said. "Although even the floor of the valley is pretty high. Maybe six thousand feet."

"Gol— Gosh. How high shall we be staying then?"

"Higher than that. We'll be at the foot of

104

the Aberdare Mountains. Didn't Mrs. Ragg say eight thousand feet?"

At the bottom of the grade we came to a halt in a small town on the shore of a lake. This actually looked like a proper town, although the streets were not paved and many of the buildings had the same corrugated iron roofs. But there were motorcars parked outside substantial-looking bungalows, complete with English-style gardens. A Union Jack fluttered from a flagpole outside a bigger building. Nakuru, the sign at the station said.

"We are in the White Highlands at last," Darcy said.

Several people left the train and there was much shouting as porters were instructed to carry loads of luggage. Then on we went again. It was now late afternoon and the sun was dipping lower in the sky, shining directly through the carriage window and making it unbearably hot. The track went along the edge of the lake and again I cried out aloud. The lake was covered in what looked like pink blossoms. But at the sound of the train they rose into the air — thousands of flamingos, flying in a dense pink cloud. This was truly a land of wonders. I was now really glad we had come.

We passed another lake, then signs of

cultivation. Then we were starting to climb again on the other side of the Rift Valley. The train slowed and we stopped at a tiny station called Gilgil.

"This is where we get out," Darcy said. He helped me to climb down. Our traveling companions were also disembarking. The station was little more than a platform and a hut beside it but beyond was a large stone bungalow that proclaimed itself to be the Hotel Gilgil, as well as a school, a market and several substantial-looking white buildings. A sleek Hispano-Suiza whisked away Mrs. Simpson. An estate car was there to meet Pansy Ragg. Another took the Hartley twins.

"Why, there you are, you old devil," said a voice and a young man in a khaki bush jacket came hurrying over to us. He had red hair and his face was so freckled he looked like a walking orange.

"Welcome, welcome." He pumped Darcy's hand. "Long time no see, old chap."

"How are you, Freddie?" Darcy said. "You're looking awfully fit."

"Well, one has to be fit here. It's one long round of safari, polo, racing, tennis. Oh, and a little work thrown in." His gaze moved to me.

"This is my bride, Georgiana." Darcy

slipped his arm around my shoulder and gave me a sweet little smile that melted my heart.

"Lady Georgiana. How splendid to meet you," Freddie Blanchford said, holding out his hand to me. "I do hope you're going to have a good time here. Now, let's chivvy up those dratted porters, shall we?" He shouted words in what I supposed was Kiswahili and several men picked up the bags we pointed to.

"I've got the old jalopy standing by," he said as he led us to the road. "I wouldn't make you suffer by staying in my bungalow here in town. Government issue, you know. It's all right for a single chap like me, but certainly not what you'd describe as luxurious. So I've wangled an invitation for you with friends. And I'd invite you for a drink at the hotel before we set off, but I'd prefer not to drive once it gets dark. The road is a bit of a bugger."

As we approached the car he said to Darcy, in a lower voice, "It was good of you to come. I can't tell you how glad I am that you're here."

CHAPTER 9

Friday, August 9
Kenya at last!

After a horribly bumpy flight we have arrived in Kenya. I've seen all sorts of wild
animals already. But something in the
way that Freddie Blanchford greeted
Darcy has made me uneasy.

The motorcar really could be described as
an old jalopy. It was open-topped and liberally flecked with dust and mud. Darcy
insisted I take the front seat beside Freddie
while he perched on the luggage in the rear.
We set off, leaving the town behind. The
condition of the road was awful — it was
unpaved with great ruts in it and we
bumped around so much that I thought it
wiser not to open my mouth to talk. Freddie
didn't seem to notice it and chatted away
happily.

"Had a good flight? Good show. You were obviously on time to meet the train, which was lucky as spending the night in Kisumu is not an experience I recommend. Three million mosquitoes waiting to suck your blood. It's much better where we are, because of the altitude. Too cold for them at night."

I nodded and smiled. He realized I wasn't saying anything. "Sorry about the road. The long rains have been over for a couple of months but they were bad this year and the oxcarts really wreck the surface when it's muddy. It will be better up above in the valley."

"Isn't that a contradiction of terms?" Darcy asked from the backseat. He seemed to have no problem speaking.

Freddie chuckled. "We're still close to the floor of the Rift Valley here. The Wanjohi Valley, the one they have dubbed the Happy Valley, is at the top of the escarpment." He glanced back at Darcy. "It's all right. We're all crazy in Kenya, you know." He fell silent for a moment. "So who was on the flight with you?" he asked. "I saw Pansy Ragg, and Major Eggerton, and the Rutherfords, but I didn't recognize the others."

"Son and daughter of Lord Cheriton," Darcy said.

"Interesting. I knew he had children with his first wife but we've never seen them out here. I didn't even know he was in contact with them. I wonder what brings them out exactly now?"

"Their father wants to get to know his heir, so they say," Darcy replied.

"Oh, of course. That makes sense. So who else?"

"An American lady called Simpson."

"*The* Simpson?"

"That's the one."

"Gracious. Then the rumors one hears are true. The prince is currently with Delamere. That's a long way to come for a short romantic tryst."

"Love knows no obstacles, obviously," Darcy said.

"You think it's love and not infatuation?"

"I've no idea. But I do know he's serious about her."

"Then let's hope he gets her out of his system before his father dies," Freddie said.

He turned back to me. "Enjoying what you see so far?"

I nodded again. I remembered that we had also traveled with Jocelyn Prettibone, but I hadn't seen him at the station. I supposed he was traveling on to Nairobi, where he'd have more chance of finding a job. Darcy hadn't even bothered to mention him. We were now on a road winding up a hill. Sometimes the road hugged the side of a steep drop and we had a view across the whole expanse of the Rift Valley. The wide grasslands and lakes of the valley floor were now being replaced with a mixture of trees and green grass, a parkland that looked a lot more like England. And the sky — I had never seen such a vast sky before — an enormous arc of blue with a line of clouds building over the far side of the Rift Valley. The breeze that blew in our faces was fresher too, tinged with the smell of eucalyptus. The road led along the top of a ridge and the sight of a group of round mud huts with thatched roofs and some naked African babies playing outside reminded me that we were actually far from home.

"A Kikuyu village," Freddie said. "Most of them have now moved to work on the settlers' farms. Good employment, you know."

Ahead of us was a line of soft blue mountains, looking hazy in the slanting light. "That's the Aberdares," Freddie said. "That's where we are heading."

Then the road dipped downhill again and crossed a rushing stream over a rickety bridge made of logs. "You can see why I'm not too keen to drive this in the dark," Freddie said. "There are several more bridges like this. And you never know what you're going to meet on the road. You certainly know it if you hit a buffalo. Or an elephant for that matter."

"I think you'd probably notice an elephant before you hit it," Darcy said dryly.

"You'd be surprised how fast they move," Freddie said. "And how silently. If one steps out of the bush in front of you, there's not that much you can do."

"Are there many elephants around here?" I asked, because the landscape looked so tame and civilized.

"Enough. They've mostly retreated to the Aberdares since the valley's been cultivated. They're a bloody nuisance, pardon my language. They come out of the forest and do damage to crops and gardens."

We crossed several small ravines with streams flowing through them. Each bridge was more precarious than the last.

"How much longer?" Darcy asked. I suspected he was getting even more bounced around in the back.

"Half an hour or so, if we don't meet anything on the road." As he said this the sun was dipping behind the black line of western hills, bathing the world in pink light. I sat up, feeling tense now, and expecting an elephant to step up from behind every bush. We rattled and bumped across another rushing stream.

"You'll be staying with Diddy Ruocco," he said.

"Italian?"

"True-blue British, but her husband was an Italian count. Bit of a bounder. She's much happier without him," Freddie said, turning to address us and making me grip the armrest as we narrowly missed a giant pothole. "You'll like her. She breeds horses . . . polo ponies and racehorses too. Been in the colony since the early days. She's a good egg. One of the few who will actually speak to me. She'll make sure you're taken care of. And of course everyone will invite you to dine. We're always curious about visitors here. It can be bloody boring talking to the same handful of people all the time."

"Where does this Diddy live?" I asked as we were now approaching a tall conical mountain, almost like the kind of mountains that small children draw. "Is this the Aberdares?"

"This is Kipipiri, our lone mountain; the Aberdares are to our right. We've got a few miles to go yet. Diddy lives up at the north end of the valley. Next-door neighbor to Bwana Hartley, or Lord Cheriton I suppose one should say now. Which is convenient."

I was about to ask why it was convenient when Darcy said, "Why won't people speak to you? I've always thought you were an easygoing sort of chap, the kind people would want at their dinner parties. Tell a good story. Like a good laugh . . . Has Africa changed you?"

"Not at all," Freddie replied. "But I'm the bloody government official. Settlers don't like the government. Rules and regulations, you know. So I'm lucky if I ever get invited to dinner. Diddy likes me because I play polo. That's the only reason I'm tolerated around here — my polo skills." He laughed, a little bitterly, I thought.

We were now seeing more signs of cultivation: fields of crops, of what looked like maize, wheat, rows of small trees, and the occasional glimpse of a large house up a long driveway. The mountains to our right had now come closer to the road and were clothed in thick forest. The air felt decidedly chilly. I was tired, uncomfortable and hungry. We had been up since five. Stands of tall trees now grew beside the road, and from time to time we passed between great rocks. I remembered again what Freddie had said about elephants stepping out in front of the car. Then I saw a sign, *Wanjohi Polo Club.* A splendid field surrounded by a white picket fence and a pavilion such as would grace any cricket pitch in England. This definitely lifted my spirits.

"Almost there," Freddie said.

"Where do they keep the horses?" I asked, not seeing any in the paddocks.

"Ponies," Freddie corrected. "You play polo on ponies." He smiled. "They keep them safely on their estates, and shut them up in their stables overnight. Big cats like the taste of horsemeat."

"Golly," I said. The very British polo club had made me forget that we were in the wilds of Africa. "There are lions here?"

"Mainly leopards. Not too many lions, actually, since they prefer to hunt in open savanna. But the occasional lion does learn that we keep cows and horses up here and they are much easier pickings than gazelles and zebras in the open. You'll find the farms all have high hedges or walls to protect the livestock. But they don't keep out the leopards, of course. Too wily. So just be a bit careful after dark, won't you?"

He turned to grin at me, as if enjoying all of these dire warnings. Then he added, "All of the farms keep guards. You're probably quite safe." Then he added, "Ah, here we are."

He swung the motor through a tall white wooden gate above which hung a sign with *Hastings* written on it.

"Hastings?" Darcy asked.

"Funny how so many of the settlers name their estates after their old haunts in Britain," Freddie said. "Does this remind you of a sedate seaside town? In fact did you ever see anything less like Hastings in your life?"

Darcy chuckled. We drove between green pastures dotted with great eucalyptus trees, then came to another gate, this time in a tall hedge. A skinny African boy leaped out to open the gate in the hedge. "Welcome, bwanas," he said, smiling shyly. "Welcome, memsabu."

And to my surprise we were driving through what looked like a lovely English garden. Manicured lawns, a fountain in the middle, even rosebushes. On the far side of the lawn was a low stone bungalow with a steeply sloping shingle roof. At the sound of the motorcar several big dogs ran out, barking furiously.

"Quiet, you brutes, heel," shouted a female voice as a slender woman, wearing riding breeches and an open-necked shirt, stepped out of the shadow of the veranda that ran around the whole front of the building. "They don't listen to a word I say," she said, rolling her eyes in exasperation as the dogs now surrounded the motorcar, tails wagging furiously. "Hello, Freddie. Had an easy drive, then? No mishaps?"

"Perfectly easy, thank you, Diddy, old bean." He had jumped out and came around to open my door as Darcy attempted to climb over the mound of luggage. "Diddy Ruocco, may I present Mr. and Mrs. O'Mara."

"How do you do?" We shook hands. "It's very kind of you to have us to stay."

"Well, I couldn't have left you to the mercy of Freddie, could I?" she said. "My dears, you'd have been eaten by mosquitoes and poisoned by that rotten cook of his. Anyway, much more fun up here in the valley. Lots of parties, and safaris, and polo, of course. We've a match on Sunday. Do you both play? We have mixed teams up here, you know."

"I play," Darcy said.

"I've never tried," I confessed.

"Well, you wouldn't. Women don't in England, do they?" Diddy said. "But I take it you hunt."

"Oh rather." I grinned. "I adore hunting."

I realized this sounded rather strange for someone who was reluctant to shoot things on safari. But one in my position is brought up to hunt and what I loved was the thrill of the chase, jumping over fences and ditches. And actually I was glad if the fox got away at the end of it!

"Then you'll get the hang of it. I'll give you a lesson tomorrow. But we shouldn't keep you standing out here. Let me show you to your rooms, then you'll have time to take a bath and change for drinks before dinner." She clapped her hands and called out some words in a local language that was either Kikuyu or Kiswahili and several servants wearing red fez hats and immaculate white uniforms rushed out to retrieve our baggage.

"I should be getting back then," Freddie said. "It's almost dark."

"Nonsense. Stay and have dinner and spend the night. You're not wanted until morning, are you?"

"No, but I didn't bring any things. . . ." Freddie looked doubtful.

"Dear boy, we certainly have spare pajamas and a shaving kit," she said. "Everyone does up here. You never know who will be spending the night, after all." And she gave a hearty laugh. "You may stay as long as you've brought the requisite gift."

"I have a case of claret in the boot, if that's what you mean," Freddie said.

"I hope it's good claret."

"Only the best for you, Diddy darling," Freddie said.

"Splendid. You're a good chap even if you are a bloody government official," Diddy said. She clapped a hand on Darcy's shoulder. "Then let me show you your room. The houseboys should have taken in the bags by now."

She led us along the veranda while the dogs still swarmed around us and opened a door at the end onto a large and pleasant room. The electric lights had already been turned on and the bags were stacked beside the wardrobe. In the middle was a four-poster bed and a good-looking antique chest of drawers and dressing table. A fire was burning in the fireplace. It looked like any English bedroom.

"There's plenty of hot water for a bath," Diddy said. "It's heated from a bonfire in the back. All mod cons here, you know!" And she laughed.

Now seen in the harsh electric light she was not as young as I had thought. Her hair, pulled back into a chignon, was streaked blond but her face was weathered from constant exposure to the sun. I put her at over forty. Her figure, however, was as slim as a girl's.

"I'll leave you to it, then," she said. "Come down for drinks when you are ready. Oh, and make sure you close the shutters at night. We should be quite safe here, inside the hedge, but one does get the occasional baboon, or even a leopard. One of the neighbors had her little dog taken from the foot of her bed during the night last week. Didn't hear a thing. Only deduced what had happened by the trail of blood." With those cheerful words she went off, leaving us alone.

"That's nice to know, isn't it?" Darcy said. "How do you feel about having your toes nibbled off by a leopard?"

Tension inside me had been building during the drive from Gilgil. Suspicions had been growing. Things needed explaining. And now this talk of leopards made me blurt out, "Why are we here, Darcy?"

He looked surprised. "I wanted to give you a special honeymoon, a honeymoon you'd always remember."

"It must be horribly expensive to fly to Africa," I said.

"One puts by money, here and there," he replied with a shrug. He had put his suitcase on the bed and was already unpacking clothes, his back to me.

"So why was Freddie Blanchford terribly glad that you'd come?"

"We're old pals. I expect he's a bit lonely. It's good to see a friendly face."

"And he invites you now? Conveniently when you need a honeymoon?"

Darcy spun around, frowning. "Look, what is this? The Spanish Inquisition? He saw the wedding announcement in the *Times,* all right?"

"No, not all right," I said. "I know you too well, Darcy O'Mara. There is something more to this. You have no clear honeymoon plans and then suddenly you announce to the Queen that we are going to Africa. Out of the blue. Just like that. If Freddie had invited us, why didn't you tell me?" I went across to the dressing table and smoothed down my hair, staring at myself in the mirror, trying to control my words and sound calm and rational. I didn't want this to be a hysterical outburst. "You know what I think? I think this is a trip that we couldn't possibly afford unless someone paid for it. A honeymoon in Africa? Who does that apart from film stars and millionaires?"

I turned back to face him. "This is some kind of assignment for you, isn't it? You were being sent here and you thought it was a brilliant idea to have me tag along."

He came over to me and slipped his arms around my waist. "It wasn't like that at all," he said. "I really wanted a special honeymoon for you but to be frank I didn't know how to pull it off. When this trip was suggested I thought it would be perfect."

I was still standing like a statue, resisting his attempt to pull me toward him. "Ah, so you admit that it was an assignment for you. You're out here on some kind of shady business, right?"

"Quite the opposite, actually," Darcy said. "Not at all shady. If you really must know — and this must be strictly confidential, of course — I'm here on the trail of a jewel thief."

CHAPTER 10

Friday, August 9
At Diddy Ruocco's house in the Happy Valley

Well, we've arrived safely but frankly I
don't know what to think. I should have
guessed it was too good to be true that
Darcy had planned this dream honeymoon for us. Now part of me wants to
be angry with him for deceiving me, but I
have to remind myself that, whatever the
reason, I am here in Kenya and that this
is the trip of a lifetime.

I was still glaring at Darcy. "A jewel thief?"
I asked.

Darcy put his fingers to his lips. "You
never know who might be listening," he said
softly. "This is a close-knit community. I
wouldn't want word getting around why I'm
actually here." He went over and closed the
windows, looking around first to see that

123

nobody was hovering outside, listening.

"Why would a jewel thief come to Kenya?" I asked. "To steal ivory?"

"We're dealing with much bigger game than ivory," he said. "There have been several daring and spectacular burglaries in London in the past couple of years. Items missing from society parties — and the conclusion we have come to is that the thief has to be one of them."

"A member of high society, you are saying?" I said. "But why Kenya?"

"It's just a hunch. Scotland Yard has always felt that on every occasion the thief left the country almost immediately after the gems were stolen. Once a certain wealthy Arab who is known to trade high-value stones showed up in Baghdad right after the theft. And then the necklace appeared, with the stones suitably refashioned, in America. And this time a Mr. Van Horn, an Afrikaner, from South Africa, arrived in this part of the world a couple of days ago and is staying at the hotel in Gilgil, for a safari holiday, he claims." He paused and wagged a finger at me knowingly. "Mr. Van Horn is in the diamond business. And the gem that was stolen this time was a fabulous diamond necklace."

"I see." I sank onto the edge of the bed.

"So there has just been another jewel theft, then?"

He nodded. "The day before the royal garden party. A necklace with a priceless central diamond was stolen from an Indian maharani while she was at Glyndebourne for the opera festival."

"Was she staying at Glyndebourne House? It should be easy to find out who else was staying there and whether one of them was on our flight."

"She was staying there, but it was the day of one of the picnics. Everyone was out on the grounds. Hundreds of people. The maharani's servant was distracted by some kind of commotion going on outside — someone a little too drunk on champagne, perhaps — and while she was looking out the window and not paying attention the jewel case was raided."

"So someone sneaked into the room without her hearing them?"

"Apparently. She swears the door was locked, and she was looking out the window so nobody could have come in that way."

"Do you think she was telling the truth? Maybe she was in league with the thief."

Darcy shook his head. "She had been with the maharini all her life. The epitome of the loyal servant. And she spoke no English.

And she was distraught when questioned."

"I see."

"Only the one necklace was taken — the one with the fabulous center stone — which makes it clear it was no ordinary thief. It was a thief who knew where there was a buyer for what he had stolen."

"Crikey." I sat, staring at the flickering flames of the fire, trying to digest all this information. "So you suspect that the thief was someone on our flight?"

"Most probably," Darcy said. "It was the first flight to Africa after the burglary. It's highly unlikely the thief would come by ship, which would take several weeks. And Mr. Van Horn would have no valid reason to stick around for several weeks."

"Why didn't you have the luggage of the passengers searched?" I asked.

Darcy grinned. "We did. At least, all the luggage of the Kenya passengers that was left on board the plane was searched during that overnight stay in Khartoum. Unfortunately not the hand luggage."

"Couldn't you search the actual passengers?"

"My dear girl, you can't go around searching people without due cause and a search warrant. We are not Nazi Germany. Peeking at their bags was highly illegal, although customs is allowed to check baggage."

"So how do you know that the culprit got off in Kisumu? He might have gone on to Rhodesia or South Africa."

"Because Van Horn is here. And for that very reason our suspect is most likely staying in this area or Van Horn would have gone to Nairobi and stayed at the New Stanley Hotel."

"Unless he wanted to put people off the scent," I suggested. "But if he's South African, why not have the burglar come down to South Africa to meet him?"

"Because he is well watched in South Africa, also because I suspect our thief wants it to look like a legitimate journey."

"There weren't too many people who disembarked from the train in Gilgil, were there? Only a handful. Ourselves. Mrs. Simpson . . ." I paused and chuckled. "I'd like to discover that she is a jewel thief as well as a gold digger but I think it's highly unlikely. I can't see her climbing up drainpipes in her haute couture."

Darcy smiled too. "That leaves the Hartley twins, who have apparently never been out to Kenya before. So one asks oneself, why now?"

"Because Daddy has just inherited the title and wants to get to know them," I said.

"And apart from them there was Pansy Ragg and those older people. One of the men was decidedly stout. I can't see him climbing drainpipes either. But Pansy Ragg does like to buy expensive clothes. Could it be a woman?"

Darcy frowned. "I doubt it. Simply because of the risks taken in previous burglaries."

"Well, that's all the people who got off in Gilgil," I pointed out. "I suppose our burglar could have gone on to Nairobi and then come back for a quick meeting with Mr. Van Horn. Or he could travel up to Nairobi for the meeting and then head home."

"All possible," Darcy said.

A question mark had been flying around my head, fighting with all the other information, for some time. Now the question took shape. "Darcy, why you? Why not send a real policeman, from Scotland Yard, over here. He'd have the authority to actually search and arrest."

Darcy nodded. "You're right. Why me? I suppose because I've done undercover jobs for them before. I'm a good observer and I have the perfect cover story. Nobody doubts I'm out here on my honeymoon."

"But I don't see how you can possibly

keep tabs on all the suspects and Mr. Van Horn," I said. "You've seen how difficult it is to get around. You can't keep popping down to Gilgil."

"Freddie's taking care of that part," he said. "He's been thoroughly briefed by Scotland Yard and he is the law in these parts. He has his spies shadowing Van Horn. My job is to watch for interactions if Van Horn comes up to a party in the valley or one of the settlers decides to take a little jaunt down to Gilgil. Everyone knows everyone else's business up here."

Suddenly I jumped up, waving my arms excitedly. "Jocelyn Prettibone. We forgot all about him," I said. "He went on to Nairobi, didn't he? But he could be back. And he's the sort of person other people overlook. Perfect for your thief."

"You're not wrong there," Darcy said. "Plays the idiot. Everyone ignores him. Yes, you may be right. We'll have to see if he comes back to the valley or if Van Horn takes a sudden trip to Nairobi."

"So it's a working holiday now," I said. "You have your spying and I have mine."

"Meaning what?" he asked sharply.

"The queen asked me to keep an eye on the Prince of Wales, in case Mrs. Simpson joined him, which she has. She's terrified they will get married in secret and present her with a fait accompli."

"You can hardly stop them if they do," Darcy said.

"I know that. The queen just likes his activities reported back to her."

"He's been out here several times before, you know," Darcy said. "On those occasions he had affairs with local women."

"I don't think the queen minded that as much, because they weren't serious," I said. "It's the dreaded Simpson she fears because the woman has such a hold over him. If they really married could the king dissolve the marriage, I wonder? She could never be queen, could she?"

"I've no idea," Darcy said, "and at this moment I don't care. I don't know about you but I'm tired and frightfully hungry and I want my bath and a drink. So let's put other people's business aside and remember that this is our honeymoon, all right?"

"Sounds like a good idea," I said. "Shall we toss a coin for first bath?"

CHAPTER 11

Friday, August 9
At Diddy Ruocco's house in the Happy Valley

It's lovely here but I'm still coming to terms
with the fact that we are on the trail of a
jewel thief.

A half hour later we were clean, dressed in
evening attire and making our way along
the veranda to the main entrance. Having
come from the warmth of a bath and a room
with a fire I was horrified how cold it was
outside. Icy breezes drifted down from the
mountain and I was glad I had brought
Mummy's mink stole with me. She had
insisted I take it. "As if I will ever have any
use for such things again," she had said
dramatically. "The lonely widow woman.
That's how I shall be known from now on."

"Which of your husbands has actually
died, apart from Daddy?" I asked with a

cheeky smile.

She gave a dramatic shrug. "Isn't that enough? The widow of a duke. That's what I am."

I thought of her now as we walked along the creaking boards and I wrapped the mink stole more firmly around me. I should have brought her with us. I'd have given anything to see her interactions with the infamous Lady Idina Sackville . . . or whatever her last name was at present.

A Kikuyu servant had been standing guard at the front door and stepped forward to open it for us. "Memsabu is waiting for you in the back room by the fire," he said and led the way through.

It was not a big room by the standards of one who has grown up in a castle, but it was an impressive room. The walls were paneled in a dark wood, the ceiling was high, with an enormous fan in the center, and the whole of one wall was composed of windows that during daylight must look out over a splendid view. A rising moon played with shadows across the lawns but no lights were visible in the inky distance.

I took all this in rapidly before Diddy rose from an armchair beside the fire. "Ah, there you are," she said. "Come and get warm. You must be freezing. And you've brought a fur — how sensible of you. So many people come out here expecting Africa to be hot and steamy jungle. But we're at eight thousand feet here and the cold comes down the mountainsides at night. Now, G and Ts all around? We've already had a couple but we don't mind joining you, do we, Cyril."

I was surprised as a man rose from the other armchair — since Freddie had told us she lived alone. He was small and wiry with a neat little blond mustache and round glasses that made him look like an owl. He bobbed his head too, birdlike. "You must be Lady Georgiana and Mr. O'Mara. How do you do," he said. "I'm Cyril Prendergast. I'm also a guest of Diddy at the moment."

"At the moment!" Diddy gave a loud laugh. "I can't get rid of the fellow. He goes, then he turns up again, like a bad penny."

"Well, your house is so jolly comfortable, darling Diddy," Cyril said. "How can one resist, especially when you are so free with the spirits." And he took a glass from the tray that one of the house servants was presenting.

"Cyril is a big-game hunter," Diddy said.

This was the last occupation I would have predicted for him. He was immaculately turned out in a white tuxedo jacket and black bow tie with a purple silk handkerchief

133

in his top pocket. I would have expected schoolmaster, accountant, even government tax collector. But big-game hunter? I couldn't see him facing a large cat, let alone a lion.

"You make that sound very daring, Diddy," Cyril said. "Actually what I do is lead safaris. Business was better in the twenties, of course, before everyone lost their money in the crash, but there are still enough people with money to burn and the desire to shoot something. I always pray it's not an elephant or a buffalo. I do hate to send a client home in a pine box."

He took a big gulp of his gin and tonic. I took a tentative sip of mine. It was jolly strong. I noticed that our hostess and Cyril knocked theirs back as if it was water they were drinking. Darcy, however, was also taking his time.

"Drink up, drink up," Diddy said. "You must be jolly thirsty after all that travel today. All the way from Khartoum in an aeroplane, Cyril. Imagine that."

Cyril gave a dramatic shudder. "I really can't. Too frightening for words. I went up in a plane with Beryl once. Never again."

"Beryl?" Darcy asked.

"Beryl Markham, of course. She's taken up flying as well as horse training."

"Oh right," Darcy said. "Didn't she once have an affair with one of the royal princes?"

"With all of them, darlings," Cyril said, chuckling. "Except for that upright little Duke of York, who is quite the family man, one hears. But then he does stutter badly. So off-putting in bed when he tries to whisper sweet nothings."

"And Queen Mary banished Beryl Markham, didn't she?" Darcy was also grinning. "Must be quite a woman. I shall enjoy meeting her."

I remembered I had heard some sort of gossip about Beryl and affairs with members of the royal family when I was too young to really take in what it meant. It crossed my mind to wonder whether the Prince of Wales might want to rekindle the relationship and thus make Mrs. Simpson jealous enough to leave him. One could only hope!

"And how was your flying experience?" Diddy asked.

"It was rather a bumpy flight," I said.

"It always is," Diddy responded. "You're lucky the propellers didn't clog with sand and dust. Then you would have had to put down somewhere in the Sudan, and God knows how long you would have been stuck there."

I glanced at Darcy. He was studying his drink.

"And Diddy tells me you're on your honeymoon. How splendid," Cyril said. "I've never been married myself and poor old Diddy here is a widow."

I looked across at her. She laughed again. "You make it sound so tragic, Cyril. I was married for six months . . . he was an Italian count. Giovanni Ruocco. His name sounded so glamorous that I was dazzled. But the stupid man had at least six affairs during that time. I was about to dump him when a rhino did the job for me. Best thing that could have happened. I got rid of the husband, kept the property and was overwhelmed with sympathy." She took another swig of her gin. "Now I can focus on my horses. Cyril and I now lead a quiet and chaste life compared with the rest of the inhabitants of the valley. In fact I think we're the only ones who aren't cavorting with someone else's mate."

"Is it as bad as that?" I asked.

"Oh yes. The main sport around here isn't polo. It's musical beds," Diddy said. "You'll see if you're invited to Idina's. Or our next-door neighbor's, for that matter."

"Lord Cheriton?" Darcy asked, looking up from his drink.

"I still think of him as Bwana Hartley," Diddy said. "Can't get used to this new-found elevation to the peerage."

"He has an American wife, so we're told?"

"He does. Angel Trapp. Father owns steel mills. Rich as Croesus. You'd think all that money would make Bwana toe the line, wouldn't you? But he's quite open about his mistresses."

"More than one mistress?" I asked.

"Not usually at the same time. This time there has been a slight overlap, one hears." Cyril gave a malicious little smile. "For the longest time it was Pansy Ragg. In fact we thought they might divorce their respective spouses and make it permanent, but then Tusker Eggerton brings home this hot little piece from Birmingham — the aptly named Babe." Another wicked grin. "And now we hear that Pansy is no more. Silly woman should not have gone home to England for so long. And silly Tusker should not have left his new wife behind."

"He was one of the men we saw on the plane, wasn't he?" I asked. "Looks like an ex-military type."

"That's Tusker all right," Diddy said. "Was a major in the war. Never lets anyone forget it. He came out in the soldier-settlement scheme right after the war and has done rather well for himself. He grows pyrethrum for insecticide. It's much in demand these days."

An African houseboy arrived offering a tray of sausage rolls. They were warm and delicious.

"These are marvelous," Darcy said. "So you raise pigs in Kenya?"

"This sausage is actually kudu," Diddy said. "Cyril shot it for me as a present, but it makes good eating, doesn't it? I have a really good Somali chef. Bwana is always trying to snag him from me."

I was trying to resist my second gin and tonic when Freddie joined us, looking uncomfortable in his bush jacket when we were all in evening dress. "I should have thrown a formal outfit into the back of the car, just in case," he said.

"Don't worry about it, dear boy. It's only us," Diddy said. "And Cyril here won't dare to mention it in his wicked little column, will you, Cyril."

"Not if the claret is good enough," Cyril said. He turned to Darcy. "So what sort of business are you in, O'Mara? Do you have a profession? I take it you're not a spoiled aristocrat like so many of them around here."

"I'm an aristocrat but in no way spoiled,"

Darcy said. "My father has just about managed to cling onto a drafty castle in Ireland and now trains racehorses for a Polish princess. So I've always had to make my own way in the world — although I can't say I have an actual profession."

"A man after my own heart," Cyril said. "Surviving on his wits alone. With only a meager castle in Ireland for security." He grinned. "So what do you do to bring in a crust? Or have you married a rich wife like Bwana?"

"Really, Cyril." Diddy slapped his hand. "That is too nasty, even for you."

"I'm afraid I'm as penniless as my husband," I said. "But Darcy accepts occasional assignments —"

"To locate people overseas — that kind of thing," Darcy said, cutting me off and making me realize that he did not want his profession known. As if I really knew the full extent of it myself!

"And you help your father buy racehorses, don't you?" I chimed in rapidly, not wanting him to be angry with me that I might have given away anything I shouldn't.

"Then you've pulled out all the stops for this honeymoon, haven't you?" Cyril went on smoothly, a little grin curling his lips.

"Or is some friendly benefactor springing for it?"

"I think who is paying for my honeymoon is my own business," Darcy said. "I was brought up not to discuss money."

"Touchy," Cyril said, still smiling.

"You should learn early on that Cyril's main sport is to needle people," Diddy said. "He means no real harm by it. Just slap his hand and ignore him. I always do."

Luckily at that moment we were summoned through to dinner. The dining room was also paneled in dark wood and had some impressive trophy heads on the walls — a buffalo with magnificent horns, an antelope with long curly horns. Not unlike Castle Rannoch where I had grown up with stags' heads around our walls. I supposed I had to face the fact that shooting was the norm among my kind of people! I was wondering what sort of game would be on the plate for supper when a plate was put in front of me with a fish on it. Darcy reacted with surprise. "This is trout."

"So it is." Diddy grinned. "Caught this morning. When the first settlers came to this area they stocked the rivers with trout. Trout fishing is a major sport here, when we are not shooting things or rolling in the hay with someone else's wife. I, on the other hand, have sensibly constructed a trout pond so I can have trout whenever I feel like it."

"The streams coming down from the mountains are a godsend here," Cyril said, already tucking in hungrily to his food. "You must let Diddy show you her dams that give us electricity. And constant fresh water for the house, and the fountain."

"And Bwana next door has the most impressive waterfall at the top of his estate," Freddie added.

"Naturally," Cyril said. "Everything Bwana has is the most impressive. The biggest and best, so they tell me." And he gave me a naughty wink.

"So what brought you out to Africa, Mr. Prendergast?" Darcy asked.

"My dears, I came out to be a writer," Cyril said. "I was going to write wonderful books about life in the bush, but somehow the books never materialized. I became a gossip columnist for the *Nairobi Times* instead. And when that didn't pay enough to take care of the bills, I took up leading safaris. I'm rather good at it, actually. I spin a good tale of the dangers. My clients are frightfully thrilled and we usually manage to shoot something. I'm a surprisingly good shot."

"He is." Diddy nodded. "You wouldn't think it from looking at him, but nerves of steel."

Cyril smiled modestly this time. "People always underestimate me," he said.

"It's a pity Cyril wasn't on the plane with us," I said to Darcy as we went back to our room. "I'd say he'd be the ideal cat burglar. Too harmless and innocent looking but apparently a crack shot and a big-game hunter."

"And a gossip columnist." Darcy laughed. "What a dangerous combination!"

I had a sudden brilliant thought. "Darcy, remember what Cyril said about flying with Beryl? The thief could have come out here by private plane. Zou Zou offered to fly us herself, so it would be possible for a good pilot."

"So we should have Freddie check for us on aeroplanes that might have flown in from Europe this week," Darcy said. "Good thinking."

I grinned to myself. I was not just the little wife who had been brought along. I was jolly well going to be useful in this investigation!

CHAPTER 12

Saturday, August 10
At Hastings, Diddy Ruocco's estate, the
  Happy Valley, Kenya

I think I'm going to enjoy myself after all.
On the trail of a jewel thief! Doesn't that
sound romantic and exciting? Darcy will
see that I am a huge asset to his work
and maybe he'll include me in the future.
Wouldn't that be fun?

I woke at first light and lay there, listening
to unfamiliar birdsong. Darcy was still blissfully asleep, looking so young and adorable.
I resisted the desire to kiss him, slipped out
of bed and stood looking down at him for a
moment, thinking how jolly lucky I was.
Then I was curious to see what kind of birds
might be making those various sounds. I
pulled on trousers and a jacket over my
pajamas, put on my shoes and crept out. It

was freezing cold and I almost retreated to the warmth of the bedroom again. There was a delicious smell of wood smoke in the air, mingled with the scents of eucalyptus, jasmine and honeysuckle. Nobody was about. The dew lay thick on the lawns and white mist crept down from the mountains above us so that we were in a hazy world. Then through the haze I saw flashes of bright gold. Brilliant little birds with iridescent heads and golden wings flitted around the rosebushes, hovering to drink nectar from the flowers, chirping in tiny voices to each other. I followed them across the lawn, entranced. Behind the house the land rose in a series of terraces. I saw the mountain stream that provided the electricity, and the trout pond. Then a loud honking made me jump. I couldn't identify what might make such a noise — an ancient lorry? — until two ungainly birds with giant bills flapped from tree to tree ahead of me. Were they hornbills? I followed them, as the ground rose steeply.

I found I was out of breath and had to pause, feeling my heart racing. Was this the result of a long flight? I wondered. As I stood there, gasping for breath, I examined my surroundings. This part of the grounds was more like the sort of parkland of grass

144

dotted with trees and bushes that you'd find in the wilder parts of English estates — not unlike my own Eynsleigh. Then suddenly I realized that I was at the edge of the forest. Ahead of me tall trees rose, their tops lost in the morning mist. Creepers trailed from their branches, some flowering with bright splashes of color, and among them fluttered brilliant butterflies, larger and more colorful than I had ever seen in England. I stood there watching them, not daring to go into that forbidden realm, until suddenly there was a movement among the trees. I froze, realizing I was now far from the safety of the lawns. But it's still Diddy's estate, I told myself, even if it is a wilder part. And as I stood quite still two small antelope crossed the path ahead of me. I couldn't believe what I was seeing. They picked their way daintily, pausing to browse occasionally on a leaf.

I wasn't going to go up into deeper forest but these two were moving across the parkland, not up it. I followed them, until I stepped on a twig, it snapped and they bounded away. I glanced around and realized I had come farther than I intended. I could only just catch a glimpse of the house through the trees.

I should go back, I thought to myself.

I nearly jumped out of my skin when a deep voice right behind me said, "Don't move. Don't take another step."

I wanted to turn and see who was speaking, but I did as I was told and remained frozen.

"Now slowly step backward," said the voice, "and slightly to your left."

I took one step backward, then another, until a pair of hands landed on my shoulders, making me jump again. This time I turned around and saw a large middle-aged man with a weathered face and a strong jawline looking down at me. In his youth he would have been extremely handsome. He was quite good-looking still, a powerful man with deeply tanned skin and bright blue eyes. His sun-streaked hair he wore rather long so that it curled over his collar. In spite of the cold he was wearing an open-necked shirt.

"You should look where you are walking and not take the forest lightly," he said. "All sort of things live here that would love to kill you."

"Was I in danger?" I asked. I scanned the trees, trying to spot a lurking lion or elephant, but could see nothing.

"You really were," he said. "One of the most deadly encounters you could have is right at your feet."

He pointed to the forest floor. A foot or so ahead of me was a wide black ribbon and it was alive and moving.

"Siafus," he said.

I peered at them. "Ants?"

"Driver ants. They can kill anything that is weak or can't move. If you tripped and fell down they'd swarm all over you in seconds and even if you managed to run away their bite is extremely painful. In fact the soldier ants at the outside of the column bite and won't let go. The Maasai use them for sutures when they are gashed in the bush."

I was still staring in fascination at the black moving ribbon of ants. Then I remembered my manners and turned to my rescuer. "Thank you so much. You obviously saved me from a nasty fate."

"Glad to be of service," he said. "Even though I should shoot you as a trespasser on my land."

"Your land? Golly, I thought I was in Diddy's back garden," I said.

"Up here at the edge of the forest our estates merge," he said. "We don't put up fences. No point. The elephants would just knock them down. You're also lucky you didn't meet an elephant, by the way." He held out a large hand. "I'm Lord Cheriton. They call me Bwana around here. And you are?"

"Lady Georgiana Rannoch — I mean O'Mara," I said. "I'm sorry, this has quite unnerved me. I've just got married. I keep forgetting."

He laughed then. "Lady Georgiana. Of course. How delightful to meet you. My daughter mentioned you were on the same flight as they were. Come and have some breakfast."

"I should get back," I said. "My husband will be worrying where I've got to."

"Then let me escort you back," he said. "You never know what other dangers might be lurking. Here, take my arm."

I could hardly refuse although to be honest I wasn't quite happy with the way he was looking at me. Rather like the big bad wolf when Little Red Riding Hood stepped into the cottage. I half expected him to lick his lips. Before I could take his arm he had slipped a hand around my waist. "What a delectable little creature you are," he said. "I shall enjoy getting to know you better. Most of the women out here are tough as old boots and look at your lily-white flesh. Mm-mm." And he nuzzled at my shoulder. Crikey. I had an urge to slap his face but one can hardly turn on the person who has saved one's life, can one?

Instead of taking me back the way I had come, through the fringe of the forest, he steered me down toward his own estate. Again I didn't see how I could break away from him without seeming awfully rude. We came to a flight of steps leading down to gardens even more impressive than Diddy's — lawns and ornamental pools with water lilies in them, rows of Italian cypress standing like sentinels and two giant magnolia trees in full blossom. Bougainvillea spilled over walls and shrubs, making the gardens blaze with a riot of reds, pinks and oranges. It really was quite remarkable. And I would have enjoyed exploring the garden, except as we went down the steps, Bwana's grip tightened. I felt the hand around my waist move upward until it was distinctly touching the underside of my breast. I could sense him giving me an inquiring look as to whether I was enjoying this or not. Now I was completely embarrassed and not sure what to do. This might even have been considered normal, friendly behavior in the colony, but I certainly didn't intend for the hand to do any more wandering. I was about to channel my great-grandmother and let him know that I was not amused when we heard fast-moving footsteps heading our way. We both looked up to see a slim young African man running toward us. One might have described him as beautiful. His face was finely sculpted with high cheekbones and flashing dark eyes. He moved with the grace of a gazelle.

"Bwana," he called. "So there you are. I didn't realize you were going to rise so early this morning. I have been looking everywhere."

His English was perfect, almost as if he had been schooled in England.

"Sleeping in again, eh, Joe?" Bwana said, releasing his grip on my person, and he chuckled. But it wasn't a kind sort of chuckle.

"Not really. I'm not to know you are going to rise at six unless you tell me in advance," the young man said. I was interested that his tone was not completely deferential.

"Well, no matter. You can make yourself useful and escort this young lady back to Diddy's. Go by the shortcut. Her loving bridegroom may be looking for her."

"Yes, Bwana, of course." The young man turned and gave me a dazzling smile. "If you will please come with me, memsahib."

"This is Joe, my right-hand man," Bwana

said. "He'll take good care of you. There's nothing he doesn't know about this estate." He put a hand on my shoulder. "I look forward to continuing where we left off, Lady Georgiana." And he gave me a wink.

I was glad to fall into step beside the young Kenyan.

"Your name is Joe?" I asked as we crossed a grassy area together.

"Joseph is my Christian name, memsahib," he said. "I also have a Maasai name, but you could not pronounce that."

"So you're a Maasai? That's different from a Kikuyu, is it?"

"Very different," he said. "We are the first owners of this land. Before Kikuyu. Before white people. We are warriors. To be a Maasai warrior a boy must prove himself by fighting and killing a lion with his spear."

"Goodness," I said. "Have you done this?"

"Oh yes, memsahib. I did this," he said. "I killed the lion and may wear his skin as a cape."

"But you don't wish to be with your people now? You prefer to live with Bwana?"

"There is not enough land for my people and their herds of cows. And I need to provide for my mother. I help Bwana to run this big estate. My people have shown him our ways with cattle. He has listened and now has a fine herd."

I nodded, feeling a little awkward about what he had just said.

We came to the edge of the grassy area. A row of native gardeners were now hard at work, clipping the lawns, pruning the shrubs, although everything already looked immaculate to my eyes. Ahead of us were several outbuildings behind a long white-washed bungalow with a steep shingled roof that had to be the main house. As we came close a white-clad servant came running out of one of the buildings carrying a silver serving dish.

"Is that the kitchen?" I asked.

"Yes, memsahib," Joseph said. "In Kenya we build the kitchen far enough away from the big house so that a fire cannot spread and burn it down."

"Are there often fires?"

"Sometimes," he admitted.

"And are the rest of these buildings where the servants live?"

"Oh no, memsahib," he said. "Only the Somali houseboys live behind the kitchen. The Kikuyu workers live in their own village, on the estate, far from the main house. They like their own ways. The rest of these buildings are sheds and a place for Bwana to store his motorcar and tractor."

"And the Maasai servants?"

"The Maasai do not like to be servants, memsahib," he said in a way that was putting me in my place. "They advise on the care of cattle, but most of my people would rather starve than work in the house of a white person. We are a proud people."

"So the preferred servants are Somali?" I asked, quickly changing the subject.

"Yes, memsahib."

"Because they are good cooks?"

"That and because they are smart. They learn quickly and they look better. Their features are more appealing to Europeans."

"Goodness," I said. "I'm glad I don't have to run a household out here. There would be too much to learn and too many people to offend."

"White people do not mind if they offend Africans," Joseph said.

That was the end of that conversation. There was nothing more to say.

We left the outbuildings behind and I saw the hedge around Diddy's property was now ahead of us. And beside the hedge there was a small cottage such as one would see in an English village. It had a shingle roof, a low fence around it and sunflowers in the garden. As we came close the net curtain was drawn back for a moment. Joseph looked up and waved. The curtain was hurriedly dropped again.

"Who lives there?" I asked. "Is that for guests?"

"No, memsahib. Nobody lives there now. The person who occupied it has left and moved away."

"But somebody was there. Somebody waved."

"That is just one of the servants cleaning it," Joseph said. "Bwana wishes to make it ready in case his son wishes to move in there."

I tried to imagine the spoiled, effete Rupert moving into that cottage. It might be attractive in its own way but it was tiny.

We came to a small gate cut in the hedge. Joseph opened it for me. "Now you can find your way home, I think."

"Thank you," I said. "You are most kind. I hadn't realized I had strayed onto Bwana's estate and he saved me from stepping into a line of ants."

"Siafus are very bad, memsahib," he said. "Many bad things in the forest. You should not go alone."

"You're quite right," I said, then looked up as I heard a voice shouting my name.

"Georgiana? Where are you? Are you out here?"

154

I hurried toward the sound of his voice.

"Over here, Darcy," I shouted back. "Just coming."

Darcy was in his dressing gown and pajamas, looking white and worried. "Where the devil did you get to?" he demanded. "You scared the daylights out of me. I saw your shoes and coat had gone but I couldn't find you on the grounds. I thought some animal must have taken you."

"I'm perfectly all right, Darcy," I said. "I was just exploring the estate. I didn't want to wake you and there were these pretty little birds, and butterflies, and I saw two antelope. And then I met Lord Cheriton and he warned me about siafus."

"What's that?"

"Driver ants. They swarm all over you and eat you alive."

"Charming." He put his arm around me. This time I didn't object. "You're freezing cold. Come inside and have something warm to drink."

A little later I had dressed and was drinking a hot cup of tea when Diddy showed up. I told her about the encounter with Lord Cheriton, omitting the graphic details. She gave me a knowing look. "You'll find there are some things around here more dangerous than the animals," she said. "I'd watch my step in future if I were you."

Freddie joined us, already dressed and about to leave. "No, I won't wait for breakfast, thank you, Diddy," he said. "I should be off. Plenty to do today, but I'll see you tomorrow at the polo field." Then I heard him say quietly to Darcy, "I'll be checking out the local airstrips and I'll be in touch."

There was no sign of Cyril, who only got up on mornings when he had to go hunting, so Diddy said. We enjoyed a splendid breakfast of eggs, kidneys, bacon, and then Diddy gave us a tour of the estate.

"These are my racehorses," she said, pointing at four lovely animals in the first field. "My pride and joy."

"Where do you race?" I asked.

"We have race meetings in Nairobi all the time. And down in Nakuru. We're big on betting in the colony." She strode on, so fast it was hard to keep up with her. "And over in this field are the polo ponies. Some are mine; some I stable for other people. Polo is a big part of our lives up here: our main social event. We play polo every Sunday morning and then Idina entertains every Sunday evening. You will play tomorrow, won't you?" she asked, looking back at us. "I'm counting on both of you."

"I'm game," Darcy said. "Georgiana has never played polo before."

"You'll pick it up instantly," Diddy said. "If you want to get your riding breeches on, I'll give you a few pointers now."

I had to confess then that I hadn't thought to bring riding breeches. One doesn't normally on one's honeymoon, does one? I thought this would get me out of the embarrassment of having to play polo but she said, "I expect I can find a pair that will fit you. Come on. Let's go and see."

The rest of the morning was spent with me trying to negotiate a mallet while riding full tilt on a pony. It wasn't easy. I dropped the mallet a few times, hit the pony's leg once and tried to convince Diddy that I'd be a liability to her team. But she wouldn't hear any of my excuses. "You'll find it much easier when you're actually playing," she said. Privately I thought that the sight of a large man charging toward me on a galloping horse would not encourage me to try to get the ball away from him. When we finally went inside for coffee there was another piece of news that didn't thrill me.

"Angel has just sent round a boy with an invitation to dinner tonight," Diddy said. "I told you that everyone would want to get a look at you."

"Lord Cheriton's wife? We're to dine there?" Darcy said. "That's good."

"It will be interesting." Diddy shot me a warning look. "I'm dying to meet these twins of his, and you never know who else will be there. Quite a lively gathering. Not as lively as Idina's party on Sunday night, of course."

"Are we invited to that?" Darcy asked.

"Naturally. Everyone is invited to Idina's parties. I'm pretty sure it won't be your sort of thing, but I do recommend you go once. It's an experience not to be missed."

"Shall you be going?" I asked.

"God no," she replied. "Not my cup of tea at all. Idina and I aren't the best of pals . . . not since we fought over the same man once. And she won. But she'll expect you to be there. It will give you a chance to see the rest of the valley in action."

"It seems as if our honeymoon is turning into one mad social whirl," I said.

I was going to tell Darcy about Lord Cheriton and his advances to me this morning but I thought he might leap to defend my honor and do something rash like punching the man in the nose. We were, after all, only here for a short while. I'd make sure I was never alone with Bwana again!

CHAPTER 13

We are about to go to dinner with Lord
Cheriton, aka Bwana, and his rather
unpleasant children. Darcy seems quite
keen and I can't really tell him why I'm
not. I did tell him about Rowena and her
behavior at school but he thought that
was a lame reason not to want to meet
her now. "You're one up on her," he said.
"You've already snagged a husband, and
a good one too."

So here I was, putting the finishing touches
to my hair and makeup, about to leave for
Lord Cheriton's estate.

"You look very nice," Darcy said, admiring me. "Very chic."

I was wearing the evening pajamas that
Zou Zou had brought me from Paris.

"Thank heavens they are backless," I said,

"because Diddy doesn't seem to have a maid to help me get dressed. I certainly wouldn't want a house servant to do up my buttons."

"That's what you have a husband for." Darcy came over to me and slipped his arms around my waist. "A willing volunteer to dress you, and undress you."

"Darcy, stop it." I slapped his hand as he was getting a little too amorous. "You are spoiling my hair."

"It's all right. It can wait until later," he whispered and let me go. I grabbed the mink stole. We joined Diddy and Cyril, and we set off. The African night was absolute darkness. One of the houseboys went ahead of us, carrying a lantern. Even so there were rustlings and strange noises that filled the night air. I think I heard the distant roar of a lion. I was glad I was with a group of people, even though I told myself I was safely on Diddy's estate.

I had expected Lord Cheriton's bungalow to be grander than Diddy's. But it really wasn't — only bigger. Joseph met us at the front door.

"Welcome, welcome," he said, beaming at us. "Come in. Bwana and memsahib are expecting you."

The room we entered was large but quite

plain, with whitewashed walls, small windows and wooden floors. It was very much the hunting lodge with animal skins on the floor instead of rugs, and impressive animal heads all around the walls, along with native spears and shields. However, there had been an attempt to beautify things, probably by the current Lady Cheriton. There was some good antique furniture — not all from the same period — a couple of large gilt-framed portraits and mirrors on the walls, and vases of flowers everywhere, which created a sweet, almost sickly fragrance that competed with the wood smoke of the fire burning in an enormous rock fireplace. Over the fireplace a pair of impressive tusks was mounted. A line of white-clad servants stood against one wall, while Rupert and Rowena were standing with their father beside the fire. Lord Cheriton looked up as we entered then headed toward us, his arms outstretched. "Here you are. Splendid. Splendid. How are you, Diddy, old chum? And Cyril too. Looking peaky, Cyril. Haven't been out in the sun enough recently, I suspect."

"If you are implying that my safari business is not doing as well as it should you are absolutely wrong, Cheriton," Cyril said. "I've just become rather more choosy with my clientele. And if you really must know, I've already been hired to take the Prince of Wales and his lady love next week."

"That should give you something to put in your gossip column," Bwana said.

"I wouldn't dream of it. One must keep up the pretense that the royal family is beyond reproach." Cyril looked indignant and Bwana laughed.

"You weren't always so noble about what you put in your columns, I seem to remember." He didn't wait for Cyril to reply but turned his attention to us. "And here is the happy couple. How do you do, O'Mara. I've already met your lovely wife. Come and meet Angel and have a drink."

Bwana's wife, the former Angel Trapp, was reclining on a sofa that was covered in zebra skins. "My dear, this is Rowena's old school chum and her new husband, Lady Georgiana and the Honorable Darcy O'Mara."

Angel held out a delicate hand to us. "Delighted to make your acquaintance. Actually delighted to meet anybody from the outside world these days."

"That's what we need, new blood," Bwana said heartily. "I said so to Lady Georgiana this morning. New blood. That's what this colony needs. You should think about it, O'Mara. Still plenty of land to be snapped up and money to be made. You could try coffee or tea. We're a bit too high for coffee but tea should do well here." He didn't wait for Darcy to respond but went on, "I'm thinking of starting a tea plantation myself. If I get it going then Rupert can run it. He'll need to learn how things work around here, since he's my heir." He gave Rupert a hearty slap on the back. "All this will be yours one day, my boy. Not that I intend to go anywhere soon, but you need to get the feel for it while I'm still around. Learn to love it as I do."

"You want me to take over out here, Father?" Rupert looked horrified. "But what about the estate in England? You have just inherited Broughton, you know. Don't you ever think about going home?"

"It's a bloody great monstrosity of a castle on a godforsaken moor," Bwana snapped. "If it wasn't entailed I'd bloody well sell it. And as for going home — my home is here in Kenya. I made that choice long ago when I first arrived and I was the only white man for fifty miles. It was damned hard work, but I stuck to it. I made a life for myself. A damned good life and I expect my son to take over what I've achieved." He looked up angrily. "And from what I see England has gone soft. Lost too many men in the Great

War and has simply given up." He waved a finger at his son. "What England needs is a damned good shaking up. That chap in Germany has the right idea."

"Hitler?" Rupert said. "You think Hitler has the right idea?"

"Of course he does. Pride and military might, that's what a country needs. And being governed by the right people. Those born to rule. No bloody socialists and lower-class intellectuals."

"Hitler seems to me to be a fanatic and a bully," Rupert said. "Britain would never tolerate a leader like that."

"He's a pathetic little man," Rowena agreed. "And he shouts too much."

"Better than that weak and wet Stanley Baldwin who has just been elected," Bwana said. "You wait and see. Hitler is going to shake up Europe."

"Enough politics, Ross," Angel said. "You know that politics bore me. And anyway whatever is going on in Europe means nothing to us, stuck in this backwater."

"On the contrary," Bwana said. "You'd be surprised how important backwaters will be." He looked up suddenly. "What happened to those bloody drinks, Joseph? Come on, boy. We're dying of thirst over here. Bring on the drinks trolley, for God's sake. I think you're half-asleep these days."

Joseph said nothing. His face was impassive as he wheeled the trolley into the center of the room.

"I think it's jolly unfair that Ru should inherit everything," Rowena said. "We are twins, after all, and actually I am older by twenty minutes."

"He's the male, you know that," Angel said in her languid voice that reminded me of Mrs. Simpson. "Everything goes to the eldest male. That's the stupid law everywhere. If I'd had a brother I wouldn't have had a penny of family money. Luckily I didn't." And she smiled.

I studied her. She was not beautiful, a little too skinny with hollow cheeks, also like Mrs. Simpson, but her makeup and hair were flawless. Unlike everyone else I had seen here, she didn't look as if she'd ever been out in the sun. She was wearing an interesting dress with a cape, the sort of thing my friend Belinda might design, and she was dripping with jewels. Her necklace was a mixture of rubies and diamonds and there was a large diamond rock among the many rings on her fingers. The thought crossed my mind that if Rupert were the jewel thief he would have no need of Mr. Van Horn to dispose of his stone. It would be happily welcomed and paid for right here.

She reached out for my hand. "Come and sit next to me."

I took the offered hand and she pulled me down to the sofa beside her. "I love the pajamas," she said. "Are they from Paris?"

"They are," I admitted.

"Chanel?"

"Schiaparelli."

"My dear, I'm impressed."

"They were a wedding present from a very rich friend," I said. "I don't normally dress this way."

"I've stopped keeping up with the latest fashion," she said with a sigh. "What is the point out here? Most of the women dress like men and they have skin like old leather boots. I keep begging Bwana to let us go to Paris or London but he's always too busy with his . . . various pursuits." She shot a critical glance across at him. "We are so far from everything here. You can't imagine how boring it is stuck in the middle of nowhere with only animals to shoot, and only the same few people to talk to. The same boring people. The same corny jokes over and over again."

I didn't know how to answer this. I was sure what she said was true. I glanced across at Darcy. I just hoped he had not been enticed by Bwana's offer to come out here and make a new life. The trouble was that he was exactly the type of person who would flourish out here. A new wave of worry flooded over me. Was the jewel theft just a story, an excuse to get us out here, and was the next surprise he'd spring on me be that he wanted us to settle here? I snuck a glance at him. He was deep in conversation with Lord Cheriton, Diddy and the twins. His head was thrown back and he was laughing heartily, clearly enjoying himself. I pictured a future in which he took to this life like a duck to water and I became like Angel, bored, angry and out of place.

I don't have to agree to anything, I thought. If I don't want to move I'll tell him so. He wouldn't go against the wishes of his wife.

This made me feel a little better. I downed the gin and tonic I had been given. It seemed to be mostly gin with just a hint of tonic and I stifled a cough. Angel drained the last of hers and held out the empty glass for a refill.

"Memsahib wants another?" Joseph asked. "It is almost time for dinner."

"If Memsahib wants another drink, Memsahib gets another bloody drink," Angel said belligerently. I realized she might already have consumed a few. Was this the way she fought off the loneliness and boredom? How awful it must be to be so far from home, so far from the lights and action of America, and to be stuck with a husband who juggled two mistresses. No wonder she drank.

We were called in to dinner. A houseboy waited behind every chair, ready to serve us. I had grown up with servants at Castle Rannoch but never with this many. They were addressed as "boy" but from their faces I could see these were grown men. And it made me feel uneasy the way Bwana barked commands at them, as if he was talking to dogs. The first course was brought — a clear consommé with croutons. This was followed by a fish course in a white sauce, and then large steaks. I didn't think they were beef, but chose not to ask. Not that I would have dared to interrupt! Bwana dominated the conversation, expressing opinions on everything in that big deep voice of his. "Time to toughen you two up," he said to the twins. "Look at you, white as lilies, soft as my best butter. I'd take you on safari but I'm introducing a new bull to the dairy herd. You can come and watch the action if you like. Nothing like watching a good bull in action."

"Really, Ross, is this dinner table talk," Angel said. "Lady Georgiana is used to civilized company."

"Lady Georgiana grew up on a big estate. I'm sure she's seen animals mating before now."

"That may be, but she doesn't want to talk about it at a dinner table."

"And what would you talk about? The latest fashion?"

"As if there would be any point here where nobody would notice if I wore Molyneux or Woolworth."

There was an awkward pause.

"The young couple has been invited to Idina's tomorrow night," Diddy said.

"That will be more of an eye-opener than the bull," Bwana said with a great guffaw of a laugh.

"Shall you be going?" Diddy went on.

"Wouldn't miss it. Don't think I'll bring my offspring, though." He turned to Darcy. "So do you have a safari lined up yet?"

"We've only just arrived," Darcy said. "And we are on our honeymoon. We'd like some time just to ourselves and to explore."

"Safari is perfect for that. In a tent in the middle of nowhere. What could be more romantic? And then bagging your first elephant together? You must take them,

Cyril. And you can take my two along as well."

"Safaris are expensive, Bwana," Cyril said. "Are you planning to hire my services?"

"If you damned well insist," Bwana said. "Not that you're much of a great white hunter. With you around all they'll bag is a wildebeest and only because wildebeests are so stupid that they walk right up to you and don't run when you fire a shot at them."

"I'll have you know I'm a damned good hunter," Cyril said. "One of these days I'll take you on, see who can shoot the most animals."

"I might just take you up on that. Down in the Serengeti." He nodded happily and motioned the waiting servant to fill his plate with another helping and Joseph to refill the wineglasses.

We ate and drank very well that night, then we went back to the room with the fireplace and brandies were served with the coffee. With the warmth of that fire I felt overwhelmingly tired and fuzzy headed. I remembered Diddy's warning about the altitude and going light on the alcohol. We certainly hadn't been doing that this evening. I decided I should go to the bathroom and splash cold water on my face before I passed out or fell asleep. I rose from my chair and whispered my request to Angel.

"Use the one in my bedroom, honey," she said. "That's the closest. Second door on the right."

I followed her directions. The bedroom was not exactly tidy, with various outfits thrown over the backs of chairs. Clearly a lady's maid was not a requirement up here. Queenie could get herself a job and be appreciated, I thought with a smile. I went through to a bathroom with a large claw-footed tub and splashed water on my face.

When I emerged I was startled to see Lord Cheriton standing outside the bathroom door.

"Oh, I'm sorry," I said. "Were you waiting to go in?"

"No, I was waiting for you, you sweet creature," he said. "I haven't had a chance to be alone with you all evening."

"That's because you're the host and I'm with my husband," I said, trying to sidle past him. He was looking at me rather, I imagine, as a lion would be examining a zebra. I glanced uneasily at the door and tried to move past him.

"But you still owe me for saving your life this morning." He blocked off my exit, backing me into a corner. "I always expect debts to be repaid." And he forced his big body against me, half crushing me while his hands took both sides of my face as he attempted to kiss me.

"Oh, come on," he said as I turned my face away and we bumped noses. "Don't play the little innocent with me. You're in Kenya now. You have to learn to play the games our way. A quickie on the bed here and we'll be back before we're missed."

His hands were now definitely wandering as he kept me pinned in place. I had had enough of being polite. Anger overtook any thought that he was my host and I was a guest in his house and it might not be the done thing to bring my knee up where it would hurt most.

I pushed him away with all my strength. "Shame on you," I said. "You have a wife in the next room and two children to whom you're supposed to be setting an example."

He was laughing at my efforts. "That namby-pamby pair? I can't believe they are my spawn. And let me tell you that Angel's not much fun between the sheets either. I meant what I said about new blood, young blood."

"And what makes you think that I'm attracted to you?" I demanded. "I've just married a handsome, young and virile man. Do you think I'd want someone who is old, fat and boorish like you?"

It was lucky I was wearing pajamas and not a long tight-skirted evening dress, which would have restricted my movement. He might be pinning my body but my knee was still free enough to come up sharply and make contact right where it would hurt. He gave a surprisingly high-pitched yowl and doubled over. I pushed past him. As I stalked out of the room I bumped into Rowena, hovering in the hallway outside.

"Still up to your old tricks, spying on other people, Rowena?" I said. "Most of us have outgrown our schoolgirl ways."

I stalked down the hall to rejoin the group, my heart thumping in my chest.

"Darcy, do you mind if we go home now?" I said. "I have an awful headache. I'm afraid the altitude is getting to me."

Darcy gave me a look that understood immediately there was more to this than a headache. Angel and Diddy were kind and solicitous. Angel offered to fetch me aspirin but Darcy said, "I think the best thing for her is to sleep, Angel."

"Of course it is," Diddy agreed. "I'll take her home. We'll have plenty more occasions to meet while they are staying with me. You must come over to lunch when Bwana is showing the twins the estate. We'll have a good chin-wag, just us girls."

As soon as we were alone in our bedroom I told Darcy what had happened. His face flushed with anger.

"The bastard," he said. "We were told he had that sort of reputation. I'm sorry. I should have noticed that he left the room after you did. Don't worry, I'll shadow you every second from now on. And if he tries anything again, I'll kill the bastard."

When I told him my response he burst out laughing. "That's my girl! Good for you, Georgie." He pulled me down to the bed beside him. "I can see I'll have to be careful in making my advances in future. You are clearly a formidable foe."

"You don't ever have to worry," I said. "Your advances will always be welcome!"

CHAPTER 14

Sunday, August 11
At the polo field. Yikes.

I am absolutely dreading this. I know I'll
make a fool of myself. Why can't I learn
to be more assertive and just smile
sweetly and say thank you, but I prefer
not to play. And yet Diddy is our hostess
and she is so jolly insistent.

At ten o'clock on Sunday morning, wearing
breeches and boots that were both too small
for me and one of Darcy's open-necked
shirts, I mounted one of the polo ponies, a
bay called Squibs who seemed to have an
evil gleam in his eye. They are called ponies
but this one looked an awfully long way
from the ground. We followed Diddy's
mount down her driveway as she led a string
of ponies for the other participants. There
was already a lively scene when we arrived

175

at the polo field. Bunting had been draped across the gateway. Several motorcars were parked and their owners, dressed in smart riding gear, were standing around a table, drinking what seemed to be champagne and cocktails — at this hour in the morning. African servants, dressed immaculately in white uniforms, hovered in the background, ready to wait on us.

Diddy was greeted and Darcy and I were scrutinized with interest as we dismounted and tied up the ponies.

"You've brought more players — jolly good show." The speaker was one of the men who had been on the plane with us. Tusker Eggerton, if I remembered correctly. The one whose wife was now, if rumor be correct, fooling around with Bwana. There was no sign of any wife at the moment. Diddy introduced us all around.

"Splendid. Glad you've come. We definitely need fresh blood to improve the quality of our polo," the other man from our flight said. His name was Chops something — Chops Rutherford, that was it — and his wife was smartly kitted out in her riding gear, ready to play polo with us. "I'm afraid we can't start until His Royal Highness gets here."

"The Prince of Wales is coming to play?" I asked.

"Wouldn't miss it for the world," Chops's wife said. "Loves his polo, so he said when we dined with them last night at Tom Delamere's."

"The lady friend is not so keen," Chops muttered. "She proclaimed it to be boring but he begged her to come along and cheer for him. I suppose I shouldn't say it, but he's like a little boy when she's around. She bosses him terribly."

"Be careful what you say. Georgiana is related to him," Pansy Ragg interjected, coming over to join us with her husband in tow.

"Oh, of course you are," Chops's wife, whose name I was desperately trying to remember, said to me. "I read about your wedding in the newspapers. What exactly is your family connection?"

"We're first cousins once removed, I believe," I said.

"Good God, then we're supposed to be curtsying or something," she said.

I laughed. "I'm afraid not. Since my grandmother was not a prince, her offspring didn't keep the HRH."

She laughed too. "That's a relief. I never quite know what to do when one meets royals informally. Although he's jolly nice, isn't he? Easy to get along with."

"Yes, he's really nice," I agreed. "I've always been awfully fond of him."

"Here they are now," someone said, as an open-topped Rolls-Royce came through the gateway.

"Anyone seen Babe?" Tusker said, scanning the scene with a scowl on his large red face. "Is she still in that damned pavilion fixing her hair? Damned bad form not to be here when the prince and Delamere arrive."

The big motorcar came to a halt and I was surprised to see that a young man was driving. He too was dressed ready to play polo and he came around to open the rear door for the prince and Mrs. Simpson. I had heard of Lord Delamere and always thought of him as an older man — a grand old gentleman, unofficial leader of the colony.

"Who is that?" I whispered to Diddy.

"That's Tom Delamere — the new Lord Delamere. His father died and he's taken over the ranch. Awfully nice chap. I'll introduce you."

There was actually no need. The prince spotted me. "Why, it's young Georgie," he said, his face breaking into a big smile. "What a lovely surprise. Wallis tells me you're out on your honeymoon. Congratulations."

This, of course, made me the center of attention, which I hated. I was introduced to Tom Delamere and his wife. Out of the corner of my eye I saw Bwana Hartley come out of the pavilion, followed, after a suitable pause, by a young lady with brassy blond hair and a shirt that was a little too tight and opened a little too low. As she emerged into the sunlight she gave a small self-satisfied smile, like a child who has just raided the biscuit barrel and doesn't think anyone else has seen. Babe, I thought, and glanced around to watch Tusker's red face turn two shades redder. I looked around some more, but I couldn't see Bwana's wife. His children weren't there either. I did, however, notice Pansy Ragg shoot Babe a look of pure venom. I also spotted an older man, dressed rather formally, sitting on the veranda of the pavilion with a drink in his hand.

"That man on the veranda?" I asked Diddy.

"Never seen him before in my life," she replied. "He looks rather lost. Someone's visitor I suppose. I'd better go up and talk to him."

I watched her exchanging pleasantries

with the man and then she came back. "He's visiting from South Africa, so I understand. He rode up from Gilgil in Freddie's car. A Mr. Van Horn. Very strong Afrikaans accent."

Clever Freddie, I thought. Now he and Darcy will be able to see any interactions with all the local residents. Cyril had now arrived too, but refused to play. "Such a brutal game, polo. All that clashing of mallets."

"Darling, you have no compunction in shooting large animals," Diddy said. "And yet you think polo is brutal."

"Put it down to being innately lazy," Cyril said. "Besides, if I am on a team against Bwana I am always tempted to clobber him by mistake."

"Don't you like Bwana?" I asked.

He gave me a pitying look. "Dear girl, who does? The man is poison. He sued me once over a column I'd written about him — all truth, you know . . . well, slightly exaggerated, but he won and I had to pay him damages. It's been mutual loathing ever since."

"If you're not playing you can go and keep Mr. Van Horn company," Diddy said. "Freddie felt sorry for him stuck all alone at the hotel in Gilgil and brought him along."

180

"Then I shall be delighted," Cyril said. "Cape Town. So civilized."

"He's from Johannesburg," Diddy replied with a chuckle.

I watched Cyril slide into the seat beside Mr. Van Horn. Then my attention was turned to the arrival of another motorcar and a collective whisper went around the crowd. "It's Idina."

The object of my mother's loathing climbed out of her car. She was certainly not the vamp I had expected. In fact she was an ordinary-looking middle-aged woman, wearing trousers and an open-necked shirt with a red bandana around her throat. But when she was greeted and her face broke into a smile I could tell why men found her fascinating. You often hear of eyes sparkling. Hers really did. They positively flashed with sex appeal. Fascinating.

"Darlings, I'm sorry I'm late. Awfully bad form, I know," she said. "But we had a touch of trouble with the motor today. Wouldn't start for some reason. But my new chauffeur eventually got it working, didn't you, sweet boy?"

Her chauffeur had also come out of her motorcar and my jaw dropped open when I saw that it was none other than Jocelyn Prettibone. Pansy Ragg was the first to go over to him.

"Well, you've landed on your feet, haven't you?" she said. "Lady Idina's chauffeur? How did you manage that?"

"Rather lucky, what?" he said. "She was in Nairobi yesterday and I was hanging around the club, hoping to meet someone who might offer me a job, and she asked me if I could drive and I said of course I could and she said she had a terrible hangover and was in no condition to drive herself home. So I drove her and she said she liked the look of me so why didn't I stay and make myself useful around the place. So here I am."

He gave a delighted grin.

"You better watch yourself," Pansy said. "Idina eats little boys like you for breakfast and spits out the bones."

"Heavens, she doesn't look the carnivorous type," Jocelyn said. "Besides, she apparently has a chap living with her. A strong and rugged bush pilot. I wouldn't be in the running."

"So where is Langlands?" someone asked Idina. "Don't tell me you've chucked him already?"

"He's off flying somewhere." Idina waved her hand indifferently. "And of course I haven't chucked him. I haven't even broken him in yet!" She had a delightful laugh.

When she was introduced to me she took both my hands. "I know all about you," she said. "Your mother has been as naughty as I have. Rather naughtier, I think, because I've confined my bolts to Englishmen whereas I believe your mother has spread her favors liberally across the globe."

She said this in no way maliciously but rather with a twinge of envy in her voice, so I had to smile and agree she was right. "Her current chap is German, is he not?"

"You're quite well up on things in Europe, Lady Idina," I said.

"Oh, Idina, please, or I'll have to call you 'Lady' too and it's so tiresome, isn't it? Well, one does pop home from time to time, or to Paris. And one hears gossip."

"Except you won't have heard the latest on my mother. The German has broken off the engagement. His father died, he's taken over the business and his mother disapproves of Mummy."

"Goodness, so he's a mama's boy at heart. Then she had a lucky escape." Idina paused, grinning. "One thing I can say about all my husbands is that they have left their mothers nicely far away." She gave my hands a squeeze. "You will come to my party tonight, won't you? I'm counting on you.

You'll have such fun. We always do."

I found myself agreeing that I would. She wasn't the sort of person one could say no to — just like the queen.

The gentlemen had tired of small talk and were keen to get on with the polo. I was assigned to the prince's team, along with Diddy, Darcy, Freddie and Harry Ragg. Be grateful for small mercies, I told myself. At least I wouldn't have to risk tackling the heir to the throne and inadvertently knocking him from his horse. Squibbs bucked and tried to bite my toe as I mounted. I had been right in thinking him to be bad tempered. My heart was beating rather fast as we went out onto the field and lined up facing the other team. Four chukkers of seven minutes. I just hoped I could survive that long.

The referee's whistle blew. Ponies surged forward. There were great thwacks as mallet hit ball and shouts of "Good shot. Well played," from around the field. My strategy was to hover in the background and hope that the ball never came near me. Squibbs had other ideas. He hurled himself into the fray and no amount of tugging on the reins would stop him. We were heading straight for two members of the opposing team. I actually closed my eyes, felt my arm jerk and heard a thwack.

"Oh, well done, Georgiana," called Babe's voice. "That's the ticket."

Apparently I had stolen the ball. But Squibbs would not rest on his laurels. He charged against the opposition again. This time my mallet caught up with Tusker Eggerton's.

"Steady on, old girl," he shouted as I nearly toppled him from the saddle.

"I'm frightfully sorry," I called back.

"Don't apologize," Harry Ragg shouted. "Brilliant play. Perfectly legitimate." He swung his pony close to mine. "I must say you're a little firecracker. Glad you're on our team."

I managed to stay in my seat and we won the match. By a miracle I didn't unseat the heir to the throne and have him trampled to death. I was congratulated as I slid gratefully from the saddle.

"Well played, young Georgie," David said as he led his mount beside mine. "Too bad girls aren't welcome at our club in England."

I gave a silent prayer of thanks. Mrs. Simpson pushed her way through the crowd and the horses and took his arm. "Let someone else take care of the horse, David," she said. "I've been without you for too long, and

I'm dying of boredom. Such a stupid infantile game."

"Oh no, Wallis, it's jolly good fun," David said as she dragged him off.

As they walked away I thought I heard her say, "Well, make the most of it because when we're married . . ." And the rest of the conversation was lost in the crowd.

I found, to my embarrassment, that I was absolutely exhausted. I was finding it hard to breathe and was quite dizzy. For a horrible moment I thought I might faint. Diddy came to my rescue. "Are you all right?" she asked.

"I don't know why I'm so wiped out," I said.

She smiled. "It's the altitude. It takes a while to get used to. We are at eight thousand feet after all. Just take it easy for a couple of days and go light on the alcohol. Here, let me take care of your pony. You go and join the others and have some lunch."

I let her lead Squibbs away. A long table had been set up with a magnificent spread on it: salads, smoked trout, cold meats, fruits that were unknown to me. And at one end were glasses of champagne. I watched Mrs. Simpson lead David up to the veranda, away from the rest of us, and I remembered that I had been commissioned by the queen to keep an eye on them. I went over to Lord Delamere.

"Lord Delamere," I began hesitantly.

"Tom, please," he said. "We're quite informal here. Otherwise I'd have to call you Lady Georgiana and that's such a mouthful. Besides, you outrank me. And I don't like being reminded of that."

"I'm only the wife of an Honorable these days," I said and he smiled.

"Good chap, your Darcy. I've met him before."

The fact that he knew Darcy and everyone spoke highly of him made me decide to take him into my confidence.

"I have a favor to ask," I said in a low voice. "When the queen knew I was coming out here she asked me to keep an eye on the Prince of Wales."

He looked amused. "What did she expect you to do — guard him from wild beasts?"

"Exactly," I said. "At least one wild beast. It's his lady friend. The queen fears that her divorce from her latest husband has now gone through and she's terrified they will get married in secret and then present the marriage as a fait accompli."

Tom Delamere actually laughed. "And you're supposed to leap in and stop it?"

I laughed too. "I can hardly see myself doing that, can you?"

"Anyway, you don't need to worry," he said. "Because I'm the justice of the peace around here so they would need me to marry them. And that's just not going to happen. So relax and enjoy your honeymoon."

"I hope so," I said. "It all seems rather . . . unsettling out here."

"The wildlife, you mean?"

"Both human and animal."

He laughed again. "Yes, we are rather wild. At least some of us. But you have the dashing Darcy to protect you. You don't need to worry."

"That's true," I said and suddenly I felt a whole lot better. Darcy was here. I really did have nothing to worry about.

CHAPTER 15

August 11

Heading for Idina's house, called Clouds. I'm a little worried about this. Even Darcy seemed reluctant and he normally loves a good party. But Idina seemed very nice and if other people drink too much then we don't have to. Furthermore I've just discovered that one stays the night so we don't have to drive back in the dark, which had been one of my concerns. So all is good.

"Is Idina's house far away?" I asked Diddy.

"Right at the other end of the valley. A good fifteen miles I'd say."

"Oh, so how are we going to get there?" I asked. "It's a long way for one of your staff to drive us."

"Darlings, I'll give you the motorcar for the night. I won't be going anywhere and

Cyril has declared he has had enough of Idina's high jinks."

"Always the same high jinks, which makes it terribly boring," Cyril said. "Not my cup of tea, at all. Besides, I promised I'd show that Mr. Van Horn a little of our Kenyan wildlife."

I saw Darcy look up sharply. "You'll be driving him?"

"Freddie Blanchford has volunteered to drive. I'll just be the knowledgeable guide. Nothing too taxing: a few elephants, hippos, that sort of thing. Nothing he doesn't already have in South Africa, but he made a comment that their wildlife was superior so I felt the honor of Kenya was at stake."

"What was he like?" Darcy asked. "It was good of you to talk to him."

"A little pedantic, if you ask me. As so many Afrikaners are. And opinionated on the virtues of South Africa and its treatment of the native tribes versus our handling of them. He thinks we're too soft."

"Did he talk to you about his work at all?" Darcy asked. "What line of business is he in?"

"Real estate, I believe. He travels to Europe selling properties to rich Europeans."

"Real estate?" I started to say, and got a

warning look from Darcy.

"Oh, so he's come here to speculate on our property, has he?" Diddy asked.

"He claims it's a holiday, but one never knows." Cyril smiled. "I must say young Freddie is taking good care of him. I told Freddie I'd be happy to drive him around in my ancient safari vehicle but Freddie said he was on the spot and it would save me driving down to Gilgil."

We went to our room to pack for the night.

"I thought you were sure he was in diamonds," I said to Darcy as soon as we had closed our door. "Is it possible you've got the wrong man?"

"Not at all. He clearly doesn't want to reveal his true identity. Smart of Freddie to volunteer to drive them."

"But Cyril can't be mixed up in your jewel theft, can he?" I asked. "He's been here all the time."

"That's true," Darcy admitted thoughtfully. "But he seemed rather eager to chat with the man this morning, which I felt was a little out of character."

"If he had the jewel he could have passed it over while we were playing polo," I said. "Then they wouldn't want to meet again."

"Again that's true. But there is something going on I'm not quite sure about."

"Perhaps Freddie has enlisted Cyril to work for the government."

Darcy chuckled at this. "Cyril is probably the last man who would want to work for the common good. He's out for Cyril. That's patently obvious."

I packed my nightgown and Darcy's pajamas, our robes, slippers and toilet bags.

"What are we going to wear?" I asked. "Proper party clothes?"

"I think so. White tie for me and long frock for you."

"What about those evening pajamas?"

Darcy frowned. "I'm not an expert on women's fashions but I'd say they'd be perfect."

"But driving back in the morning? It will be cold," I said. "Should we take along trousers and a jersey, do you think?"

"Good idea." He nodded. "You see, you don't need a maid after all."

"If Queenie were here she'd probably pack one shoe and no stockings," I said. "And a suit jacket but no skirt."

"At least she's turning into quite a good cook," Darcy said. "I know you'd hate to give her the sack. Now you don't have to."

"Your uncle and aunt would love to have her back," I said. "How funny that people are now fighting over her."

We were not expected at Idina's until eight. Diddy gave us a late high tea with a boiled egg and watercress sandwiches. "You probably won't eat until ten or eleven," she said. "And you'll need something in your stomachs for all the alcohol."

The night air flowing down from the mountains felt icy as we climbed into Diddy's open-topped Riley. I have to confess I was feeling apprehensive about this — not just the journey in the dark on a horrendous road with the possibility of elephants stepping out from behind bushes, but the party itself, which was too wild for Diddy. I told myself not to worry. Darcy was with me. He wouldn't drink too much or behave in a silly fashion.

And so we set off. The headlamps cut a small beam of light into absolute darkness. Darcy drove carefully, swerving to avoid the worst of the potholes and boulders lying on the road. Even so we bounced around a bit and I held on to the dashboard and side door to steady myself. After a couple of miles the headlamps picked up a huge dark shape in the road ahead of us.

"Elephant!" I grabbed at Darcy. We jerked to a stop. I had seen elephants in the London Zoo but this one was enormous. It turned its head with its big curving tusks toward us and gave us a long stare. We sat holding our breath, not knowing what to do if it charged at us. I felt horribly vulnerable in the open motor. It seemed as if hours passed. I could actually hear its stomach rumbling. Then it crossed the road as if we were a minor annoyance not worth bothering with and disappeared into the darkness. I could hear foliage being trampled as it went on its way.

"Well, now we've got a good tale to tell when we get home," Darcy said. We looked at each other and gave a relieved chuckle.

About halfway there we came to a place where the road narrowed as it passed between large boulders. A small stream flowed over the roadbed and we had to slow to a crawl to negotiate it. Again I held my breath expecting a leopard to leap down on us. But we made it safely through and came to Idina's house without further incident. Several other motorcars were parked outside the entrance. We found ourselves arriving at the same time as Pansy and Harry Ragg.

"Hello, my sweets," Pansy called, waving merrily. "Come to be naughty with the rest of us?" She turned to Harry. "Don't scowl, darling. It will give you wrinkles and I don't want to be stuck with an old husband."

"It looks as if you are stuck with me,

whether you like it or not, my darling," he said. "So I'm supposed to smile and say what ripping fun, am I?"

"That's exactly what you are supposed to say," Pansy went on. "You know I adore you."

She put a hand up to touch his cheek. I couldn't see his expression in the dark.

A tall Somali servant admitted us at the main gate. The house was another long, low bungalow, but this one was built around a courtyard with rooms around three sides. We were shown to one of the bedrooms and told to deposit our things there before we were received by Idina. The bedroom was furnished in a more feminine style than Diddy's: satin drapes tied back at the windows, satin quilt and pillows on the bed and . . .

"Golly," I said, quite forgetting again. "There's a mirror on the ceiling."

Darcy looked up, amused.

"Why would anyone want a mirror on the ceiling?" I went on. "You can't actually see how you look from there and you'd get a frightful crick in your neck looking up."

Darcy laughed now. "You really are a sweet innocent, aren't you? You'll notice it's right above the bed. There are some people who like to look at themselves when they are engaged in . . ."

"Golly," I said again and turned bright red. Darcy ruffled my hair.

"Don't worry, I promise we'll turn the lights off — unless you want to?"

"No!" I said, making him laugh harder.

"I was going to say you were just like your royal great-grandmother, but from what I've heard she really enjoyed that sort of thing."

"She adored Prince Albert."

"And her Scottish lad? And what about Abdul the Indian?"

"I'm sure her relationship with them was one of mistress and servant," I said, making him laugh harder.

"Not exactly the best choice of words there, my sweet."

I went to hit him. He grabbed my wrist. "Careful or we might be making use of that mirror," he whispered.

Further exploration revealed a bathroom with a huge tub big enough for two people and plenty of hot water. We took off our coats and I spruced up my hair and makeup after the drive in the open motorcar, then, feeling apprehensive, we were led to Idina. Instead of being taken to the double doors at the center of the quadrangle we were led past them to a door on the right. Pansy and Harry Ragg appeared from another bedroom and were also led to this same door.

"So Idina is receiving visitors the way she always does?" Harry said, with a derisive chuckle.

"Yes, Bwana Ragg. Please enter," the Somali servant said.

We entered a larger and more opulent bedroom. Lots of wine-colored satin and another mirror on the ceiling, but the room was empty.

"Through here, darlings," a voice called, echoing as if in a cave. Pansy and Harry obviously knew the drill. They gave us a knowing look and went ahead. The bathroom was enormous and now quite steamy. On the far wall was an enormous green onyx bathtub with water pouring from a bronze lion's head on the wall. And in the bath lay Idina, completely naked. I swallowed back the word "golly" before I could say it this time.

"Well, here you all are. Welcome!" she said. She stood up and reached for a towel. "Darcy and Georgie, how lovely that you came. We're going to have such a good time, aren't we, Pansy?"

"I'm not sure yet," Pansy said. "Is that Babe person coming?"

"Tusker and Babe always come. You know that."

"Bwana's coming, is he?" Pansy asked and I detected a note of wistfulness in her voice.

"He promised to. But not his offspring, apparently. He claims it wouldn't be their sort of thing, but I rather think it's because it would hamper his own style." She was still holding the towel in one hand and she danced it over the surface of the water.

"He's bringing Angel?"

"I assume so. Annoying, as it makes the number uneven . . . but then again . . ." Idina finally put the towel around her and tucked it over her breasts like a sarong. "Go through to the drawing room. The drinks table is ready and waiting."

Darcy and I exchanged a glance when we were safely outside in the dark again.

"I'm not sure this was such a good idea," he whispered to me. "I was afraid it might be like this, from the rumors I'd heard. But it seemed churlish to refuse at the time, didn't it? At least we have the motorcar and we can escape if we have to."

"Imagine receiving your guests in your bathtub," I whispered.

"Yes, but I have to say she has a damned good figure for a woman her age," he whispered back. "You must tell your mother. It will make her livid."

"I don't know about that. Mummy has a

good figure too. But I don't think she's ever received her guests in her bath. I must ask her. Perhaps she's kept her wilder exploits from her daughter." I remembered some very explicit photographs I'd once had to retrieve for her.

CHAPTER 16

August 11

> At Clouds, the home of Lady Idina. I'd give
> her a surname but I haven't been able to
> find out who she is married to at the mo-
> ment. I'm not sure I'm ready for this. If it
> starts with a mirror on the ceiling and a
> hostess naked in her bathtub where on
> earth can it go from here?

Darcy was chuckling as the central front
doors were opened and we followed Harry
and Pansy Ragg into a big room dominated
by a great marble fireplace. No expense had
been spared on this house. It was furnished
tastefully with plenty of soft sofas and
chairs, as well as the required animal skins
on the floor and trophies on the walls. In
the center of the room a well-stocked drinks
table had been set up, around which several
people were already standing. There was

already a fug of cigarette smoke and I blinked a little as I looked around, recognizing Tusker and Babe, Chops and Mrs. Chops, whom I seemed to remember was called Camilla.

"Jolly good. The newcomers are here," Tusker said, nodding approval at us.

"Brave of you to come, darlings." Camilla Rutherford gave me a knowing look. "I suspect you'll learn more tonight than you have on your honeymoon so far."

I didn't know what to say to this and glanced around the room. There were two couples I hadn't seen before — a sophisticated-looking pair, the man with a thin Ronald Colman mustache and the woman small, slim and dark, not unlike Mrs. Simpson. In a gloved hand she held a cigarette in a long ebony holder. The other pair looked larger and more countrified, not as fashionably dressed, as if they might be farmers.

"And who do we have here, then?" Harry Ragg asked. "I don't think we've met. Not one of Idina's normal crowd."

"Mr. and Mrs. Atkins and Mr. and Mrs. Tomlinson," Chops Rutherford said. "All the way out from Nairobi."

Hands were shaken and polite how-do-you-dos muttered. When the larger man demanded, "What about a drink, then?" he spoke with a northern accent, reinforcing that this was not one of the Happy Valley aristocrats. I wondered why he was here. "I can't stand here any longer with no drink in my hand," he said. "We've had a long drive, you know."

It took me a moment to notice that the attendant at the table was not a smartly dressed African servant but Jocelyn Pretti-bone, now wearing evening dress and looking extremely uncomfortable.

"Oh rather. What can I get you?" he asked.

Mr. Atkins, the man with the mustache, who was standing closest to the drinks table, stepped in to be served first.

"Make mine a pink gin and the memsahib will have a white lady." The man barked the orders and I saw Jocelyn wince.

"Sorry, I've no idea what those things are," he said.

"What sort of bartender are you, for God's sake?" Mr. Atkins demanded.

"Actually I'm not a bartender at all," Jocelyn said, his accent several degrees higher in social standing than the red-faced man's.

"Are you taking the mickey? Aping your betters?"

"Gosh no," Jocelyn said. "I'm actually

202

here only because I helped Lady Idina out with her motorcar and she seems to have taken a fancy to me."

"Has she, by George?" The man shot his wife a horrified look. "Snatching from the cradle now. I told you that pilot chap wouldn't last two months."

"Oh, no, crikey, not that way," Jocelyn stammered. "Not like that at all. Just that she felt sorry for a poor lost chap in Nairobi and is letting me help out here, driving her around and things, until I get on my feet."

"Well, you won't get on your feet in a hurry if you can't make a decent drink," Mr. Atkins said. "What are you doing out here anyway? You don't seem the type."

"Got kicked out by the pater. Third son, don't you know, and not much use at most things. So here I am for the moment."

"For heaven's sake, Harry, put the poor boy out of his misery and make us all a drink," Pansy said, not unkindly. "Show him how to mix a cocktail. Then at least he can get a job in a London nightclub when he goes back home."

I watched as Jocelyn tried to follow instructions and mix cocktails. It was amusing to note the various expressions from the assembled guests — amusement, frustration, annoyance and superiority. Definitely the last. I also had time to note that the whole party was frightfully well-dressed. The outfits came from Paris and the women were sparkling with impressive jewels. Any one of them might have been interested in what the jewel thief was bringing to Kenya, I thought. Then I glanced at Mrs. Rutherford and did a double take. What I had taken for a scarf around her neck suddenly moved and I saw that it was a live snake. A large, fat snake.

Darcy noticed at the same moment. "Good God. Do you always wear a snake as an accessory?" he said. "Is that sort of thing expected in Africa?"

Chops Rutherford chuckled. "It's Idina's pet python. Camilla has grown rather fond of it, but Idina doesn't want to part with it. So I suppose I'll have to catch her one when I'm next on safari."

"A little snake, darling, so I can tame him like this one. Although Idina feeds hers on baby mice. I'm not sure I could do that. I'd feel too sorry for the mice."

"Camilla is a great animal lover," Chops said. "You can't take her on safari or she won't let you shoot anything! We've a lion cub in the house at the moment as a pet. I don't know what we are going to do exactly when it grows up and starts eating the servants."

"Get more servants, old man," Tusker Eggerton chuckled, coming to join the conversation. "Ten a penny around here. And they are always breeding like rabbits."

This statement seemed to be accepted by all of them. I tried to conceal my shock. I wondered if the African servants, standing in attendance around the room, spoke enough English to understand and what they thought of the settlers' rudeness.

With Harry's help Jocelyn was able to hand everybody a cocktail, with only one accidental showering of ice by Jocelyn. It was unfortunate that the ice showered over the testy Mr. Atkins and his Mrs. Simpson look-alike wife.

"The boy's an idiot," I heard the man say as they removed themselves hastily from the table, brushing the ice from his white evening jacket. "In all probability he's Idina's long-lost child from one of her affairs or marriages, come back to haunt her!" And those around him laughed nervously, knowing this might well be true. I studied Jocelyn and wondered if it was. Kenya did seem an unlikely place to send someone as hapless as he.

Darcy and I settled on gin and tonics. It

seemed simpler that way. While they were being poured Idina joined us, looking absolutely stunning in emerald green silk pajamas, with a front so low-cut that it plunged almost to the waist and left absolutely nothing to the imagination. She was certainly not wearing a brassiere. And around her neck a string of emeralds that sparkled in the candlelight. "You've started drinking without me, you naughty children," she said. "Now I'll have to down them quickly to catch up. A sidecar please, Jocelyn, my darling."

Jocelyn shot Harry a quick look of desperation and Harry stepped in to whisper instructions.

"Ah, you've met the Tomlinsons and Atkinses?" Idina went up to both couples and bestowed kisses all around. "Lovely. Splendid. I bumped into them at the Muthaiga Club when I was last in Nairobi. They'd heard about my famous parties, naturally, and wanted to see for themselves." She went over to the drinks table, accepted the cocktail Jocelyn offered her and downed it in one go, holding out her glass for a refill. "I'm sure Nairobi is too dull for words these days. Since old Lord D died. He was such a live wire, wasn't he? Remember when he rode his horse into the dining room at the club? And leaped the tables? His son is a little too straightlaced for me."

"We hear the Prince of Wales is staying with him." Mrs. Atkins, the woman who resembled Mrs. Simpson, gave a knowing smile. "Is he not coming tonight? I sort of hoped it might be fun if . . ."

"I'm sure the Prince of Wales would have adored to come, darlings — been here like a shot — but he was reined in by a certain woman. She doesn't like to share."

They all laughed at this.

"And the new Lord Delamere is decidedly stuffier than his father. We hear he is keeping the prince suitably captive," she went on.

"That's an awful pity," Mr. Atkins said. "We only came because Diana was hoping to meet the prince again."

"We had such a jolly time in Nairobi when he was here a few years ago," the wife said. "But he traveled alone in those days, didn't he? And he knew how to party as well as any of us. Remember when he threw all those gramophone records out the window because he couldn't find the one he wanted?"

"And he went off for a quickie with Beryl in the middle of dinner?" Her husband gave a dry little chuckle, such that I wasn't quite sure whether he approved of this or not.

"And now he's shackled by that dreadful American woman." His wife sighed. "I wonder if it was his idea or Mrs. Simpson's for her to fly out to join him?"

"He was pining for her, poor little boy," Idina said. She had absently removed the python from Camilla Rutherford's neck and was draping it around her own. The forked tongue flicked as the python regarded the company with its black beady eyes.

"The queen will be furious," she continued. "Remember how she banished Beryl from England after she heard about the prince's carrying-on with her?"

"And his brother," Harry Ragg chimed in. "Don't forget his brother George who came with him. He was another wild one, wasn't he? I don't hold out much hope for the future of the monarchy."

"The Prince of Wales will shape up when he has to," Idina said with confidence. "They always do. Look at dear old King Edward VII. He was the most profligate playboy but then was dearly loved the short time he was king."

"Where's Bwana Hartley?" Mr. Tomlinson, the stocky farmer, looked around. "You said he was going to be here. Sheila wanted to see him again, now that he's become a lord, don't you know. And we hear he's the life and soul of the party, what?"

"Oh, you know our Bwana, do you?" Pansy asked.

"Oh yes. We've met on several occasions," the man said. "Long ago now, when he was just another simple farmer like me." He glanced at his wife. She gave him what seemed to be a cold stare. "Looking forward to seeing him again."

"He should be here," Idina said. Then her face broke into a big smile as the front door opened, sending in a blast of cold air. "Ah, here he is now, the naughty man, keeping us waiting."

Bwana came into the room, looking somehow out of place in white tie, like a wild beast suddenly domesticated. I was still taking in what Mr. Tomlinson had said — that his wife wouldn't come unless Bwana was there. It seemed that Bwana spread his favors over a wide circle.

"Sorry, Idina, my love," Bwana said as he crossed the room to her. "I know I'm late. Please forgive me. But I have brought a case of your favorite bubbly in the back of the car, so I hope I am forgiven."

"How could one resist you?" Idina gave him a more-than-friendly kiss. "And where is Angel?"

"Wouldn't come. She wasn't feeling well. She's been off her food lately and really did look peaky tonight. So it's just me. I'm sorry if that's messed things up."

"On the contrary, it makes our numbers even, which is splendid. Although of course sometimes it's a little more fun if we have to share, isn't it?" She went over to the bar where Jocelyn was still trying valiantly to be a bartender. "This lovely young man could always take Angel's place," Idina said, stroking Jocelyn's hair. "I'm sure he'd look divine in makeup and a brassiere."

"I say, steady on." Jocelyn turned bright red. "I may look a bit poncey but actually I'm quite a normal sort of chap, you know. Fancy the girls and all that."

"Isn't he a peach?" Idina chuckled.

"Enough of that talk. You know me, Idina. I don't share." Bwana scowled at her.

"Sometimes you do, sweetheart," she said. "I'd say you were very good at sharing. Always have been. Has Angel found out yet? And under her very nose." She gave him a mischievous grin, her eyes flirting with him.

"You are a wicked and dangerous woman," Bwana said. "Anyway, there are times when I don't feel like sharing. There are certain delicacies that I want all to myself. I'm a bit greedy that way." Babe giggled, Pansy glared at her, the new farmer's wife, Sheila, looked coy but I saw to my horror that he was looking at me. I glanced across at Darcy but he didn't seem to have noticed. Hadn't I made it absolutely clear that I was not interested in his attentions? Surely that wasn't the reason he hadn't brought Angel with him!

He seemed to notice the rest of the crowd now and I saw him react with surprise. "Well, well, Tomlinson. You are the last person I expected to see here. Shouldn't have thought this was your sort of thing."

"It probably isn't. But Sheila was curious."

Bwana's gaze turned to the farmer's wife. "Hello, Sheila. Faring well, I see. Put on a bit of weight but haven't we all?" And he patted at his own paunch. His gaze moved on. "Pansy? How are you, my sweet?"

"Oh, just peachy, thank you, darling. Never been better." Her voice was icy and smooth.

"Harry, old man." Bwana nodded to him.

"Come and have a drink." Idina slipped her arm through his and dragged him toward the drinks table, maybe sensing tension ahead. A gramophone was wound up and dance music was played. Darcy whisked me to dance before anyone else could, for

211

which I was truly grateful.

"They are a rum lot, aren't they?" he said. "Most of them are middle-aged. You'd have thought they might have moved past this sort of behavior by now."

I still wasn't quite sure what they had meant about sharing. Sharing what?

"If you're tired of booze there's food in the dining room or if you prefer something a little more piquant you'll find it in the library at the back," Idina said.

I was realizing that I was hungry and wanted to see what the delicious things in the library might be, but Darcy held me back. "Don't go through. It's bound to be drugs."

"Drugs?" I tried to peek through that open door, where some of the participants were now going.

He nodded. "Cocaine. It's a major sport out here. In fact . . ." He put his mouth to my ear. "I was wondering whether Van Horn might be a supplier and not in the diamond business at all. Why else would he have come to a polo match? It's not something the Afrikaners are fond of."

"Oh, I see." Of course immediately I found myself wondering whether the whole reason for this trip had not been a jewel theft after all, or whether Darcy was after bigger game — international drug smuggling. It had always seemed to me that a local policeman could track down a jewel thief better than Darcy could, especially when we were essentially trapped at Diddy's estate.

Several of the couples had now gone into that back room and the door closed behind them. Darcy was still holding me close to him, dancing with me.

"Do you think one of them is the jewel thief?" I asked. "And do you think the jewel might change hands in there?"

"I don't think any of them could afford that sort of stone," Darcy whispered. "Besides, what would be the point out here in the middle of nowhere? You couldn't wear a bloody great stone without attracting attention."

"Angel does," I said.

"Yes, I noticed that," Darcy muttered, swinging me around as other people came too close. "If her stepson, Rupert, is our thief and brought the jewel out to her, there's not much anyone can do about it, unless we get a search warrant or she wears the damned thing."

"What if he's not really her stepson?" I asked as the thought occurred to me.

Darcy gave me a look of surprise.

"Bwana said he hadn't seen them in ages. What if they are imposters — jewel thieves who chose to come out here, knowing that Angel would buy the precious stone?"

Darcy digested this, then shook his head. "Frankly, my darling, she may be rich but I doubt she has the sort of money to buy that diamond. It's one of a kind. Either the buyer is going to be a sheik or a film star or someone like Van Horn is going to have it cut into several new stones and sold that way."

"That would be an awful pity if it's a fabulously rare stone," I said.

"I agree. But thieves generally don't care."

"So you don't think that the stone is going to be passed on at this party?"

He shook his head. "If I were selling it, I'd do so in private. There would be no need to take a risk at a party like this. You drive to an estate, you do the deal and nobody sees."

"Nobody sees what?"

I hadn't realized we had drifted close to Chops Rutherford and his wife. "You're talking about what goes on here? We all have conveniently bad memories the next morning. It's only harmless fun, you know. But I don't approve of what's going on in that room now. Can't abide the stuff myself."

He downed the contents of the glass he was holding. "It's not natural. And what's wrong with getting blotto on gin? Good stuff, gin." The way he slurred his speech indicated he was halfway to getting blotto.

"I don't know about you, but I'm starving," his wife said, tugging at his arm. "One does need to work up a little stamina for what's coming, doesn't one?" She gave a nervous giggle then dragged her husband toward the dining room.

"Shall we get something to eat too?" Darcy asked.

"Oh yes. Good idea." There was safety in food, I thought. We followed the Rutherfords. There was a fabulous cold meal on the table: trout in aspic, game birds, salads, fruits. We both helped ourselves to large plates and ate happily, washing it down with glasses of ice-cold white wine. I was feeling quite content by the time we rejoined the company. Idina emerged from that back room, now very animated and laughing loudly. "Such fun," she was saying, "Such bloody good fun." Then she clapped her hands. "Games! It's time for party games."

Bwana came out of the back room right behind her.

"How's the dairy business, Bwana?" Mr. Tomlinson asked, almost belligerently. "Going well, is it?"

"Splendidly, thank you. I've got a damned fine bull, as you know."

Mr. Tomlinson's face, already red from years in the sun, turned several shades redder. "Of course I damned well know," he said.

"But I'd say it was tit for tat, wouldn't you?" Bwana said with a grin. "Damned fine milk cow?"

Tomlinson took a step forward. His wife grabbed at his sleeve and put herself between the two men.

"That's enough, Dickie. Calm down. Where are these children of yours, Bwana?" she asked. "We heard they'd come out to visit."

"And we wanted to see for ourselves what kind of creation you've spawned," her husband added. "Didn't we, Sheila?"

"Not sure I can answer that yet, old chap," Bwana said. "Certainly not chips off the old block. Refused to come with me tonight after Angel told them about our little get-togethers."

"That woman is a spoilsport," Tomlinson muttered, clearly drunk or high on cocaine, or both by now. "A killjoy. That's what she is. Time to show the young'uns a bit of life, that's what I say."

"I suppose she's got a point," Bwana said, grinning. "After all they don't know me from Adam. I don't want them to think their old man is a cad."

"Even if he is," Pansy muttered.

"Stop talking and let's start playing," Idina said, sounding now like a spoiled child. "So what shall we play?" she asked. "The sheet game? The feather game?"

"Not the sheet game. Too humiliating," Tusker said. "I still remember one of the comments about me from last time."

There was general laughter and derisive remarks about this.

"What's the sheet game?" I asked Pansy Ragg, who was standing beside me.

"Oh, great fun, darling," she whispered into my ear. "A sheet is held up with holes in it. And the men display a certain part of their anatomy through the holes and we women have to guess who is which. Poor old Tusker. He was having a bad night and we made rather rude comments. I think it put him off his oats for weeks."

I was confused. What were they talking about? A foot? A nose? Then suddenly I remembered that mirror on the bedroom ceiling. Golly. Even though nobody was looking at me, I felt myself blushing bright red. Was this really what I thought it was?

Surely not, I thought. People didn't really . . .

"Let's play the feather game," Babe said. "I've heard about it but I haven't yet seen it in action."

"Oh yes, the feather game. Such fun," Idina agreed with enthusiasm. "One of my favorites. So deliciously random."

"How do you play it?" I asked.

"You have to blow feathers across the table," Harry Ragg said. He still didn't look as if he was enjoying himself; more like he wished himself somewhere else. "Rather silly, if you ask me."

"Men on this side, women on the other," Idina instructed. "Jocelyn, bring the box of feathers from my bedroom, darling. It's on my bed."

"Oh, that sounds like fun." I went to take my place at the table, but Darcy grabbed my arm and yanked me back. "Georgiana, no. It's not our sort of thing."

"But blowing feathers sounds harmless enough," I said, giving him a questioning look. "What's wrong with it?"

He leaned closer and whispered to me. "The person the feather lands on is the person you sleep with. The men compete by blowing their feathers at the woman they want."

"Oh golly." I gave him a horrified look and stepped away from the table.

He took my arm firmly and marched me over to Idina. "Idina, Georgie and I are newlyweds. I don't think we want to participate, so if you'll excuse us, we'll be off to our own room."

Idina draped her arms around his neck. "Oh dear, and I was so hoping to score you tonight, darling boy. I can tell you've been around the block a few times and I'm sure it would have been absolutely divine." She was pressing her body up against him in the most provocative way. I resisted the urge to yank her away. She was our hostess after all. "What a pity, but I do understand. I didn't want anyone else for at least a month or so after I married each of my husbands," Idina said. Then she put a hand to her mouth and giggled again. "I tell a lie. I had a quick go with an old boyfriend when I was supposed to be changing into my going-away clothes after the wedding ceremony once. But that was just for old times' sake." She released Darcy, turned to me and stroked my cheek. "Anyway, my sweet innocents, off you go then and have some wild and unbridled sex in your own room. We usually meet around ten for breakfast, but if you want to eat earlier the boys will take care of you." She left us and took her place at the table, saying, "The man who gets me tonight is a lucky fellow. I'm feeling very randy."

I can't tell you how jolly glad I was when Darcy led me from that room. I was in a state of shock. I had no idea such things went on.

CHAPTER 17

Monday morning, August 12

On the way home from Idina's party. I have
to confess I'm still in a state of shock
and embarrassment. Either I am completely naïve or this is not normal behavior in polite society!

I'm sure it doesn't go on all the time in
England. Well, apart from my mother, of
course! It must be because we are so
isolated and far from civilization here.

I have to report that Darcy and I did not
have wild and unbridled sex that night, or
any kind of encounter at all, for that matter.
I felt far too inhibited, knowing what was
going on in the rooms around us, as well as
with that mirror on the ceiling above us. I
wondered where Bwana's feather had
landed. Pansy would be livid if it landed on

Babe, I thought. And what about Sheila, the farmer's wife? She didn't look the type to be swapping partners, and that solid farmer husband did seem rather jealous. I tried not to imagine all those people making love to someone else's wife, and I thanked my lucky stars that I was with Darcy. He might have had some wild flings in his previous life but I didn't think he'd ever want to behave the way those people were acting now. At least I jolly well hope he wouldn't!

I don't think either of us slept much. I was conscious of distant noises — not just the strange animal noises of the African night but other kinds of unsettling sounds. A shout, a laugh, a door slamming. Footsteps on the veranda outside our room. Someone running.

"Are you asleep, Darcy?" I whispered as the burst of birdsong told me that it was almost day.

"Not really," he confessed.

"Can we just slip away and go home now?" I asked. "I really don't want to face those people at breakfast and I don't want to wait until ten to say good-bye to Idina. If we go now we can write her a little thank-you note."

"For once I don't think that it should say the customary 'Thank you for having me,' "

Darcy said with a chuckle.

" 'Thank you for not having me'?" I suggested and we both laughed. I snuggled against him. "Oh, Darcy, I am glad I'm with you. What awful people they are. Surely married couples don't behave like that in England or Ireland."

"Of course they do, my sweet," he said. "As soon as our honeymoon is over I'll be all for swapping you at every soiree."

"You won't, will you?" I asked and he burst out laughing.

"Just pulling your leg," he said. "Don't worry, I aim to keep you jealously to myself forever and a day."

"Oh good. That's a relief." I sat up. "So we can go now, then? I don't even want to wait for a cup of tea."

"I think that's a good idea," he said. "On any other occasion it would be frightfully rude, but given the circumstances . . ." He let the rest of the sentence hang in the air as he jumped out of bed. "Come on then. Get dressed. We won't bother to wash until we get back to Diddy's place."

I put on my jersey and slacks as quickly as possible and we crept out like two naughty schoolchildren playing truant. As we crossed the compound a group of small monkeys scattered and leaped up onto the roof, chittering at us. The air was icy cold and the upper slopes of the lone mountain called Kipipiri were hidden in cloud. The leather seat of the motorcar was equally cold and I hastily wrapped the travel rug around my knees. Darcy started the motor and we were off. The moment we passed under that gate and were on the road I felt a great weight lifting from me. We were going back to the safety and sanity, or relative sanity, of Diddy's house, where the worst thing one had to worry about was the odd elephant or lion. Thank heavens Freddie Blanchford had selected her for us to stay with and not someone like Idina. I almost sang out loud.

The sky brightened as we started along the road. I have found that there is no such thing as twilight or dawn in Africa. One minute it is dark and then instantly the sun comes up and the whole countryside flames with brilliant light. That's how it was that morning. Tall trees cast shadows across the dusty red dirt of the road. Birds swooped ahead of us in bright flashes of color. A small animal scurried across the road too quickly to identify. I caught a glimpse of black and white monkeys bounding through the trees. It really was quite enchanting. Then suddenly we came to an area where the road swung closer to the mountain slopes. On the other side the river flowed swiftly over rocks and a light mist hung over the valley. The trees and rocks became ghostly shapes. Darcy drove carefully, ready for an animal to step out in front of us.

We came to the spot where the road narrowed as it passed between huge boulders. Darcy slowed to a crawl as we were about to negotiate the little stream that crossed our path. It was lucky he was already going slowly as we came around the bend because he had to jam on the brakes. I put out my hands to the dashboard to steady myself.

"What is it?" I whispered, peering through the mist ahead, expecting him to say "elephant" or "lion."

"Some damned fool has left a motorcar parked on the road."

We stopped and Darcy got out. The mist was already clearing with the heat of the sun, so that it swirled in strands, revealing a convertible motorcar, with nobody inside and the driver's door wide open.

"The driver might have broken down and gone for help," I said.

"And just left the road blocked?" Darcy still sounded annoyed. "If the mist had been any thicker we would have slammed right into it."

"Well, if the motor cut out suddenly he

wouldn't have had much choice, would he?"
I asked.

"I wonder if there is a property close by
where he might have gone. . . ." Darcy
looked around. "I don't remember any
houses or driveways on this part of the road,
do you?"

"It was dark," I reminded him. "I was so
concerned about elephants that I wasn't
looking for driveways."

Darcy shook his head impatiently. "I really
don't want to wait until he reappears with
help. Do you think you can help me move
it? If we both push?"

"We can try," I said, getting out to join
him. "Although we'd have to push it for a
good way before we could get around it.
The road is narrow here for quite a while, I
remember."

"Let's see how easy it is to move," Darcy
said. He walked toward the motorcar, then
he stopped suddenly.

"What is it?"

"Listen," he said. "The motor is still running."

The daylight had brought the screech of
cicadas that had drowned out other sounds
and, of course, our own car engine was still
running so I hadn't heard the purr of this
motor.

"He can't have gone far, then. Hello!" he called. "Anybody there?"

His voice echoed from high rocks, causing a flapping of wings somewhere in the bushes. But nobody answered.

"What an imbecile," Darcy said. "You don't get out in the middle of nowhere and leave the engine running. I hope he didn't just heed the call of nature and meet a lion or leopard lurking."

I was feeling more and more uneasy. I sensed something was very wrong. I could feel a watchfulness, eyes observing us.

"Do you think we should go back?" I asked. "We could tell the others and send help."

"I don't want to turn around and go all that way unless we really have to," Darcy said. "I could drive his car until I can pull off the road and we could get around it. That would be the simplest thing to do. I'd rather get on home, wouldn't you?"

"But we can't just drive away. Not like this. Shouldn't we look for the driver?"

"And if he's just stopped off to deliver something at a house nearby? We don't know — there might be a property right beside the road and the driver wouldn't have expected any other vehicle to come along at this hour."

"But what if something awful has happened to him?"

"Then we might be stepping right into danger ourselves," Darcy said. "If he met a lion or a leopard there's nothing we can do right now."

"If he's lying injured nearby?" I said. "If a lion has dragged him off into the bushes."

"If he's met a lion or a leopard there is little chance he'd still be alive." Darcy's face was grim as he scanned the terrain beside the road. "And if we come upon a feasting lion . . . I don't rate our chances highly. I don't suppose he left a gun in the car?"

We looked. A dinner jacket had been dropped carelessly onto the front seat, along with a bow tie. A suitcase and a pair of evening shoes rested on the backseat, along with a neatly folded scarf.

"At least let me drive this out of the way," Darcy said. He started to get into the idling motorcar. I was conscious that we were horribly vulnerable, standing there. Then to my left there was a movement among the bushes. I jumped up onto the running board beside Darcy, expecting a wild animal to spring at me, until I saw it was only a large black bird.

"It's all right," I said. "Only a bird."

Darcy got out again. "A vulture," he said.

"That's not good."

The vulture reluctantly flapped out of his way as he started to walk into the tall grass and shrubbery beyond.

"Darcy, be careful," I called after him as he pushed his way between bushes.

"Ow," he called. "These bushes have wicked thorns on them." Then he said, "Oh my God. Stay where you are."

But I was already following, carefully trying to avoid the worst of the thorns and getting my hand scratched in the process. "What is it? Have you found him?"

"Oh yes," Darcy said. "I've found him."

I came out between the bushes to where an area had been flattened down. All I saw to begin with were the vultures — lots of them. Some hopped away reluctantly, some rose into the air in a black cloud of flapping wings as Darcy approached. A body, or the remains of a body, was lying sprawled facedown on the grass.

"Who is it?" I asked. And then I saw. Something had already fed on the body but I recognized that blond hair and how it curled, a little long, at the back of his neck. Something had eaten Bwana Hartley, Lord Cheriton.

CHAPTER 18

August 12
On the road in the Wanjohi Valley

I feel awful. I didn't like Lord Cheriton, but
nobody should die like this, eaten as if
he was a joint of meat.

"We must go back to Idina's," Darcy said.
"She's closer than Diddy, and she has a
telephone. She can call the police and get
Freddie before he sets off on his safari."

"She won't be awake. None of them will,"
I said.

"Too bad. We'll have to wake her." He
went back to Bwana's motorcar and turned
off the engine. "No point in leaving that
running," he said. "And I don't want to
waste time trying to move it."

I suddenly realized I was going to be sick.
The alcohol from the night before had made
me feel queasy since I woke up, but the sight

of that body was a final straw. I rushed into the grass beside the road and emptied my stomach. Darcy came up to me and put a comforting hand on my back. "It's only natural," he said. "It was a pretty gruesome sight, wasn't it?"

"It was horrible," I said, reaching for a handkerchief to wipe my mouth. "That poor man. I didn't like him but I wouldn't have wished this on my worst enemy. What an awful way to die."

Darcy stood staring back toward the place where Bwana lay. "It doesn't make sense to me. He had been in this country for years. I would have said he knew it better than anyone else. So why would he have let himself be caught unawares by a big cat — if that's what it was."

"What else would have eaten part of his body?"

"Hyenas. They are the scavengers, aren't they? If they'd smelled him lying there dead they would have had a good feast."

"Don't." I shivered. "We should get help as soon as possible so that those revolting vultures don't eat the rest of him."

Darcy held up a hand to show he'd just had an idea, then pointed toward our own car. "There is the rug in our motorcar. At least we can cover him so that the vultures don't destroy the evidence for when the police get here."

"Good idea. We can weigh the edges down with stones to stop them from pulling it off in a hurry." I started picking up rocks from the roadbed. In truth I was glad to have something to keep me busy so that I didn't have to think too much. Darcy retrieved our rug and we made our way back to the body, Darcy holding the thorny branches aside for me. The vultures were even more reluctant to leave it this time. The way they stood and looked at us in that sinister hunched-over manner of theirs made them seem like the epitome of evil. Darcy had to shoo them away by waving the rug at them. Even so they retreated only a few feet away and stood there, patiently waiting for us to leave again. He stood looking down at Bwana's remains, frowning. "What is he doing over here?"

"What do you mean?" I asked.

"I mean what made him get out of the car and come so far off the track?"

"Perhaps a lion dragged him off before it ate him."

"A lion wouldn't have opened the car door," he said dryly. "And if a leopard had leaped down on him from one of those rocks, it would have killed him in the car seat. And there would be signs of a struggle, blood in the car, and there's none. He opened the door and got out, leaving the engine running. Why?"

"You said it yourself — he needed to heed the call of nature. He went into the bushes to relieve himself and some kind of wild animal was lurking there and attacked him."

Darcy nodded, still frowning. "Yes, I suppose so. But would he have risked getting out of his car here, of all places, where an animal was most likely to ambush him in the dark? Why not drive on a little until the valley opens out again and there are fields of crops beside the road?"

"The call was desperate?"

"In the middle of the night there would have been no reason to go so far into the bushes. They are thorny, for one thing. He'd risk getting badly scratched in the dark. And there was certainly nobody to see." Darcy sighed. "Anyway, I just don't think he'd be stupid enough to stop here, unless he had to."

"If a lion was blocking the road, ready to spring?" I suggested.

"He is in a powerful motorcar. He revs the motor. He drives straight at it. Lions aren't stupid. It would get out of the way."

"Or the lion crept up from behind and

leaped into the car and he jumped out to save himself?"

Darcy shook his head. "There is no sign of a lion in the motorcar. There would be paw prints, ripped leather seats. And his travel bag and evening shoes were on the backseat, undisturbed."

I helped Darcy lower the blanket to cover the body then place rocks to hold it in place.

"At least hopefully the poor chap will remain undisturbed until we can get help," he said.

As we picked our way back to the road suddenly Darcy froze. "Look at this," he said. He pointed to one of the thorny bushes. "Doesn't that look like a scrap of lion's fur, caught on this bush?" He pointed to a tuft of yellowish hair. It definitely did look the right color to be from a lion. "Well, at least it confirms one thing, doesn't it? But it doesn't appear that the lion dragged him from the car. There would be more signs of grass and branches being disturbed."

"Would he have got out of his car if he spotted a lion and decided to kill it?"

"Where is his gun?" Darcy asked. "I didn't see one lying beside him."

"No," I agreed. "And I would have thought it was rather silly to try and kill a lion in the pitch-dark."

"Very silly," Darcy said. "Look around his car. There are patches of mud and soft earth between the rocks. Do you see any pug-marks?"

We both looked but there were none.

"Look! There is his footprint where he stepped down from the car," I said. There was a clear print of a man's shoe in a muddy patch. And close to it another one.

"So he got out and just stood there," Darcy said. "Why?"

"He heard a noise in the bushes? He got out, went to investigate and the lion got him?" Even as I said the words they made no sense. "He wouldn't ever have done that." I shook my head firmly. "He saved me from those ants. He spotted them right away. I didn't. He knew this place, Darcy. He wouldn't have taken silly risks."

"Unless . . ." Darcy paused. "We don't know how much booze and cocaine he took last night. And we don't know when he headed home. What if he was still really tipsy, which gave him stupid bravado. You know — 'I'm going to kill this lion with my bare hands.' "

"It's possible, I suppose. The only good explanation, really. And the other question is, why did he leave Idina's so early? Did he have to get back home for something this morning?"

"Maybe he had promised Angel that he wouldn't spend the whole night there. He realized he'd stayed a little too late and was speeding home," Darcy suggested.

"Until something made him stop here of all places." I looked around. The mist had now almost lifted and the boulders rose, dark and forbidding, on either side of the road. "It's almost like a perfect place for an ambush."

Darcy nodded. "It certainly seems that way. I wonder if the ambusher was animal or human."

"Human?"

"It's a possibility," Darcy said, thinking this through. "Someone with a grudge against Lord Cheriton waits until he has to slow to negotiate this narrow part of the road. He gets out. The other man shoots him."

I looked down at the ground where I was standing. "There's only one flaw with that," I said. "There are no other tire tracks but ours and Lord Cheriton's. His tires are extra wide and knobbly. See, here are his marks from last night . . . the last car to come along this way from the direction of his house toward Idina's after us. And here are ours this morning, covering his as he returned. Besides, everyone else was still at Idina's when we left."

"You're turning into quite a detective," Darcy said, giving me a nod of approval. He walked a little way ahead along the track. "No vehicles came after him from the top of the valley last night, as you said. And it doesn't appear that any vehicle followed him from Idina's. If someone — a human — was lying in wait to ambush him it would have to be from a nearby house. Otherwise it's a good six or seven miles in either direction."

"We certainly didn't see any lights as we drove past last night," I said. "And anyway, weren't all the inhabitants of the valley at Idina's?"

"Except his wife and children," Darcy pointed out. "Also Diddy and Cyril. But I can't see how any of them could have managed six or seven miles in the dark on foot. After all, we have Diddy's car."

"They couldn't and they wouldn't," I said. "And why would they want to? If any of them wanted to bump him off they could do so on his own property."

Darcy nodded. "You're right. And there is that tuft of lion fur caught on the bush. A lion figured in this somehow. We need to get back to Idina's and try to make sense of this. See what might have happened last night that might be relevant."

"I did hear a lot of doors slamming and feet running," I said.

"Perhaps he had a row with someone," Darcy said.

"If so, they didn't follow him," I pointed out. "I can't see other vehicle tracks, can you?"

"I suppose we could have driven over them, if we took exactly the same route, and we had the same sized vehicle," Darcy admitted, staring at the red earth of the track. "But I really don't see . . ."

"Another person might have ridden in the motorcar with him," I suggested.

Darcy bent to examine Bwana's car. He sniffed at the air. "No expensive perfume. No dropped gloves or other clues. Anyway, that wouldn't make sense. If someone had ridden with him and killed him then where are they now? Are there any estates nearby? If not, the person would not have gone home on foot. It's several miles to anywhere. And I don't see any footprints on the track, do you?"

I checked in both directions. "No," I admitted.

He sighed. "This is very perplexing,

Georgie. I hate it when things don't make sense."

I stood beside the motorcar, helping him to reverse down a tricky stretch of road until we came to a bit of a clearing where he could actually turn around. I climbed in and we drove like the devil back to Idina's house.

CHAPTER 19

August 12
At Idina's house again

> I am still shaking. I've seen dead bodies
> before, but not like this. Bwana's body
> was a horrid, bloody mess with great
> chunks taken out of him. I really wish I
> was safe at home.

Only a couple of African servants were up
and about when we arrived back at Idina's.
They came to the front door on hearing our
motorcar drive up.

"Bwana O'Mara, you forget something?"
the head servant asked, coming over to the
car.

"No, there has been an accident," Darcy
said. "You need to wake up the memsahib
right way."

"Wake her now?" He looked worried. "Oh
goodness gracious, sir . . . She doesn't like

240

it if we disturb her after one of her parties."

"Then I'll wake her," Darcy said. He strode in the direction of Idina's bedroom and banged on the door. "Idina, wake up. Emergency."

"Bugger off!" came a muffled and grumpy voice.

"Idina. I need you to call the police. It's an emergency. Lord Cheriton is dead."

There was a long pause then the bedroom door opened. Idina definitely looked the worse for wear . . . bleary-eyed, blinking like a mole in the daylight and with her robe hastily thrown onto a naked body.

"Is this some kind of joke?" she demanded. "It better not be someone's idea of a joke."

"No joke. We found his motorcar parked on the road and his body in the bushes," Darcy said. "We have to call the police and notify Freddie Blanchford."

"Oh my God. Was it an accident?" she asked. "Was he driving too fast and hit something?"

"I don't know what it was yet. He didn't hit anything. He stopped his car and got out and his body is now half-eaten by animals of some kind. We need to get hold of the police as quickly as possible."

"How absolutely horrible." Idina looked

as if she might throw up. "Bring me coffee," she barked at one of the servants who were hovering as close as they dared, not wanting to miss any excitement. She turned back into the room. "Get up, Pixie. You'll need to be decent before the police get here."

I couldn't resist peeking past her into the bedroom. The other occupant of her big bed was the supercilious little man with the mustache. He didn't look quite so polished now with his dark hair all tousled and his eyes still half-asleep. I found myself wondering why Idina had chosen him. Surely she would have had her pick. Then the thought occurred to me that he might not have been the first visitor. Didn't Diddy say that they played musical beds? Oh crikey. I was cringing with embarrassment, wishing again that we had never come in the first place.

"What the deuce are you talking about? Police?" Mr. Atkins jumped out of bed, realized he was naked and grabbed at one of the pillows, holding it in front of him. If it hadn't been so deadly serious it would have been funny. I swallowed back a desire to giggle. "Look here, Idina. People can't know I was here. If word got back to Nairobi . . . I'm a bloody representative of the Crown, you know."

"Nobody needs to know anything," Idina

said calmly. "You and your lovely wife came to dinner and stayed the night because one can't drive back to Nairobi in the dark."

Idina tied her robe more firmly around her waist. She turned to one of her servants, waiting behind me. "Go and wake Mr. Jocelyn, Farah. Tell him I need him immediately."

"Yes, memsabu," he replied and darted away to one of the outbuildings. So Jocelyn was not granted a bedroom in the main house, I thought. That must mean that Idina did not have any designs on him. He was housed with the servants.

"How far away is the body?" Idina asked us, as we left the bedroom and made our way along the veranda.

"I'd say about six miles," Darcy said. "You know that spot where the track becomes really narrow as it passes between those big rocks?"

"Of course. Near the Eggertons' place."

"The Eggertons?"

"Yes, darling. Tusker and Babe. Their estate is just before you get to the narrow part. You must have noticed their gateway. It has their name over it."

I tried to glance at Darcy but he was still focusing his attention on Idina.

"I wonder if they saw anything. . . . They

must be told." She shook her head. "I can't believe he's gone. You're sure it was him? You said the body was partly eaten."

"I'm sure," Darcy said.

She reached the main front door and a houseboy leaped to open it for her. I was relieved to follow her into that big central room. The fire was already roaring in the stone fireplace and it was delightfully warm. I had been so shocked by what had just happened that I hadn't noticed until now how jolly cold I was. The morning air was icy and I was shivering — from shock as well as the cold air, I suspected.

"It's impossible to believe." Idina put a hand up to her mouth. "My dear Bwana. What on earth would have made him stop along the way? An elephant? They don't like motorcars."

"There was no sign of an elephant and no damage to the motor," Darcy said. "We did see a scrap of what looked like lion's fur on one of the thorns."

"Lion? In that part of the valley? That's most unusual." She frowned. "It must be a rogue man-eater that has decided to move in on human territory. I suppose it lay in wait and pounced on him when he slowed to cross that little stream."

"In which case it was a dashed clever

lion," Darcy said. "It opened the car door and let Bwana Cheriton step out. His footprint is quite clear."

"How extraordinary. Nobody knew this country better than him. He'd never have got out in the dark if he saw a lion. Perhaps it was blocking the road, and he took a shot at it and only wounded it and it came for him."

"We didn't see a gun near the body," Darcy said.

"He always carried his gun with him. We're never without a weapon in this part of the world. You never know."

"We didn't exactly search the car carefully," I pointed out. "Or look under it or under the bushes. He could have dropped a gun, I suppose."

"It could have been a leopard," Idina said thoughtfully. "Yes, that's more likely. If it leaped down from one of those rocks, right onto him. He'd be hampered by the steering wheel, not able to move, so he'd open the car door and get out, trying to shake the thing off him. But the leopard managed to bite into the back of his neck, as they like to do, and he fell and died." She nodded with satisfaction as if she was pleased with this diagnosis. "Yes, that would have been it. Even a smart hunter like Bwana can't always predict the behavior of a leopard."

"Idina, for God's sake take me to the telephone," Darcy said. "We need to try and catch Freddie Blanchford before he sets out from Gilgil. He's taking a chap on a safari jaunt with Cyril Prendergast."

"I really don't see why you're so keen to have the district officer here. What good can he do? It's the doctor you need. He'll give you the cause of death and sign the certificate. And I'm sure you'll find it was a leopard."

"I'd really like Freddie Blanchford to see the body," Darcy said patiently. I was impressed how calm he was remaining. "He should be the one to decide if the police need to be called. If we don't hurry he'll have left."

"Don't fret so, darling. If he's already left I can have Jocelyn drive out to the spot where the road comes up from Gilgil and intercept him," Idina said. "But all right. We'll try to get him on the old blower first."

I had not joined in most of this conversation because I was thinking about something Idina had said. Now I decided to ask. "Idina, you said the Eggertons need to be told. Aren't they still here?"

"No, darling." She turned back to me. "They went home in a huff. Or at least Babe was in a huff because Bwana's feather landed on another woman. She thought he was deliberately snubbing her. And then Tusker's feather landed on Pansy and Babe thought he'd done that deliberately to spite her. So there was a big blowup and they went home."

"And who did Lord Cheriton's feather land on?" Darcy asked.

Idina smiled. "Why, me, darling."

"A smart move on his part," Darcy said. "Not wanting to choose between either of his mistresses or the woman from Nairobi who was hoping to snag him for the night."

Idina gave him a cold stare. "I rather like to think he chose me because he's always liked me best. He wanted to marry me once, you know. But I had a new husband at the time and it seemed like too much trouble to go through another divorce. I'll tell you one thing: I'm a hell of a lot better in bed than that little shopgirl Babe, or Pansy Ragg for that matter."

"If he was with you, then what time did he leave? And when did Mr. Atkins take his place?" Darcy said. I was glad he asked this and not me. I had been thinking the same thing but would have been too embarrassed to say anything.

Idina frowned. I could tell she was taking

this as an insult to her feminine attraction — that Bwana might have tired of her and wanted to leave her.

"Well, that was just it, darling. We never got very far, did we? We had just retired to my bedroom and he was undressing me when Jocelyn knocked on the door and said that Bwana's wife had telephoned. She was feeling much worse and wanted him home right away."

"So he went?" Darcy asked.

"Not exactly right away." Idina gave a little smile. "We did . . . finish what we had started. But then he went."

"And what time was that?"

"Couldn't have been much later than midnight."

"And had the Eggertons already left at that stage?"

"Yes, they went right after the feather game."

Two servants appeared carrying pots of coffee and arranged them on the table that had previously housed the drinks.

"Help yourselves," Idina said, going over to pour a cup. "You must need it as much as I do. The telephone is over here on the wall. Do you want to make the call or shall I?"

"If you don't mind I'd like to speak to

Freddie Blanchford myself," Darcy said. "He's a good friend of mine. And he'll know the protocol in such a case."

"What protocol?" Idina asked. "Bwana made a stupid mistake and got himself killed by an animal. I keep telling you: what you need is Dr. Singh to come up and sign the death certificate."

"We need to verify that it was an accident," Darcy said.

"What on earth do you mean?" Idina said. "You're not suggesting it was suicide, are you?"

"Certainly not. But I am suggesting we need to rule out murder."

"Murder? Don't be ridiculous," Idina said. "Who'd want to murder Bwana? His workers love him. And everyone else in the valley was here."

I seemed to remember that not everybody agreed with the statement that Bwana's workers loved him, but I said nothing.

"You said the Eggertons drove home," Darcy pointed out.

Idina laughed. "Oh, come on. You don't think that Tusker Eggerton waited to ambush Bwana because he was having a fling with Tusker's wife? That makes no sense. He couldn't have known that Bwana would leave my place before midmorning. And it's a foolhardy man who would spend the night in that particular spot. He also might have found himself facing a leopard or an elephant in the dark."

"I'm not saying it was Tusker Eggerton," Darcy said, "I'm just pointing out that not everybody was at your house all night."

Idina sighed as if this was all rather difficult, then picked up the telephone mouthpiece and handed it to Darcy. "I think you're making more of this than necessary. Call Freddie. He's a sensible enough young man. And tell him to bring Dr. Singh with him."

I watched as Darcy talked with the operator, asked for Freddie, got a reply then put the telephone down in disgust.

"He's already left. That was his house servant. He's going to see if he is still picking up Van Horn at the hotel and he can stop them before they leave Gilgil."

At that moment Jocelyn came bursting into the room. He too looked rather wild, with bloodshot eyes. I wondered if he might have joined in the festivities after we left or this was just a result of testing the various cocktails. "Your boy said it was an emergency, Idina. Are you all right?" he asked. He was buttoning his shirt as he spoke, then looked around and reacted with surprise as he saw us. "Good heavens. You're already up and dressed."

"They were on their way home, but they came back because Bwana met with an accident," Idina said.

"Oh crikey, is he all right?"

"He's dead," Darcy said.

"Dead? Lord Cheriton is dead?" Jocelyn stared at Darcy, his mouth open. "Are you sure? He's not just passed out after too much . . . you know."

"He's been half-eaten by an animal," Darcy said. "I'd say I'm pretty sure he's dead."

"Oh crikey." Jocelyn looked as if he might be sick at any moment.

"And it's imperative that we get in touch with the district officer, Freddie Blanchford," Darcy went on. "He's driving up from Gilgil at this moment."

Idina stroked Jocelyn's cheek. "So what I need you to do, my darling, is to take my motorcar and drive it to where the road from Gilgil joins our road and intercept Freddie as he comes past."

"Golly. Suppose he's driving fast and doesn't see me?" Jocelyn said.

"Oh, for God's sake, Jocelyn." Even Idina sounded frazzled now. "Use your initiative for once. That spot is quite open. Stand in the road. Wave something at him. He'll see you."

"I hope so." Jocelyn didn't look too sure about this, as if he could picture being mown down by a speeding motorcar. He sighed. "Righty-o, then. I'll be off. Did you leave your car keys in the ignition?"

Her expression softened again. "Of course, sweet boy. Here. Take a cup of coffee with you. And grab a jacket. It's freezing at this time of the morning."

She thrust a cup of steaming coffee at Jocelyn, who tried to carry it without spilling as he hurried out.

"Such a willing child," she said. "I rather think I might have to give him a few lessons — show him the joys of what he's been missing until now." She gave her wicked little smile. "But my dear beloved Chris might not take kindly to a live-in rival."

"This Chris is your new husband?" Darcy asked.

"Chris Langlands, darling. The new love of my life. But we're not actually married. I decided to live in sin this time and it works well as Chris hates being tied down. He's a pilot, you know. They are quite flighty in more ways than one. I had to promise he could come and go as he pleases when he

252

moved in."

"And when will he be back?"

She shrugged. "I've no idea. He appears. He disappears. It's really quite fun. And between you and me I was rather glad he was away last night. He gets touchy about certain things."

That was interesting, I thought. She had spent the first part of the night with Bwana, before he had been summoned home. What if her current lover, Chris, had returned unexpectedly, found Bwana in her bedroom, then followed him and killed him in a fit of jealousy? At least we now had one motive, if it did turn out to be murder.

CHAPTER 20

August 12
At Clouds, Lady Idina's house

I think I must be suffering from delayed
shock. I can't stop shivering. It was awfully cold out there, but I can't seem to
get warm again. And I can't get the vi-
sion of that body out of my mind.

In a way I hope it was an animal, and not
a person, who killed Lord Cheriton. That
would be tragic, but so much simpler.

One by one the other visitors appeared in
the great room, moving like silent ghosts,
pouring themselves coffee and huddling
around the fire for warmth. Some of them
were still in pajamas and dressing gowns;
others had dressed hastily. They all looked
pretty haggard and sleep-deprived. I was
amused to notice that married couples now

stayed close together and scarcely acknowledged other couples, with whom they had presumably been cavorting all night.

"What's this all about, Idina?" Harry Ragg demanded. "Your boy was babbling some kind of nonsense about Bwana being eaten by an animal."

"True, darling, I'm afraid."

"Don't tell me a leopard got into the house somehow. Don't you have guards?"

"Of course, but . . ."

"But wasn't he with you?" Pansy glared at her.

"He was, but he was summoned home by She-who-controls-the-purse-strings, claiming she had become very sick and needed him. So he went like a good boy."

"And was attacked on the way home?" Pansy asked. Of all of them she looked the most upset. "An elephant?"

"We don't know yet," Idina said. "These young people were on their way back to Diddy when they found his motorcar abandoned on the road."

"Door open. Engine running," Darcy said. "And his body in the bushes some feet away."

"How extraordinary," Chops Rutherford exclaimed. "That doesn't sound like Bwana. He'd never get out of his motor in the middle of the night. Bloody stupid."

"Unless some animal leaped down onto him," Idina suggested. "It was apparently at that narrow part where the road passes between the rocks."

"Have the authorities been called yet?" Mr. Atkins asked. He was now dressed, his hair combed with its neat central parting so that he looked quite respectable. "A death certificate will be needed."

"I've sent the boy off to intercept Freddie Blanchford, who is on his way up to Diddy's house."

"Blanchford?" Chops demanded. "The damned government chappie? What's he got to do with anything? He has no authority over a body. He's not the doctor or the police, is he?"

"You know very well that the nearest policeman is that dim-witted constable in Ol Kalou, and he couldn't get here because Bwana's car is blocking the road. And the district commissioner is actually the final law around here." Idina looked uncomfortable. Presumably her sentiments about district commissioners were the same as her neighbors'. "If we needed to have a senior policeman sent out from Nairobi, he'd have to put in the request."

"Police?" Atkins snapped the word, looking up from his coffee. "What have police got to do with some damned man being attacked by a damned animal? It seems quite simple to me. He was drunk, he was careless and he didn't take the usual precautions one might when driving alone at night."

Others were nodding agreement.

"That sounds exactly right," his wife said. "Of course that's what happened."

"All things considered, I think my wife and I should head home before this damned district officer chappie takes it into his head to ask too many questions," Atkins said. "One can't be too careful in my position with the present governor being so holier-than-thou."

At that moment the Tomlinsons came in. Mrs. Tomlinson looked as if she had been crying.

"We've just heard the shocking news," Mr. Tomlinson said. "I couldn't stand the chap myself but that's no end for a man who practically built this colony. And I'm afraid I'd better take the wife home straight away. She's pretty cut up about it, as you can imagine."

Sheila Tomlinson nodded. "I can't believe it," she said. "I never thought, in a million years . . ." Then she put her hand to her mouth, shaking her head.

I noticed that Pansy Ragg looked equally distraught. Had Sheila Tomlinson once been a mistress of Bwana? I wondered. And why did he seem to have that effect on all the other women when I had found him so repulsive?

The slim Mrs. Atkins grabbed at her husband's sleeve. "I just want to go home. I knew it was a mistake to come here in the first place. Drive me home now, Pixie."

"You were the one who was so keen on coming, old girl," Mr. Atkins snapped at her. "You wanted to see your bloody Prince of Wales again."

"Oh, I seem to remember that you were the one complaining about how our life needed a little spice in it and actually angled to get this invitation," Mrs. Atkins replied, glaring at him.

"This is all totally irrelevant," Mr. Atkins said. "The point is that we are in no way connected with this man's death and I think it the wisest possible course of action that we leave immediately."

Darcy stepped between them and the door. "I'm sorry, but I don't think you should leave until Freddie Blanchford gets here," he said.

Mr. Atkins's face flushed bright red.

"What are you talking about? And who the devil are you anyway?"

"I'm a visitor from England and I know I've no right to suggest anything, but I have had some experience with crimes and it seems to me this must be considered a suspicious death until we have actually proved that Lord Cheriton fell victim to an animal attack."

"Well, of course he did," Atkins snapped, glaring at Darcy. "We were told the body was half-eaten. Do you think there are cannibals in this part of Africa, then?"

"I just expect that Blanchford needs to rule out human involvement," Darcy went on. "He may need to call in the police."

"Absolute bloody rubbish," Atkins blustered now. "Human involvement. Wasn't every human for miles around at this very house?"

"Every white human," Chops Rutherford reminded him. "Plenty of Kukes all over the valley."

"Surely the Kikuyu are not known for their violence, are they?" Mrs. Atkins asked. "Our neighbors always say how gentle their houseboys are."

"I don't think Bwana was known for being particularly kind to his workers," Chops added. "A hard taskmaster. I've seen him whipping a man for knocking over a can of milk. He had a foul temper. But if they were going to set upon him they could do so on his own estate, couldn't they? And the Kikuyu are innately lazy. They wouldn't walk all that way to ambush him."

"Even the natives have their share of rogues and criminals," Harry Ragg pointed out. "Those who have broken tribal laws and been kicked out of society."

"Robbery, are you suggesting? Bandits?" Atkins glared.

"It wasn't robbery," Darcy said. "Nothing was disturbed on the seats of the motorcar." He hesitated, looking uncomfortable. "Look, as I said, I'm an outsider here. It's not for me to make assumptions. I think someone in authority should take a look, and since there is no policeman within easy reach I just think it's up to your district officer to decide whether the case looks suspicious and the police should be called in."

"I can't see what it could do with us. We're not even local," Atkins said. "Visitors from Nairobi, that's what we are. We don't even know the man and have nothing to do with this whole business. So if you don't mind . . ." He tried to push past Darcy, who was a good six inches taller and much broader.

I don't know what might have happened after that but there were sounds outside the front door and Jocelyn bounded in, rather like an overgrown Labrador puppy, full of enthusiasm. "I found him. I managed to wave him down and he's just coming," he said.

"Well done, clever boy," Idina said, making him beam. He really was rather endearing, I thought. I could see why Idina had taken to him. It must feel like rescuing a stray.

Jocelyn held the door open and Freddie Blanchford came in, followed by a scowling Mr. Van Horn.

"How long is this business going to take?" he demanded in that strong accent. "I was promised a safari. It may be my last chance before I go home."

"There's been a suspicious death, I'm afraid," Darcy said. "And Mr. Blanchford is the government official in these parts, so I think your safari will have to be postponed. Besides, you can't get through to Diddy's at the moment. Bwana's car is blocking the road."

"Bwana? You mean that big chap at the polo field the other day — Lord Somebody?" Van Horn sounded surprised. "He's the one who has been killed?"

"I'm afraid so."

"But this is most disturbing," Van Horn said. "Do you have native uprisings here? We travel with armed guards to keep natives in their place at home. Didn't the man have a gun with him?"

"Mr. Van Horn, why don't you help yourself to a cup of coffee? The kitchen boys should be getting breakfast started soon," Idina said. "And thank God you've come, Freddie. We were about to have mutiny on the *Bounty* with my various guests wanting to go home."

"You're dashed lucky, Idina," Freddie said. "We were held up behind an oxcart on the road going up the hill for a good fifteen minutes, otherwise we'd have been long gone. I promised Cyril we'd be at Diddy's place by six thirty. I'd better telephone and explain."

"You probably shouldn't telephone anyone right now," Darcy said. "Lord Cheriton's family haven't heard the news yet and I think you should take a look at the body for yourself and be the one to break it to them."

Idina was frowning. "That's odd, isn't it? Angel telephoned him around midnight and wanted him home right away, but she hasn't rung up again to find out where he got to?"

"Maybe she didn't want to annoy him

when he was having fun," Harry Ragg said. "He didn't like to be crossed, did he? She asked him to come home. She tried her best, but she wasn't going to push her luck too far."

"Was he the sort who could be violent?" Darcy asked. "With his wife, I mean?"

"He could be a bit belligerent when he'd drunk too much," Pansy said, glancing at her husband. "He did give me a shove once. I fell and hit my head against the wall. Harry was furious. He was all set to give him a damned good hiding, weren't you, darling?"

Harry just glared.

So Bwana could be violent, I thought. That might give several people a motive, including Angel. It was a pity that she had a cast-iron alibi. There were no tire marks coming from the direction of Bwana's estate after his own motorcar. And anyway, did they have more than one motor?

Freddie stepped forward and clapped his hands. "So, ladies and gentlemen. I'm sorry to have to take up your time but this is a serious matter. So far I know very little and I hope you'll assist me in collecting the facts so that I can make a decision about what is to be done next."

"I don't see why you are needed at all,

young man," Atkins said. "Wasting your time as well as our own. The blasted chap was attacked by some kind of wild animal and killed. He was driving home drunk, and not paying attention. End of story."

"So all of you have spent the night here, is that correct?"

"We all stayed on after Idina's party, yes," Mr. Atkins said before anyone else could answer. "We come from Nairobi. It was too far to drive home in the dark. And damned dangerous too. So Lady Idina was gracious enough to offer us all hospitality."

"Atkins, isn't it?" Freddie held his gaze. "You work at Government House? Then you must have met my uncle, the former assistant governor?"

"Haversham was your uncle? Splendid fellow," Atkins said, already looking less bellicose.

Freddie turned back to the group. "So let me get this straight. Lord Cheriton was attacked by an animal while driving home." Freddie spoke the words slowly. "What time did he leave? Did anyone see him go? Was that earlier this morning?"

"No, it was only just after midnight," Idina said. "And I saw him leave. He came to tell me."

"Lord Cheriton did not stay the night, like

your other guests, then?"

"His wife did not come with him because she was under the weather," Idina said. "He got a telephone call around midnight to say she was feeling worse and wanted him home. Being the dutiful husband he left immediately." (There was a snort of amusement from one of the crowd at this statement.)

"And who discovered his body?"

"We did," Darcy said. "Georgie and I were driving back to Diddy's place when we found a motorcar blocking the road. It's that place where the road narrows to pass between boulders and it crosses a little stream."

"Oh right. About five or six miles from here, on the road north," Freddie said.

"We slowed to cross the stream and there was this motorcar, with a door open and the motor running, blocking the road ahead," Darcy said. "We hollered and nobody answered so we looked around a bit and found the body in the bushes a few feet away. There were vultures all over it and it had been clearly eaten by some large animal. We covered it with a rug and came straight back here."

Freddie looked around the assembly, clearly trying to decide what his next move should be. This probably wasn't the sort of thing he'd had to do before. Some of the guests were lounging on sofas, looking quite comfortable, while others were standing and impatient to get away.

"I suppose the first thing to do would be for me to take a look at the body and for us to call Dr. Singh to ascertain the cause of death."

"That's what I've been saying all along," Harry Ragg said. "We don't need the police to be involved. We don't actually need you to be involved. It's not a matter for police or government officials. All we need is the blasted doctor to take a look and say what killed him and we can all go home." He got up, walked over to the wall and picked up the telephone mouthpiece. "Go on, then. Call the bloody doctor and let's get this over with."

"Very well." Freddie hesitated, then took the telephone from Harry. "But I must insist that you all stay here until the doctor and I have viewed the body. I will need statements from everyone."

"Damned cheek," Atkins said. "It wasn't as if any of us were involved. We were all tucked up in bed when the man left."

This produced another snort, from Pansy Ragg, I believe.

266

"All the same, one has to follow the proper procedure," Freddie said. "Bear with me. As Lady Idina mentioned I'm sure that breakfast will be ready soon. I suggest you have some more coffee while I call the doctor and then take a look at the body. It shouldn't take too long."

As the guests began to disperse, Freddie touched Darcy's arm. "Maybe you'll come with me and give me all the details, old chap," he said.

"Georgie should come too," Darcy said. "She's very observant."

"Oh, but I wouldn't want to put a woman through something as horrid as this," Freddie said. "I mean — a partially eaten body. It's not the sort of thing . . ."

As they spoke I was debating whether I really did want to see that body again. But I was flattered that Darcy clearly wanted me to come along with them.

"I've seen bodies before," I said. "Don't worry. I won't faint or scream."

"Well, all right then, I suppose you know what you are doing." Freddie shot Darcy a worried glance. "I'll just call Singh and we'll get going. The place where the road narrows? That's where he should meet us?"

"He won't be able to go any farther because the motorcar is blocking the way,"

Darcy said. He put an arm around my shoulder. "You do want to come, don't you? I didn't want to leave you behind, unless you'd rather?"

I gave him my brightest smile. "Of course I want to come. Wouldn't miss it for the world."

CHAPTER 21

August 12
On the road in the Wanjohi Valley

As I put my coat on I can't stop thinking that I really do not want to see that body again, but pride won't let me back out. Darcy wants me with him. That is a good feeling. Also I'm not too keen to be left with Idina and all of her odd guests. What a rum lot they are. I can't believe that people act that way in England. Maybe it's the rarified air out here that takes away their inhibitions. They have apparently been hopping in and out of bed with each other all night and this morning they are acting with the politeness and civility of almost strangers.

I was feeling jolly hungry and the smell of bacon cooking wafted from the kitchen as we came out of the house. I hoped it might entice the men to linger but they were determined to be off immediately. All traces of mist had disappeared and a fierce sun shone down on those parts of the road that ran between cultivated fields. Darcy had volunteered to drive, which was a good idea as Diddy's Riley was a much smoother ride than Freddie's old jalopy. As we drove we told Freddie the details of what we had found. Darcy slowed the motor to a crawl as we approached the rocky part and stopped well before the road dipped between the boulders. Nobody spoke as we got out. I started to experience the sense of unease that had gripped me before: something I hadn't felt with any of the other bodies I had stumbled across in my life. I found myself glancing around nervously as if something was watching and waiting to pounce on me.

"Were there any animal prints beside the stream?" Freddie asked, walking ahead of us to where the rivulet crossed the road. The boulders, twice the height of a man, cast black shadows across the track.

"There were none around the motorcar," Darcy said. "We didn't check the stream."

We looked now but it seemed that nothing larger than a bird had visited the banks recently. Certainly no large cat. Blue and yellow butterflies were flitting around the water and the scene was a charming one as the stream danced over rocks. It was hard to believe that something so awful lay nearby.

"And no prints around the motorcar?" Freddie asked.

"The only footprints belong to Lord Cheriton himself," Darcy said. "Look. This is where he stood when he got out. And the other foot beside it."

"He got out and stood still." Freddie bent to look at the two distinct footprints. "That's odd, isn't it?"

"Unless he was desperate," Darcy said. "He needed to relieve himself, couldn't go on any longer, so he stood there, beside the car, and peed into the bushes."

"Possibly." Freddie nodded. "But there is no sign of his being attacked by something." He examined the ground, then peered into the motorcar. "And if he took care of things here, what would have made him go into the bushes?"

"Beats me." Darcy shook his head.

"And where exactly is the body?" Freddie asked.

"Through here." Darcy indicated the spot. "Do you want to take a look at it before the doctor gets here?"

"Not particularly," Freddie replied. He was already looking a little pale around the gills. "I don't think we should disturb it more than necessary."

It was rather comforting to realize that tough men like Freddie were equally squeamish when it came to dead bodies.

"Well, take a look at this." Darcy pointed to the scrap of fur caught on a thorn. "Does this look as if a lion passed this way?"

Freddie examined it closely. "It certainly could be. But it doesn't necessarily mean it was here last night. That fur could have caught on the thorn at any time. All the same, it is a little strange to find a lion here. This isn't normally their kind of territory. They prefer the open country at the top of the valley where there is plenty of game. And they usually hunt as a pride. I suppose this could be a lone rogue male who has found that the domestic animals settlers keep can't run away and are an easy meal. Have you heard of animals being taken?"

"We haven't been here long enough to hear much," Darcy said. "And the subject of animals never came up last night." He gave me a quick glance.

"I've never been invited to one of Idina's parties," Freddie said. "Pretty wild, I gather?"

"Let's just say it would raise eyebrows in Belgravia," Darcy said.

272

Freddie grinned. "Quite an eye-opener for you, I'd imagine?" He turned back to me.

I was tempted to pretend to be sophisticated and say that I was quite used to such things, but I'm not very good at lying. "I had no idea people behaved that way," I replied.

"Was it just alcohol or were drugs involved?" He was looking at Darcy again.

"We didn't actually go into the back room but I am pretty sure that cocaine was being offered there. They were all far gone by the time we went to bed."

"I'd love to know who supplies it," Freddie said. "The customs chaps have been keeping their eyes open at the airstrips and at Mombasa where the ship comes in, but no luck so far. All I can tell you is that there seems to be a steady supply." He turned to me. "I take it you didn't join in the festivities?" And he chuckled.

"If we did we wouldn't tell you," Darcy replied. "Georgie was game but I had to stop her."

"Darcy!" I glared at him as he burst out laughing. The sound of his laughter created rustlings in the bushes. Freddie stepped away warily.

"Probably only the vultures still waiting," Darcy said. "There were a lot of them when we first arrived and it was impossible to drive them away. We covered the body as well as we could. Let's hope they haven't been able to remove the rug."

He pushed a thorny branch aside and took a step into the bushes. "It's all right," he called back. "We did a good job weighting down that rug. They've only managed to uncover the legs."

I felt a shiver of nausea at the thought of vultures eating a leg, but quickly swallowed it back. All the same I wasn't in a hurry to see the body again. Those vultures with their hunched shoulders and evil stares were the stuff of nightmares for me. The way they hopped only a few feet away and stood patiently waiting to return to their feast was one of the most unnerving things I had ever witnessed. I found myself wishing that Darcy and I had continued to stay on that houseboat on the Thames. At least there was nothing more alarming than a swan looking in the porthole there.

"I hope Singh doesn't find himself behind another damned oxcart," Freddie said. "It is impossible to overtake them on most of the road."

"Is he a good doctor, do you know?" Darcy asked. "Indian, I presume."

"Yes. He's a Sikh. Wears a turban, but a

good chap. Trained at Barts in London."

They started to move away from the body, as if not wanting to stand too near it. Freddie leaned closer to Darcy. "You don't think this can have anything to do with —" he muttered.

"How can it?" Darcy replied, casting a wary glance in my direction in case I had overheard. "Who would know he was going to leave the party in the middle of the night? Unless one of them . . ." And he said no more, coming over to me, still standing beside Bwana's car. He put an arm around my shoulders. "How are you holding up? Shouldn't be long now."

It was probably another half hour before the doctor's old car could be heard, long before we saw it. It sounded like a cross between a sewing machine and a lawn mower. When it came into sight it was an elderly Morris 10. The doctor was particularly tall and with his turban on could barely fit inside. He extricated himself and hurried up to us.

"I received your message that it was most urgent, Mr. Blanchford. A dead body? An accident on the road? I keep telling the authorities that these roads are death traps. Only last week a car went over the edge while driving down to Gilgil. People drive too fast, of course. These big and powerful motorcars are too much for our little country lanes."

There was a pause while we were introduced and hands were shaken.

"So you were the ones who found the body?" Singh asked us. "It must have been a terrible shock for you, especially for the young lady."

"The young lady is tougher than she looks," Darcy said, giving me a wink.

We now walked together until we reached Bwana's motorcar.

"We found this with the door open and the motor running," Darcy said. "There was no sign of the driver. We called. Nobody answered. Then we heard a movement in the shrubbery there. I went to investigate. . . ."

"That was foolhardly of you, if you don't mind my saying so," Dr. Singh said. "Anything could be lurking in those bushes. Even a simple antelope can do damage if it charges at you." He wagged a finger, and his head, as he spoke. "But please continue. I should not be interrupting. I am told by my wife that I talk too much." He gave a little grin.

"There were vultures all around a body. I

276

could see it had been partially eaten by a large animal. I couldn't say immediately who it was but we recognized him by his longish hair and the way it curled at the back of his neck."

"Then who was it?"

"Lord Cheriton. The one they call Bwana."

"Bwana Hartley? That is surprising to me. Of all the people around here I would say he was the one who knew the dangers of the country best. Was he set upon as he was driving slowly between these rocks?"

"It doesn't appear that way," Darcy said. "There was no sign of anything being disturbed in the motorcar. See, his things are still folded on the rear seat."

"Very well." Dr. Singh sighed. "It is not for me to play the detective. Show me the body please."

"Through here." Darcy held aside a particularly thorny strand.

Dr. Singh followed him. I hung back this time. Vultures flapped up into the air. Some retreated to the top of the boulder and peered down in a most spooky way. I decided to follow rather than be alone on the road with the vultures regarding me with interest.

"Ah yes," I heard Dr. Singh say. "Clearly

he has been attacked by some large beast. It has taken large chunks out of him, poor man. At least that makes it easy to sign the death certificate with the cause of death as misadventure."

"But there is no sign of his having been dragged through the bushes," Darcy said. "I can't think why he would have gone so far off the trail in the middle of the night."

"Maybe he caught sight of a lion and knew it to be a marauder and decided to shoot it. He took a shot, thought he had killed it, but it was alive and attacked him instead."

"There are two things against that," Darcy said. "First, I can see no sign of a gun, and second, there is no kind of blood trail to indicate he wounded something."

"I see you are knowledgeable in the ways of the hunter, sir. I understood you to be a visitor to our great colony."

"I have hunted stag at home. The principle is the same," Darcy said.

"It is, however, possible that he fell forward and the gun is beneath him." Dr. Singh wagged a finger again, as if he had scored a point. "With your help we shall turn him over gently."

I looked away now. Frankly I didn't want to see what his front looked like. I remembered Bwana talking about those ants and how they could devour an antelope. There was a chittering noise in the big eucalyptus tree behind the rocks and a group of black and white monkeys bounded through the branches. I watched them until I heard Darcy say, "Ha. Look at this. That was never made by an animal."

Freddie whistled. "Good God, O'Mara, you're right. Your hunch was spot-on. It wasn't an animal that killed him, it was a human."

I couldn't resist taking a look for myself now. I peered through the bushes. Bwana was now lying on his back. His face had been horribly disfigured, and the front of his white shirt was covered in blood. But Darcy had opened his shirt and I could see what he was pointing to. A neat stab wound right around his heart.

CHAPTER 22

August 12
At various sites in the Not-So-Happy Valley

Okay, I'm going to say it. Golly! Somebody in this valley killed Lord Cheriton. I'm not saying I blame them completely. A man who behaved like him must make enemies. There must be a lot of husbands in Kenya who are not too happy with his going after their wives. The trouble is, they were all at Idina's house last night, weren't they?

And I thought this was going to be a wonderful, peaceful honeymoon in the middle of nature! Sigh.

"This is no longer a job for me, Mr. Blanchford," Dr. Singh said. "We need to summon the police immediately. The criminal investigation department from Nairobi. It is up to them to ascertain how this man died."

"Surely the stab wound killed him?" Freddie said. His voice was definitely shaky. Mine would be too if I was looking at a mutilated body on my territory.

"It certainly seems that way," Dr. Singh agreed. "Somebody killed him then left him here, hoping that animals would eat enough of the body that we would assume he had been attacked by a wild beast."

"Is it possible he was killed somewhere else and dumped here?" Freddie asked, looking up at Darcy.

"I don't think so." Darcy also looked paler than usual. "Certainly not in that motorcar or there would be traces of blood. And the way the ground beneath him is blood soaked indicates to me that he fell and continued to bleed here."

"The killer was unlucky, wasn't he?" I said. They looked up, as if they had forgotten I was with them. "Normally if you stab someone you'd expect them to fall backward," I said. "And if that had happened the animals and vultures would have eaten away the evidence of the stab wound."

"By George, she is right!" Dr. Singh slapped a fist into his hand. "Spot-on, young lady. That's exactly what the killer thought would happen. That indicates he did not stay around long enough to see his victim fall and die. And you say nothing was taken from the motorcar? Then not a holdup for a robbery?"

"Nothing seems to have been touched in the motorcar," Darcy said. "Of course, we haven't been through his pockets to see if money was taken."

"That will be up to the police now," Dr. Singh said. "We must not loiter here any longer. Do you know who might have the closest telephone?"

"We were told that Major and Mrs. Eggerton live not far from here," I said.

"Tusker? But surely they were at the party, weren't they? They seem like partying types," Freddie said.

"They were, but they left early. Babe was in a huff, apparently," I said. "Because Bwana was ignoring her and chose —" I couldn't go on and say the words "chose to go to bed with Idina instead of her." My upbringing forbade such utterances.

"So they are home right now?" Dr. Singh said. "Then I suggest you drive to their estate immediately, alert them to what has happened and ask that they will kindly spare some of their boys to help keep a guard on the body until an inspector can get here."

"How far are we from Nairobi?" I asked.

"At least two hours, if the road is okay." Freddie looked at the doctor for confirmation. "And I think I will need to get back to Idina's to make sure nobody leaves before the police have a chance to question them."

"I feel that I should stay with the body." Dr. Singh did not look too happy about the prospect. "We cannot risk the evidence of the stab wound being destroyed by more animal bites."

Darcy was still staring down. "That was a pretty big knife," he said. "Two inches at least, wouldn't you say? Who might carry a knife like that?"

"The natives all have pangas at least as wide as that," Freddie said, "but I think it would be hard to stab someone with a panga. The way the blade is fashioned. You slash, you don't do precise stabbing."

"No, this has been neatly done," Darcy agreed. "Whoever did it knew how to go in between the ribs. Instantaneous death if you know what you're doing — right into the heart."

"Don't," I said. This was suddenly becoming too much for me. But of course I wasn't going to admit it. "We shouldn't stand around talking any longer if you need to telephone for a policeman to come from Nairobi. Our speculating doesn't help. The

283

police will do their own detective work."

I started to walk back toward our motorcar. "You're right," Darcy agreed. "We'll go straight to the Eggertons' and then back to Idina's." He glanced at Freddie. "Someone is going to have to break the news to Lady Cheriton and his children."

"I think that should be a job for the police, don't you?"

"Unless someone at Idina's has decided to break the news without permission," Darcy said.

"I don't think anyone here is a great friend of Angel. She keeps herself apart from most of the socializing here, you know. I think she hates it, if you want my opinion. Can't wait to go back to Europe," Freddie said.

Darcy's eyes met mine for a fleeting second. A really good motive for having her husband killed. And she had the money to hire somebody to do it.

"Tell Eggerton that I am remaining on guard beside the body," Dr. Singh said. "And I need some of his estate workers to help me keep guard until the police get here."

"Of course. We'll have Eggerton bring them to you," Freddie said. "Take care, won't you. If necessary retreat to your motorcar. You'll be safe enough there."

"You don't think big cats will come after the body in the daylight, do you?" Singh sounded alarmed now.

"I doubt a big cat had anything to do with this," Freddie said. "A hungry lion would not have left this much of the carcass. And if he was killed by a stab wound it would have been hyenas that were drawn by the scent. They don't normally come back in the daylight but they can be very bold at times."

"We'll send help right away," I said. "Let's go, Darcy."

We had to do a bit of maneuvering because the doctor's little car was behind us on the narrow road, but finally we piled into Diddy's splendid motor. I let out a little sigh of relief as we left that awful scene behind us. After less than a mile we came to a track leading off to our left, up toward the mountains. A simple sign beside it read, *Lancers. Eggerton Estate.*

"Lancers?" I asked.

"Major Eggerton was once with the Bengal Lancers," Freddie said. "Very proud of the fact."

"And yet he chose to settle in Africa, not India," Darcy pointed out.

"I don't think anyone chooses to stay in India with that climate," Freddie replied.

The motorcar bumped and jerked over ruts as we drove up the narrow track. I was expecting a simple farmhouse or bungalow at the end of it but we came out of the trees and there was a palace. It was a white building with a dome in the center and columns along a graceful veranda. In front of it were manicured lawns, a pond covered in water lilies and lovely flowering trees.

"Wow." Darcy sounded as startled as I felt. "I wasn't expecting this. So the Eggertons live well, do they? Not exactly on his army pension."

"He has family money and his farm does well too," Freddie said. "You can see why Babe married him. No expense spared."

As we approached the house a giant wolfhound rushed out, barking ferociously. We hesitated to get out of the car until a house servant emerged, running up to the dog and grabbing it by the collar. It still lunged at us, snarling.

"Sorry, bwanas. Sorry, memsabu," he said. "He is a good watchdog."

"He certainly is," Freddie said. He got out, moving cautiously around the animal. "We have come to see your master."

"I do not think that he is awake yet," the man replied. "They go to a party last night and get home very late. I am sure the mem-

286

sahib will stay asleep until midday. She is not an early riser. So may I suggest that you return later?"

"I'm afraid not," Freddie said. "It is an important matter. There has been a murder. The police must be called."

"A murder? A Kikuyu has been killed?"

"No, a white person," Freddie said. "Can you please escort me to the telephone and go to wake your master?"

"Certainly, bwana. I will lock up the dog first. Please follow me."

He led us up onto the broad veranda, furnished with comfortable rattan sofas and chairs. Then we stepped into an impressive central room — the one containing the dome. Colored light spilled in from above, throwing mosaic patterns onto a polished wood floor. There were the required animal heads on the walls and an enormous tiger skin in front of the fireplace. And all around were signs of a life in India: brass trays, statues of Hindu gods. The one thing I noticed was that everything in this room reflected Tusker Eggerton. His bride's personality was quite absent. No wonder she was flattered when Lord Cheriton pursued her, I thought. And the possibility of maybe snagging herself a title must have been delicious. Poor Babe. She'd be devastated to learn that he was no more.

We were told to wait. Freddie was taken through to a telephone in the master's study and soon returned. "I have spoken to the police in Nairobi and an inspector is on his way. I have been instructed to keep all the participants at Idina's until he has a chance to get statements from all of them."

"They won't be pleased about that," Darcy said.

"I know. Another reason to hate me. Only the fact that my uncle was a respected man in the colony prevents someone from sticking a knife into my back one night, I fear."

"What an awful thing to say, Freddie," I said. "You can't mean that."

"You have no idea how antigovernment the settlers are. Those of them who have been here a long time think that this is their land, carved from virgin forest, and it's up to them to do what they like with it. And I have to admit that some of the government regulations are a little strict. You have to get permission to remove water from a stream that flows through your property . . . things like that can put backs up."

"I can see that," Darcy agreed. "I'm not too thrilled about rules and regulations myself."

"Of course you aren't. You're another

maverick. You'd do well in Kenya."

"Absolutely. Then Georgie and I could go to one of those parties every week, eh, Georgie?" He grinned as he said it.

"Don't tempt me. I might take you up on that," I replied. "When I become bored with you."

CHAPTER 23

August 12
At Tusker Eggerton's house, called Lancers

It's clearer to me now why a young woman
like Babe married a chubby older man
like Tusker Eggerton. He obviously has
buckets of money! And of course they
were the only couple who had the means
to kill Bwana. They had left the party
shortly before he did. I wonder if I'll be
able to ask questions?

We were laughing so we didn't hear the
footsteps at first. Then Tusker Eggerton
came storming into the room, tying the cord
on his robe round him as he walked. He
was a big florid man and the robe only just
covered enough to show that he was naked
beneath it.

"What the devil is this all about?" he
demanded. "I might have known it was you,

Blanchford. Exceeding your authority again, I don't doubt. Bloody government prig."

"Not at all, sir," Freddie said. "I was sent here by the government medical examiner, Dr. Singh. He needs to borrow some of your workers immediately. There has been a murder and the body needs to be protected until the police can examine it."

"Some bloody native has been topped in one of their fights?" Eggerton blustered. "I don't see what that has to do with me or mine."

"Not a native, sir," Freddie said. "One of your neighbors. Lord Cheriton."

"Bwana? Bwana has been murdered? But that's not possible. He was at Idina's party all last night. Are you sure?"

"Perfectly sure. Not far from here, as it happens." Freddie was keeping his voice calm and even. I was quite proud of him. "Where the road goes through the boulders. So if you could supply some of your workers to help stand guard. Various animals have already had a go at the body."

The big man looked shaken. "Well yes. Of course. By all means. Good God. What a shock. I'd never have thought . . . in a million years . . . poor old Bwana. Not my favorite man but what a thing to happen."

"I'll run the boys straight up to Dr. Singh,

291

then," Freddie said, "and come back for Mr. and Mrs. O'Mara."

"Right." Tusker Eggerton nodded. "Go and see about it, Sammy," he said to the tall house servant who had welcomed us. "How many do you want?"

"I think three or four should do it. I can't fit more into the motorcar."

"Three or four, Sammy. Make sure they are not squeamish about standing near a dead body. Better be Somalis, then, from the house. The Kukes have funny ideas about bodies and evil spirits."

"That is because they do not worship Allah, bwana," Sammy said gravely. "I will select some of my own. We do not fear death."

He strode from the room with great dignity. Tusker Eggerton stood staring out the door. "Bwana Hartley. Who would have thought it," he muttered, then he seemed to realize we were still there.

"Not a great introduction to Kenya, what?" he said. "We're normally such a peaceful bunch too. Get along smoothly. Let's hope the police can find the blighter who did it. Some rogue native, I expect. Kicked out of his job and determined to get revenge." He paused, tying the cord more firmly around his ample waist. "But what are you doing out and about this early? You were at the party. Everyone usually sleeps until midday."

"We left at first light," Darcy said. "My wife was eager to go back to Diddy's. She wasn't comfortable. Not really her sort of thing, you know."

"I suppose not, although her cousins in the royal family have certainly thrown themselves into our ways with enthusiasm in the past. Surprised to find the Prince of Wales wasn't there. He would have leaped at the chance before." He chuckled at his use of words.

"His lady friend keeps a tight rein on him," Darcy said.

"She was the one who flew out with us? The skinny dark-haired woman who clearly thinks a lot of herself?"

"That's the one." Darcy stifled a grin.

"Poor chap. I wouldn't want to be saddled with someone like that. But then he won't be, in the end, will he? He'll marry some dreary princess and do his duty."

He turned to look at me. "One hopes so," I said. "His parents certainly hope he'll do the right thing when the time comes."

"You know him well, do you?" Tusker asked.

"Yes, quite well. I've known him since I

was a small child. He's very kind and I'm fond of him. But Mrs. Simpson seems to have a strange hold over him."

"God knows why. She certainly isn't beautiful, or young." He seemed to realize something. "I don't suppose you've had breakfast, have you? You must be positively starving, and in a bit of shock too, I expect. Come on. Let's chivvy my boys up and get something on the table." He strode across the room and tugged on a bell rope. Almost instantly there was the sound of slippers flapping on the marble floor and a young houseboy appeared, looking agitated. "Off to the kitchen with you. Tell them we have guests so we want breakfast now and they'd better make an effort. Get cracking. Go."

"Yes, bwana. I will tell them," the boy replied and ran out of the room again.

Major Eggerton was still pacing like a caged animal. "What about a drink, then?" he said, going over to a tray of bottles on the sideboard. "I think we all need one, don't you? Brandy? Good for the nerves, although personally I always think that a good stiff G and T can cure most ills."

"Not for me, thank you," I said. "Much too early in the day."

"Nonsense," Tusker Eggerton boomed. "Hair of the dog, don't you know. Come on. Just a small one, then. A sip of brandy, for God's sake."

"Well, just a sip, then," I conceded, not because I wanted the brandy but because I thought it would cause more of a hoo-ha if I said no. Tusker took the top off a crystal decanter and poured a good two inches of brandy into a glass, handed it to me then turned to Darcy. "What about you, old chap?"

"A G and T, then, Tusker," Darcy said and got a nod of approval.

"Take a seat. Breakfast should be ready any moment. I've got the best damned set of kitchen boys in the valley. I pay them well. They know which side their bread is buttered. Although between you and me the new memsahib hasn't a clue how to deal with them. Not brought up with servants, you know. She thinks I'm too hard on them. I tell the silly cow that's all they know. They expect a master to work them hard, make them toe the line. Their own chiefs and medicine men certainly aren't kind and gentle with them." He chuckled. "Come on, drink up. There is more where that came from."

I realized that this was a perfect opportunity to get information out of Tusker Eggerton, especially now that he was knocking back the snifters. I tried to think of ways to phrase things carefully. The chance came when he asked, "So what time does the doctor think this murder took place?"

"He hadn't done a thorough examination when we came here," Darcy said, "but we know Lord Cheriton left the party just after midnight."

"Just after midnight? Are you sure? Whatever for?"

"He got a telephone call from his wife, one gathers," I said, not wanting to be left out of this conversation. "She didn't come because she was feeling ill and then she told him she was feeling worse and wanted him home."

"So he obeyed like a good little boy? That doesn't sound like Bwana." Tusker gave a derisive snort.

"His children are visiting him from England," I said. "Maybe he wanted to give a good impression to them."

"Maybe. So you think he was attacked on his way home then?" He turned back to Darcy.

"It's hard to say," Darcy said. "The body felt quite stiff to me and it didn't seem that the wounds were still bleeding. So he'd have been dead for a while. Of course, some animal had taken great chunks out of him

296

and the vultures were doing their share."

I glanced at Darcy and the matter-of-fact way he could discuss this.

"So what makes you think he was murdered, then?" Tusker demanded. "Isn't it rather obvious that he was killed by an animal?"

"There were signs that a person had done the initial deed," Darcy said cautiously. "I gather you and your wife drove home before Bwana. You didn't see anything suspicious on the road, did you?"

"Suspicious? What do you mean by that? A person lurking in the bushes?" He gave a sneer. "When I'm driving in the dark all I'm looking out for is a large animal in my path. I don't have time to check the shrubbery. Besides, it is absolutely pitch-dark. Anyone hiding two feet from the road wouldn't be noticed."

"Why did you leave so early?" I asked. "Was your wife also not feeling well?"

He looked at me, frowning, but my face was one of innocent sweetness — at least I hoped that was how I looked.

"My wife was having a minor temper tantrum, if you want to know," he said. "I thought she'd embarrass herself and me if we stayed around so I whisked her home. She had had rather a lot to drink and she hasn't learned to hold it well yet."

"Why was she upset?" I knew I was pushing my luck.

"Upset? She was bloody furious. She thought, for some reason, that Bwana Hartley fancied her. I'm sure you've heard all about it. Gossip spreads like wildfire in this community. She didn't realize that his roving eye keeps on roving and doesn't settle in one spot for long. They had a little fling and he tired of her. I knew he would; that's why I didn't make a fuss about it. She'd be dumped and then she'd return to being the dutiful wife. And if she wasn't the dutiful wife, I'd ship her back home to her mother in Birmingham." He laughed loudly as if this was a great joke he'd obviously made many times before.

"What's so funny?" said a woman's voice and there was Babe Eggerton, standing in the doorway in a pink silk robe with feathers around the edges, looking pale and rather lovely. Without her normal gash of red lipstick and powdered cheeks she had a sweet face with good bone structure and looked absurdly young. "I heard laughter. It woke me up," she said, going across to the drinks tray and pouring herself a large brandy. "I didn't realize visitors ever came this early in the morning."

Her accent was still a little rough around the edges.

"I'm sorry but this wasn't a social call," Darcy said. "Yours was the closest house to telephone the police."

"The police?" She looked alarmed. "Burglary?"

"A murder," Darcy said.

"It was your pal Bwana," Tusker said and I sensed he enjoyed saying it. "They found him lying beside the road."

Babe just stared at him with her mouth open. "You're making it up to taunt me," she said. "You're being horrid. Of course it wasn't Ross. We left him at the party, in Idina's bed."

"I'm afraid it was Lord Cheriton," I said. "His wife telephoned him to come home soon after you had left."

"And he went?" She sounded surprised. "He is not normally good at doing what women tell him." Then it seemed to hit her. "Oh my God. It really was him? He's really dead?"

"I'm afraid so," Darcy said.

She put her hand up to her face and stood there for a moment like a statue, although her hands were shaking a little. "I can't believe it. And I said some horrid things about him last night. I was angry and drunk too." She looked up, glaring. "Well, you know who must have done it, don't you?"

"No, who?" her husband asked.

"That Tomlinson fellow. Why else were they at the party? They've never come to one of our things before."

"Why would Tomlinson want to kill Bwana?" Darcy asked.

Babe gave him a pitying smile. "Because his wife used to be married to him, of course."

"Sheila Tomlinson was married to Lord Cheriton?" The words just burst out. I felt myself blushing.

"A long time ago now," Tusker said. "He went home to England after the war. He met Sheila and married her. Then they sailed back to Africa but when she arrived she didn't exactly approve of the living arrangements. Shocked her, I don't wonder. Well, it would, coming from a nice upper-class upbringing, wouldn't it? He quickly found she was no fun and his attentions turned elsewhere, so there she was, poor girl, stuck in Africa with no one to turn to. And that's when Tomlinson stepped up and took her off Bwana's hands."

"Good gracious," I said. "So he dumped her to marry Angel?"

"Oh no, sweetie pie," Tusker said, chuckling. "Angel is a recent addition, when Bwana decided he needed an infusion of capital into the farm. There have been a couple more Mrs. Hartleys in between, and I bet they are both kicking themselves that they didn't stick around to become Lady Cheriton."

"And who were they?" I asked.

"Well, one went home to England and is probably living happily with a stockbroker, and the other is Camilla Rutherford."

"Camilla Rutherford?" This was getting more complicated by the second.

"Oh yes. But she was as bad as he was. Chops Rutherford is her third husband since Bwana, I seem to remember."

"Golly." The forbidden word just slipped out. Well, it would, wouldn't it? There is only a certain amount of shock I can take.

"Is there no woman around here that has not been involved with him?" Darcy asked.

"Idina is the only one who turned him down — a proposal of marriage, I mean," Tusker said. "She hasn't been above accepting an offer for a quick roll in the hay. But I think he's always retained a soft spot for her."

I was still mulling what Babe had said earlier. "If Sheila was married to Bwana but then she married Tomlinson why would you think that he'd want to kill Bwana now? It all happened a long time ago and presumably she is happy with her current husband. Haven't things turned out for the best for both of them?"

"Bwana has taken great delight in needling Tomlinson for some reason," Tusker said. "He was like that. He'd pick on someone he didn't like and find clever ways to upset them. I think he was rather annoyed that Sheila was actually happy with someone else — especially someone as boring and solid as Tomlinson. Anyway recently Tomlinson had ordered a prize bull from South Africa. However, then Bwana ordered a bull at the same time from the same place. They both arrived together. Of course, only one was the prize animal for which Tomlinson had paid considerably more. But Bwana got there first and had the prize bull delivered to his estate. Tomlinson tried to prove Bwana had taken the animal that should have been his, but of course all bulls look quite alike in photographs and a photo can't prove which one was the better stud. He tried. He took Bwana to court, but he lost." He paused, grinning as if he appreciated this, in spite of his feelings about Lord Cheriton. Then he added, "Bwana enjoyed a good court battle. He usually won."

"But must have made a lot of enemies," Darcy pointed out.

"There have been plenty of people who wanted him dead at one time or another," Tusker said, "but you know in spite of everything it was hard not to admire him." He looked up as a servant stood in the doorway. "Ah jolly good. Breakfast is ready. Shall we go through?"

"Breakfast?" Babe looked horrified. "How can you think of eating anything, knowing that his body is so close? I doubt if I'll ever feel like eating again."

"Suit yourself," Tusker said. He headed out the door and she followed.

As they went ahead of us into a long dining room a thought occurred to me. Had we actually mentioned where Bwana's body had been found when Babe was in the room? So either she knew more than she was letting on or she had been listening outside the door before she made her entrance.

CHAPTER 24

Still August 12
At the Eggertons' estate and then
on the road back to Idina's house

I am beginning to wish we had not volunteered to drive Freddie to see the body. And especially that I had not gone with them, when I had been given the chance not to. My stupid pride again. Not wanting to seem any less brave than my husband. And now we have to go back to the aftermath of the party and face all those people again and be questioned by the police. Oh crikey — another awful thought just struck me. A crime like this could make the newspapers. Queen Mary would know all too well what sort of parties went on in this part of Kenya and if she knew that Darcy and I had attended, she'd definitely be less amused than my great-grandmother had been.

Thank heavens the Prince of Wales had been persuaded to stay away. At least he wouldn't be involved in any scandal this time!

We had only just started to tuck into an excellent array of breakfast dishes when Freddie arrived back. He tried to insist that we should head back to Idina's immediately, so that he was there when the police arrived and so none of the guests had escaped, but the aromas were so enticing that he allowed himself to be persuaded to have a quick bite. That quick bite soon turned into a plate piled high with bacon, sausage, scrambled eggs and toast.

"So has the doctor ascertained exactly what killed him?" Tusker asked. "I've been told it was murder but I still don't see how you can tell that he wasn't attacked by an animal." He leaned closer to Freddie. "Look here — the poor fellow is dead. Nothing can bring him back. I know it's a bit late now because you've called in the damn police chappie from Nairobi, and a right cock-up he'll make of any investigation too. But you realize you've opened a can of worms here and nobody will thank you for it. Dirty laundry will have to be aired, if you get my meaning. You know what they think of us in Nairobi. Damn grammar-school boys coming out and trying to boss us around. At least you went to a decent public school. You should be on our side, not getting outsiders involved. Can't we just all agree that he was attacked by an animal? So much simpler that way for all concerned."

"Would you want to know there was a murderer in your midst, Major?" Freddie asked.

"In our midst? It wasn't one of us. It couldn't have been one of us." Tusker's voice was rising now. "We were all at Idina's damned party."

I waited for Freddie to say that Tusker and Babe had left before Bwana, but he didn't. "I wasn't implying that it was one of your group of friends, Major. We'll find out from the police if there are any fugitives that may have been in the area. Or those with strong political views . . ." He stopped.

"Political views? Are there people who murder because of their politics? Everyone knows Bwana was an admirer of Mosley's. Of Hitler's, for that matter. To each his own. They have their good points, I agree. We do need to make sure that the superior races continue to rule."

"I suppose an ardent communist might decide to silence such a voice," Freddie said.

"Do you know of any ardent communists in Kenya?" Tusker laughed now. "If you believed in equality for all, you'd give the bloody government over to the natives, wouldn't you? And then what kind of mess would we be in?"

"We should be going." Freddie looked at us. "Thank you for your hospitality and for the loan of your workers. I'll bring them back as soon as they are no longer needed. I presume that will be as soon as the police arrive with their own crew."

"Have the doctor tell the damned policeman it was an animal, for God's sake," Tusker called after us. "Save us all from a lot of misery."

I climbed into the back of the motorcar and soon we were bumping our way back to Idina's house. Actually I felt a lot better now that I had some good food and coffee in my stomach. My brain was now fully awake and had banished the effects of the previous night's alcohol consumption so that I could think clearly. Tusker and Babe must be considered to be prime suspects. They left the party early because Babe was furious that Bwana was ignoring her. Was it possible that he had told her it was over between them? That he no longer wanted her as his mistress? I could sense that she might have a vengeful streak in her nature.

And Tusker could be justified in wanting Lord Cheriton dead since he was openly having an affair with his wife. We knew from the party that he was easily humiliated, after the references to that naughty game they played. How easy to have dropped Babe at home and then gone out to wait for Bwana. The only thing against that was that he had no idea Bwana would be summoned home so early. And they both appeared to be genuinely shocked by the news.

I let my thoughts move on. The one thing that had been completely forgotten was the jewel theft. I had found that what seemed like different crimes were often connected in some way. Was it coincidental that his two children came out on an aeroplane right after a precious jewel had been stolen and a few days later he was dead? But again the problem was that all the settlers were at Idina's party with the exception of Diddy, Cyril and Bwana's own family. And they could surely have killed him on his own estate if they'd wanted to. Why drive all this way and ambush him on the way home? To make it look like an animal killed him, I supposed, but the flaw in that argument was that it did not appear any vehicle had come down the road after Bwana's. He had a big

Buick motorcar and the tires were quite distinctive.

These musings were interrupted by Freddie asking, "So what do you think, Darcy?"

"About who might have killed him?" Darcy replied. "I've no idea."

"No, I meant about what Tusker said. That we should have let it go as an animal attack for the sake of everyone. They dislike me enough around here, for having to administer rules they want to break. Now I'll be an absolute pariah."

"A murder is a murder," Darcy replied. "And you have to do your duty, however unpleasant."

"Spoken like a true-blue Englishman," Freddie replied. "You know, living out here one forgets what it used to be like in England. These people act like gods in their own little universe. They think there is no law that can't be broken."

"Including getting rid of someone who has become inconvenient?" Darcy asked.

Freddie nodded. "I think you'll find that every person at Idina's has some reason to be annoyed with Bwana Hartley."

"We have plenty of people in life who annoy us," Darcy said, "but it rarely leads to murder."

As I watched them talking together in the front seats I remembered something else — a brief snatch of conversation between them when they looked at the body. Freddie had said, "You don't think this can have anything to do with —" and Darcy had shut him up. To do with what? I could sit silent and out of the conversation no longer.

"Freddie, do you think this might have something to do with the jewel theft?" I asked.

Freddie looked back with a horrified glance. "How do you know about —"

"My wife is very astute," Darcy said. "She questioned me about why we were really in Kenya. I thought it wise to put her into the picture."

"About why you were really in Kenya?" Freddie repeated.

"Yes. I told her about the jewel theft in England and the fact that the thief might have come out to Kenya to hand over the stone."

"Oh," Freddie said. "The jewel theft. Of course. Oh, I see."

I, on the other hand, did not see. I got the feeling that they had been talking about something quite different, not a jewel theft at all. Was the stolen diamond something Darcy had made up to keep me quiet? I could hardly question him about it right now. But later, when we were safely in our own room — then I'd demand to know the truth.

We drove on in silence. I tried to admire the wildlife I spotted beside the road. I wanted to talk about the murder but if they were keeping something they knew, something important, from me, then there was little point. So I sat in the backseat, feeling miffed, and tried to evaluate who might have a motive to kill Lord Cheriton. Tusker and Babe, for a start. Either one could have done it. An interesting thought came into my head. I had noted that Babe might have a devious nature. What if the telephone call had not come from Bwana's wife at all? The Eggertons had a telephone. What if she had imitated Angel's voice and begged Bwana to come home, then secretly drove to the right spot and waited to ambush him?

I supposed it was possible but Bwana was a big, powerful man. If he had got out of his car to talk to Babe and she had pulled a knife, he could easily have wrested it away from her. Unless she had lured him into a romantic embrace — "Let's do it right here, in the middle of nowhere" — and he'd take the bait, easily aroused. And as they came together she stabbed him. Which must mean there would be blood on her clothing. And maybe a bloody knife hidden on their estate.

And if it wasn't one of them? We had already been told that Tomlinson had a bone to pick about a prize bull. But did you kill because someone had got the better of you in a deal?

Sheila Tomlinson might have been harboring anger at the way Bwana had treated her all those years ago, but she seemed happy enough with her present lot and anxious to see her former husband again. And anyway, she was at the party all night. They all were . . . Pansy, who was angry at being dumped in favor of Babe; Harry, who would be angry at his wife carrying on with Bwana; Camilla, who had been married to him before . . . I couldn't think of a motive for Chops Rutherford or for the Atkinses, outsiders from Nairobi, seeming to disapprove of the Happy Valley set but ended up being willing participants. At least Idina had been fully occupied for the entire night, I suspected.

We drove up to Idina's house and as Freddie was parking the motorcar I noticed something of interest. Two other cars were of the same make and model as Bwana's. That disproved my theory that his had been the last car to drive on the road. So actually any one of them could have followed him. It could, I supposed, even have been a group effort — the whole community deciding to get rid of a man who was too annoying for some reason. Yet that didn't seem to jibe with the good-natured way he had been greeted everywhere, and the way that Tusker had spoken of him, almost as if he admired the risks Bwana took, the way he seduced other men's wives. I hoped that the policeman sent out from Nairobi would be capable and intelligent. In my experience (which had been rather more extensive than I would have wanted at my young age) I had found too many policemen were all too willing to grab the first conclusion and the first suspect they stumbled across and not so willing to admit they were wrong. At least this time we were absolute outsiders and innocent bystanders.

CHAPTER 25

August 12
Back at Idina's house

There are times I wish I had stayed put on that houseboat on the Thames. It would have been just Darcy and me and I'd willingly have gone without the cucumber sandwiches, if necessary. Now this is all becoming too horrid. These people live such sordid lives and I'm afraid all the details will have to come out now that the police have arrived. Since we are newcomers, I'm hoping we'll be allowed to escape.

"Finally!" Mr. Tomlinson roared as we came into the living room. "Of all the bloody cheek, telling us we weren't allowed to leave. Well, what have you discovered? Was it an accident? Can we all go home now, for God's sake?"

I looked at Freddie, wondering what he would say. He shook his head. "I'm afraid it was no accident. Lord Cheriton was murdered and the police are on their way from Nairobi. Everyone will just have to stay put until they arrive."

Jocelyn had been hovering by the front door. "Oh crikey. A murder? That's awful. If news of it gets to England my father will be furious. His last words to me were to stay out of trouble. . . ." He winced as if he could already picture his father's outrage.

"Don't be silly. You had nothing to do with it," Idina said. "We all had nothing to do with it. We're deeply sorry he was killed but it's not our fault if he got out of his car on a lonely road in the middle of the night. Surely the police will see this."

"But what about me?" Mr. Van Horn got to his feet and stomped toward Freddie. "How long am I to be inconvenienced here? Can we now leave, Mr. Blanchford?"

"I'm afraid I'm not at liberty to drive you, sir," Freddie said. "You'll just have to wait with the rest of us."

"But it is an outrage. I should never have agreed to let you drive me. I am being kept here against my will. A foreign national. I shall let my embassy know."

"I apologize, sir," Freddie said. "I know

315

you have nothing to do with this and of course you were far away when it happened, but I'm afraid I have to stay here until the police arrive. If I am instructed to stick around after that then maybe Mr. and Mrs. O'Mara can drive you up to Cyril for your safari."

"It is probably too late now to accomplish anything worthwhile today," Van Horn snapped. "The animals are at their best in the early morning. At least they are in South Africa, where we have wildlife in spectacular numbers. So far here I have seen only a paltry couple of antelope and monkeys. I doubt the whole thing would be worth my while anyway."

"I can run you back to Gilgil as soon as I'm free to leave," Freddie said. "If you don't wish to go on the safari."

Van Horn shrugged. "What else is there to do in this godforsaken place?"

"What made you come here?" Pansy Ragg asked.

Van Horn shrugged again. "Business, dear lady. A couple of transactions in Nairobi and then I persuaded myself to take a quick holiday. What a waste of time. I should just head for the coast and take the next steamship home."

"It really shouldn't be much longer, sir,"

Freddie said. "And I am sure Diddy Ruocco won't mind putting you up for the night, or perhaps Cyril can arrange for tents and bearers for a longer safari. If you drive far enough north you'll be in the Mara. Great game viewing there. And if you are planning to hunt — why, there are herds of such numbers that you can fire a gun with your eyes closed and you're guaranteed to hit something."

"I have no pleasure in killing something for no reason," Van Horn said. "For meat, yes. For a trophy, yes. But simply to see a beast fall? It is not worth the effort."

He subsided into his chair again, his arms folded, his face like stone. There was an uncomfortable silence. People shifted in their seats. The air was unpleasantly thick with cigarette smoke as several of them puffed away nervously. I noticed that a couple of them already had glasses in their hands as well. The "hair of the dog" as Tusker Eggerton had said.

"It's damned cheek," Chops Rutherford muttered after a while. "What can the police want with us? You can't think we had anything to do with the poor fellow's death. We were all fully occupied when he left. Although I don't think the police need to know about that either."

"Of course they don't," Idina said. Even she was looking old and strained now, puffing away at a Turkish cigarette. "You were all safely tucked up for the night with your respective spouses when Bwana was summoned home." She paused. "Isn't that right?"

"Oh absolutely." Harry Ragg nodded, glancing at Pansy for affirmation. "Sound asleep, although Pansy did murmur that a telephone bell was ringing, didn't you, darling?"

"I think I might have done."

Several members of the party stifled a grin. I could tell the police would get nothing useful out of anyone here. I was handed a cup of coffee and I perched on the edge of a sofa beside Sheila Tomlinson, who only just acknowledged my presence with a curt nod. She was looking white and shocked. In fact most of them did have a dazed look on their faces, but that could just be because of the excesses of the night before and terrible hangovers. As I studied them, one by one, I realized they were not all present. Freddie noticed at the same time. "What happened to that couple from Nairobi? The Atkinses?"

"They left, darling," Idina said. "I tried to persuade them to stay but they said that they couldn't possibly have anything to add to an investigation into the death of a complete stranger. He was absolutely terrified about his precious reputation. Peeing in his pants, you know." She chuckled. "He's hoping to become deputy governor. Very ambitious, one gathers."

"Nevertheless, they should not have left without permission," Freddie said, sounding for the first time like the government officer trying to be in charge.

"What was I supposed to do? Wrestle them into submission?" Idina asked.

"You could have removed their car keys," Freddie pointed out.

"In hindsight that might have been a good idea," Idina said, tossing her hair petulantly, "but you must remember that I was in shock. We were all in shock. We have all lost someone very close to us."

A lot closer to the women than the men, I thought and studied them all again. Sheila Tomlinson, Camilla Rutherford, both once married to him. Pansy Ragg, his mistress and obviously very attached to him. And Idina, the one who had never let herself get too close to him. Only Mrs. Atkins seemed not to have been a moth to his flame. She had dragged her husband to the party because she wanted to rekindle a relationship with bigger game — the Prince of

Wales. I wondered who would tell the prince about this, and what he would be told. Would it make the English newspapers? Might it have any ramifications for the job Darcy had been offered?

"Well, no sense in sitting around moping," Chops Rutherford said. "If we're stuck here I suggest we fortify ourselves with a decent breakfast."

"It's all laid out and ready in the dining room, darling, although I don't know how you can think of food at a time like this. I don't think I could eat a morsel." That was just what Babe Eggerton had said. So Idina had been fonder of him than she wanted to admit.

Sheila Tomlinson had been staring down at her hands. Now she looked up. "I feel the same way," she said. "I just want to go home to my children."

"How many children do you have?" I asked because she was sitting next to me nervously playing with the tassels on her jacket and I thought it might be a good idea to get onto a safe subject.

It was. She actually smiled. "Five," she said. "All boys. Although the two older ones are now in boarding school in England. I miss them terribly. Such darling boys, all of them."

320

"Absolute little monsters from what I've heard," Harry Ragg muttered to Pansy.

This caused me to look around at the assembled guests again. Did anyone else have children? They had certainly been through enough marriages, and yet nobody had mentioned a child. Perhaps they were all sent off to boarding school as soon as they were old enough so that they didn't cramp their parents' wild lifestyle. The only children I knew of in the valley were Lord Cheriton's twins. How convenient that they were here when their father was murdered and Rupert would inherit the title and everything that went with it. Rupert, who had made it so clear that he had no intention of taking over the farm in Africa. Yes, all things considered, he was the one with the biggest motive to want his father dead.

The other guests went through to the dining room and helped themselves to the food that was keeping hot on the sideboard. Although I had already eaten at the Eggertons' I did not take much persuading to have a little more. At least eating gave us something to do other than waiting and worrying or making inane conversation. We finished breakfast and still no sign of a policeman at eleven o'clock. Idina suggested we might like to play tennis or croquet but was not met with an enthusiastic response.

I moved closer to Darcy. "Diddy might wonder where we have got to with her motorcar," I said. "Do you think we should telephone her?"

"We can't tell her the real reason we are being held up," Darcy muttered to me. "It wouldn't be right that she finds out before his family. But I agree, she might have plans for the day and be annoyed if her motorcar is not returned."

I accompanied him to the telephone and heard him say, "We've been held up, I'm afraid. There's been a spot of trouble at Idina's. I'll give you all the details when we get back. It shouldn't be too long now. No — Georgie and I are just fine. You're right. The party was a bit of a shock and no, we did not participate!"

He put the telephone receiver down. "It's all right. She doesn't need her car and besides, Cyril has his old safari vehicle. He's rather miffed, I gather, because he got up early and was all kitted out for Mr. Van Horn."

"Poor Cyril," I said. "I suspect he's innately lazy."

"He's a strange fish, isn't he?" Darcy said. "The sort of man you'd expect to find in a London club or having tea and being witty in a dowager duchess's drawing room yet here he is taking people on safari — surely one of the most dangerous occupations. Doesn't make sense."

"I agree," I said. I was going to say more but at that moment Jocelyn opened the front door, an excited look on his face. "The police have arrived, Lady Idina. Do you want me to show them in?" He gave a nervous grin. "Gosh, this is rather exciting, isn't it?"

"It's a bloody nuisance," Chops snapped. "Bring them in and let's get this over with."

Jocelyn was about to leave when Idina grabbed his sleeve. "Just one thing, darling. If the police ask you any questions about last night, we were all in bed by midnight. All nicely asleep. Got it?"

CHAPTER 26

August 12
At Idina's house

No matter how many times I have been
involved with the police in the past I still
feel that awful dread when they come
into the room. I know I am innocent and
have nothing to hide but the fear is just
the same — that they will make me say
the wrong thing. Let's hope this detective inspector is brighter than most.

Harry Ragg had stood up and looked out
the window. He pulled back the curtain and
turned to the rest of us. "Oh God. It's that
Windbag fellow."

"Windrush, you mean?" Pansy corrected.

"I always think of him as Windbag. You
remember from that incident in Nairobi?
Grammar-school boy. Little upstart. Better
watch what you say to him."

Footsteps were heard on the gravel outside. Jocelyn was still standing guard at the door. He stepped back as the inspector entered. At first glance he looked rather wishy-washy compared with the suntanned occupants of this room. Sort of beige all over. He was skinny with sandy hair and a rather sad little sandy mustache that was not growing well. He was wearing the khaki bush jacket and large hat that must have been the uniform of the local police. He removed the hat on entering. It was obvious from the way he strode into the room with a look of disdain and suspicion on his face that he wanted everyone there to be guilty.

"So, we've exhausted all the other sports you people are famous for and have resorted to killing each other now, have we?" he asked.

"I beg your pardon?" Idina stepped out to block his path further into the room. "That remark was quite uncalled for and in poor taste, Inspector." She paused. "It is 'Inspector,' I take it?"

"That's right. Detective Inspector Windrush."

"And I am Lady Idina Sackville-Haldeman. I don't believe we have met." She held out her hand to him. It was the perfect rebuke of the aristocracy to the middle class, putting the inspector firmly in his place.

Of course he had to shake her hand.

"Well, Detective Inspector Windrush, we have just been told that one of our dear friends has been murdered. We are all in a state of shock. So I'd advise you to tread carefully with us. Everyone here is a friend of the governor and we don't take kindly to bombast or wild insinuations." Although she was much smaller than him she had considerable presence and I believe he took a small step away from her.

Freddie came to Idina's side. "I'm Freddie Blanchford, sir. His Majesty's district officer. I'm the one who made the telephone call. I've been taken to the body and I think it's fairly clear that it was murder."

"You're an expert in these things, are you?" Windrush asked, still with a sneer on his lips.

"No, sir, but a large knife wound is a pretty good indication that he didn't die in his sleep."

Some of the occupants of the room chuckled, making Windrush scowl.

"And where is this body?" he demanded.

"It's several miles up the road north. I'll be happy to escort you to see it."

"You've just left it there, have you? Then

the scavengers will have found it by now."

"The medical examiner from Gilgil is with it and I have borrowed men from a nearby estate to stand guard until we return," Freddie replied evenly. "I don't know if you would want to see the body first or to get statements from everyone here. They are naturally all anxious to go home as soon as possible."

"Naturally," Windrush said. "I'll have my sergeant take initial statements while I go to inspect the body but then I will want to question everyone myself."

"I don't know what we can tell you that might be helpful, Inspector," Idina said. "Everyone here was at my party yesterday evening and I put them all up for the night so that they didn't have to drive home."

"Put them all up for the night, did you?" The way he smirked indicated that he must have heard rumors about what went on at Idina's parties.

"I try to be a good hostess," she said calmly. "And it's not safe to drive in the dark here. Elephants, you know."

"And the man who was killed. Has he been positively identified?"

"He has," Freddie said. "It's Lord Cheriton."

"Lord Cheriton?" Windrush looked puzzled.

"Used to be known as Bwana Hartley in the colony," Idina chimed in. "Just inherited the title from a cousin."

"Oh yes. You lot are always inheriting things, aren't you?" He nodded. "Bwana Hartley. Oh yes indeed. So why wasn't he here at the party? Fallen out with you, had he?"

"But he was at the party," Idina said. "His wife did not come with him as she was under the weather. About midnight he received a telephone call saying that she was feeling worse and wanted him to come home. So he left and drove home. I saw him off, because he came to say good-bye to me, but I'm afraid everyone else was already asleep."

"I heard the telephone ring," Pansy said, giving the inspector an innocent smile. "But Harry was already asleep and snoring."

"So he left at midnight?"

"Just after, I would say."

I watched Idina, impressed with her composure. She was giving a wonderfully convincing performance.

"And did his wife not telephone again when he didn't arrive home?"

"That was the strange thing," Idina said.

"She did not. He had a terrible temper, you know. One did have to tread carefully around him sometimes."

"I've come across Bwana Hartley," Windrush said. "He's been involved in several court cases, I seem to remember. People are always suing him."

"A couple of times." Idina shrugged her shoulders.

"I sued him once," Tomlinson said. "He stole a prize bull from me. But that didn't mean I'd want to kill him. That's why you go to court. To let the course of law settle things."

"And did you win your case against him?"

"I did not, unfortunately," Tomlinson said. I could see from his face that he wished he had not opened up this subject.

"So you had good reason to carry a grudge against him." Another smirk from Windrush.

"On the contrary. It was through him that I met my wife, so I'm grateful to the bugger." He put a hand on Sheila's shoulder and gave it a squeeze.

"I see. Anyone else had a falling-out with him recently?"

"It wouldn't matter if we had, Inspector," Idina said, "because as I told you everyone was here, tucked up in bed and asleep."

"Tucked up and asleep. How convenient." Windrush let his gaze move around the room. "Were there any local inhabitants who were not tucked up and asleep here last night?"

"Major and Mrs. Eggerton left early," Idina went on smoothly. "She was not feeling well."

"Is something going around up here in the valley?" Inspector Windrush asked. "All these wives not feeling well."

"I believe it's not a crime to be under the weather occasionally, even here in the Wanjohi Valley," Idina said.

"And Lord Cheriton's wife, who was also under the weather — where does she live?"

"At the northern end of the valley. She was home with her two stepchildren who are visiting from England. Also her next-door neighbor did not come to the party. You probably know her — Diddy Ruocco? Trains racehorses. Is often in Nairobi."

"Oh yes. I believe I have seen her at the track. So she wasn't invited?"

"She and I are not the best of pals," Idina said. "She prefers more outdoor pursuits."

The inspector gave a snort — halfway between a laugh and a grunt of disgust. "Well, I'll be visiting them later, I suppose," he said. "But I'll be back here when I've taken a look at the body. And I'll leave you folks to think carefully about anything that might be useful to my investigation. If this man was really your bosom friend, as you claim, then I'm sure you will want justice for him and for his killer to be found."

"Of course we do, Inspector," Idina said.

Mr. Van Horn stepped out in front of the inspector. "Look here," he said. "I am a visitor to this country, on my way to a safari drive. I have nothing to do with these people. I do not know them. I wish to have permission to leave now. My day has already been ruined."

"And you are?" Windrush asked.

"Wilhelm Van Horn. South African national. In Nairobi on business and decided to take a few days' holiday in Gilgil."

"Then what are you doing here? Did you attend the party last night?"

"Good God no. This young fellow, your district officer, kindly offered to drive me to the man who will take me on safari. We were flagged down by that boy over there, informed about the murder and brought here. I have already wasted over an hour."

"If I might see your passport, sir?"

"What person is crazy enough to take a passport on safari?" Van Horn blustered. "It is in my hotel safe in Gilgil. You may come down there to view it later if you wish. But as for my alibi, if you require one, I was drinking in the bar at the hotel in Gilgil at midnight last night. I have no means of transportation. And I did not know the man who has been killed."

"Very well, sir." Inspector Windrush gave in to this attack. "Then I see no reason to detain you. But I shall need to take the district officer with me to view the body."

"This couple can give him a lift," Freddie said. "Mr. and Mrs. O'Mara. They are on their honeymoon, visiting from England. They were the ones who found the body, when they drove home early this morning."

"Oh yes." The inspector turned to me. He had surprisingly dark eyes for a man with light hair and skin and his birdlike stare was not unlike that of the vultures I had met that morning.

"Just out from England, are you?"

"That's right," Darcy answered before I could speak.

"And which of these people are you staying with?"

"With Diddy Ruocco," Darcy said. "Freddie Blanchford is an old friend from Oxford. He arranged this for us."

"I see." He paused. "You found the body. What made you do that?"

"We were on our way home, early this morning. His car was blocking the road ahead, with the motor still running," Darcy said. "We called and thought the driver must be close by. There was a movement in the bushes. We went to investigate and it was vultures all over the body. Rather a horrible sight, I have to say, especially for my bride."

"So were you attending this party?" The question was asked directly to me.

"Yes. Lady Idina was kind enough to invite us. We met her at the polo match yesterday morning."

"You go in for parties like this, do you?" He was smirking at me now. "I'm not a complete ignoramus, you know. I've heard what goes on here."

"I grew up in a Scottish castle, Inspector. I can assure you there were no parties of any sort. It was kind of Lady Idina to invite complete strangers and a novelty to be part of the smart set for once." I didn't want him to get the impression that we had actually taken part and enjoyed it, but I couldn't think of how to say this without being rude to our hostess.

"Scottish castle, eh? You don't sound Scottish."

"Neither did my great-grandmother but

she loved to be in Scotland and built herself a castle there."

"Built herself a castle?"

"Yes. Balmoral."

"Your great-grandmother was?"

"Queen Victoria," I said. I was so proud of myself that I had to stifle a grin.

"Oh, I see. You're part of the Prince of Wales's party. Why didn't you say so?" He had gone quite pink. "Well, of course you can go whenever you wish, Your Highness."

"In that case we will be happy to take Mr. Van Horn," Darcy said. "Lady Idina, thank you for your hospitality. It was most enlightening." He took her hand.

"I hope we shall see more of you before you go home," she said, her expression making quite clear the double meaning in this.

She hugged me and we kissed cheeks, a few inches apart, the way my mother always did. "We'd better go too, Inspector," Freddie said. "Or they won't be able to get past Lord Cheriton's car."

"Oh, all right," Inspector Windrush said. "So you'll please give your statements to my sergeant and I'll be back. Nobody is to go anywhere until I return. Is that clear?"

"Oh — But — Inspector —" came the entreaties after him, but he didn't stop. We followed him out and got into our motorcar.

I let Mr. Van Horn take the front seat beside Darcy. As Darcy helped me into the backseat he whispered to me, "I've never seen you pull rank before. Name-dropping indeed."

"Only when absolutely necessary," I replied. "I was afraid he wouldn't let us go. It worked, didn't it?"

"Absolutely. Well done."

He gave me a little kiss, then climbed into his own seat and we drove off, behind the inspector and Freddie.

CHAPTER 27

August 12
Back at Diddy's house

Thank goodness. So glad to escape. The party was bad enough, but a party with perhaps a murderer among them?

The sun was now high in the sky and burned down on us as we drove along the open stretch of road. I remembered Diddy's dire warnings about sunstroke and not wearing a hat. We drove without incident until we had to stop behind the police car. The officers had already got out and Inspector Windrush was talking with the doctor.

"Oh no. Not another holdup!" Mr. Van Horn growled. "Why do they not move their motorcar off the road? They are imbeciles."

"That's because the murdered man's motorcar is blocking the road on the other side of the rocks." Darcy got out of our mo-

336

tor and hurried to catch up with Inspector Windrush and Freddie.

"Do you think it might be possible to have Lord Cheriton's motor moved off the road so that we can get past?" Darcy asked.

"We'll need to dust it for fingerprints and take photographs first," Inspector Windrush said shortly.

"Then maybe you will need my fingerprints for identification," Darcy said, "because I got into the car."

"Why did you do that?" Windrush was eyeing him suspiciously.

"The motor was running. It must have been running since midnight. I was going to move the vehicle out of the way but then I realized that the police would need to examine it. So I turned the motor off. There was no point in leaving it on."

"I see." Windrush gave a grudging nod. "You were the first person at the scene of the crime, then. What else did you touch?"

"I helped turn the body over," Darcy said.

"And why did you do that?"

"The doctor and I did it. To verify who it was, and to see what might have killed him," Darcy said. He was still being remarkably calm.

Windrush's eyes narrowed. "You don't seem to be overly fazed by finding a dead body. What sort of job do you do in England? Or are you one of these aristocrats who lounge about and play polo?"

"I certainly cannot afford to lounge around. I would gladly have taken a job but in case you don't know there is still a depression going on at home. I take on the odd commission around the world when I am offered one."

"What sort of commission?"

"Anything that pays me," Darcy said, "but as it happens I have been offered a proper full-time government job when I return from my honeymoon."

This last word obviously sank in. The inspector looked back at me with a more kindly expression. "I'm sorry, yes. I forgot you're on your honeymoon and you young people have had a nasty shock. Don't worry. We'll get the road cleared in a jiffy. I'll have my men go over the motorcar while I take a look at the body."

He was about to follow the doctor into the bushes when I couldn't resist saying, "There was one thing you might want to notice, Inspector."

"Yes, Your Highness?"

I wasn't about to correct him at this moment. I pointed to the bush. "Doesn't this look like a scrap of hair from a lion? Or at least from some animal?"

He nodded. "It might well be. But if, as has been suggested, Lord Cheriton was murdered then it doesn't really matter what sort of animal had a go at his body afterward. And the fur could have been there for ages."

"That is true," Dr. Singh said. "Now if you will come this way."

They led; Darcy followed. I stayed back this time. I'd had enough of partially eaten bodies for one morning. I heard the inspector's intake of breath. "The poor bugger has been eaten all right," he said. "So what makes you so sure that —"

Then he cleared his throat. "Oh, I see. Yes. That's definitely a knife wound. We won't need an autopsy for that. Would have gone straight into the heart. Any sign of the weapon? Right. You men search the area for a possible weapon, and for any other clues."

It probably took another half hour before the vehicles were able to be moved and maneuvered so that the road was cleared. It was like one of those annoying little puzzles where you slide the pieces across to make a picture. The body was transported to the back of the doctor's car, ready to be taken to the morgue. The Eggertons' Kikuyu workers were delivered home in the police car and we were free to go.

I went up to Freddie. "What about Bwana's widow and children? Surely if they are not given the news soon it will get to them one way or another, and that's not right. You should probably be the one to break the news, shouldn't you? Rather you than the inspector." I lowered my voice as I glanced across at the policeman.

"I suppose you're right," he said. "But I also feel I should be back at Idina's in case of more questioning. It is my district, after all. I don't want my constituents bullied or upset by the Nairobi police. Could I ask you and Darcy to break the news?"

"But what if one of them was in some way involved?" I said. "Wouldn't it be important if someone in authority saw their reactions?"

I could see that Freddie was really torn. He probably hadn't anticipated handling anything like this when he signed on as a government official. He probably pictured his days would be spent making sure his district ran peacefully and rules were obeyed. He chewed on his lip in an endearingly boyish way then looked at Darcy. "You know about these things, don't you? I imagine you can interpret reactions to the news better than I. I'll come to join you as soon as I am free, but in the meantime . . ."

"That's all right, old chap," Darcy said. "Leave it to us."

We climbed back into the motorcar. Mr. Van Horn sat beside Darcy staring ahead of him in angry silence. I wondered if Darcy was going to take advantage of having a suspect in a jewel theft actually in the car with us. When he said nothing I asked, "So, Mr. Van Horn, what kind of business are you in back in South Africa?"

"I am a broker, young lady. I put together deals."

"What kind of deals?"

"For people who want to invest in my country," he said. "We have many resources, many chances to invest advantageously. Gold, for example."

"Or diamonds," I couldn't resist saying.

His expression didn't change. "Yes, diamond mines are a great investment. If you are interested I can introduce you . . ."

"I'm afraid we are not in the position to invest in anything," Darcy said, rather shortly, I thought. "We are newlyweds. Poor as church mice."

"I see."

"Have you been on many safaris?" I went on, determined to keep him talking.

"Not many. I live in the city of Johannesburg. But I have been to Kruger Park a

341

few times as a young man."

"What sort of animals do they have in Kruger Park?" Darcy asked.

"Everything I shall see here, I am sure. Lions, zebras, giraffes . . ." He spread his hands in a shrug. "When this Mr. Prendergast offered to take me, I thought it would be a pleasant way to fill in a day before I went back to Nairobi and caught the train home. Now I am sure I have wasted my time and the safari will not take place."

We went over a particularly rutted strip of road and had to be silent rather than risk biting our tongues. Then, out of the blue, Van Horn turned to Darcy. "Were you acquainted with this Lord Cheriton?"

"We only met him once," Darcy said. "We were invited to dinner at his house."

"I understand he was a powerful man in this community. A man of influence? With political ambitions, so I'm told."

"I really don't know. We are visitors here, like yourself," Darcy said.

"So you have heard no rumor about who might have killed him?"

"No." Darcy shot him a glance. "Pretty much everyone who knew him was at that party."

"Except his own family," Van Horn said. "His children have come out from England

342

for the first time — is that not correct?"

"Yes."

"The first time he has seen them in many years?"

"I believe so."

"So he wouldn't immediately recognize them."

We drove on in silence. What had Mr. Van Horn been hinting at? That his children were not actually his offspring at all, but sent out to kill him? Surely no one could believe such a wild theory. After all, Rowena was called Hartley when she was at school with me. And besides, from the tracks on the road it was clear Bwana's vehicle was the last one to come down from the north of the valley, unless the family possessed an identical vehicle. I'd have to check on that.

We made it back to Diddy's estate without incident. Diddy came running out to meet us as she heard the motorcar. "Oh, my poor dears. What an awful shock for you. Idina telephoned me with all the news. He was murdered, you say? Are the police there now? Well, I expect they'll soon track down who did it. It will be some estate worker who has been sacked and now has gone rogue." She paused, getting her breath. "Because it can't be one of us, can it?"

When we didn't answer immediately she went on. "How was he killed?"

"Stabbed through the heart with a knife," Darcy said. "A very big knife."

"Well then." She looked relieved. "That wouldn't be one of us. If any white person had wanted to kill him they would have shot him, not risked a close confrontation like that. He was awfully strong, you know."

This, of course, was true. I could picture Tusker stabbing him, but not a woman. A big man like Bwana would have grabbed a wrist and wrested away the knife.

"Do come and have some food." Diddy took my arm. "You poor dears must be starving."

"The one thing we have had is plenty to eat," I replied, smiling. "We had a good breakfast at the Eggertons' and then another at Idina's. But I wouldn't say no to another cup of coffee. Oh, and have you met Mr. Van Horn? Cyril was supposed to take him on safari."

"There would be no point now," Van Horn said tersely. He turned to us. "Wilhelm Van Horn. Pleased to make your acquaintance."

"Mr. and Mrs. O'Mara," Darcy replied.

"I'm sorry you have been inconvenienced like this, Mr. Van Horn. Come inside and chat with Cyril. Why don't you stay the night and enjoy a proper safari tomorrow?"

"Most kind." Van Horn was being incredibly civil to her, after his earlier belligerence.

Diddy's servants whisked our belongings into our bedroom ahead of us. I followed them, anxious to change my clothes and have a wash and brush-up before I faced Angel and the twins. I wished we had never volunteered to do so. . . . Well, we hadn't exactly volunteered. We had been commandeered into the task. Darcy came into the room behind me and shut the door.

"What a business," he said. "And here I was thinking it would be a wonderful escape for us. Exotic landscape, animals, fresh air . . ."

"The landscape was certainly exotic enough last night," I said. "I don't think I will ever get those images out of my mind. What awful people. They keep marrying each other and then leaping into bed with each other; I'm not surprised they kill each other as well."

Darcy looked at me with interest. "You really think it was one of them?"

I shrugged. "From what we've heard there were plenty of people with a good motive, and the means. . . ."

"The means?"

345

"Didn't you notice? There were two motorcars exactly like Bwana's? We thought it was his tire tracks on the road, but one of them could have followed him. And what perfect alibis — they were all in bed with somebody."

Darcy shook his head. "I hope we find out that it's a Kikuyu freedom fighter. At least that would make it simpler."

"You'd rather a native was hanged than a white man? That's a terrible sentiment."

"They'd never catch him. He'd hide out in the Aberdare forest and be fed by local sympathizers. There is an underground movement that is gaining traction, you know, for more power for the natives and a say in government."

"Just a minute," I said, as things that had been said formed themselves in my consciousness. "Mr. Van Horn said something about Bwana having political aspirations? Is that right? And he could have been vehemently against natives having any say in government, and one of them decided to finish him off before he was elected?"

"Actually he already had been elected to represent this district," Darcy said, "and you are not wrong in your suppositions."

I looked up at Darcy, frowning. "Wait." I held up my hand. "When you were talking to Freddie he said, 'You don't think this can have anything to do with — ?' and you cut him off. What do you know that I don't? What other?"

Darcy looked uncomfortable. "Nothing that concerns you."

"Nothing that concerns me? But something that might concern Bwana's death? Something to do with political power?" I took a deep breath. "I am your wife now, Darcy. And I'm not an idiot. Whether I like it or not I seem to be involved in this murder so I'd like the truth please."

"You are too damned astute sometimes," he said. "You're right. You are my wife now. And you're just as good at this spy business as I am. If I keep things from you at times it's because it's safer for you not to know. But this can go no further." He went across to the window and checked that it was shut. "You heard Bwana expound his views at the dinner table the other night. He's a die-hard Fascist. A big pal of Mosley. White people rule and keep the natives in their place."

I nodded. "But I'd imagine that applies to most people here."

"Probably. But he is also an ardent admirer of Hitler. He was in Berlin a couple of months ago and our man there tells a tale that is quite chilling. Bwana's job is to rise through colony politics until he can have enough control so that at the right moment the colony can declare its allegiance to Germany."

"Allegiance to Germany?" I uttered the words too loudly then realized and put my hand to my mouth. "But that would never happen."

"Wouldn't it? You've seen the British expatriates who live here. Decadent. Fueled by drugs and alcohol — which people like Bwana have encouraged, by the way. They've made themselves highly unpopular with the natives, and they have become apathetic. The native troops would follow anyone who promised them independence after a war."

"A war, here?"

Darcy put a hand on my shoulder. "My dear, I think we have to accept that Herr Hitler is arming his country at an alarming rate. Hitler is already helping stir up trouble in Spain, and Mosley is trying to get support in England. War will come and sooner rather than later. And it will spread to the colonies, I fear."

"Crikey." I realized I sounded like Jocelyn and his innocent, boyish face came into my head. If another war came then he and all like him would be sent off to fight and die.

"We've just had the war to end all wars," I said and heard my voice crack with emotion.

"That's what we all hoped. But the Germans are itching for revenge, for a chance to hold their heads up high again. And I think Hitler wants more than that. He wants to rule the world."

"That's crazy," I said. "He must be crazy."

"But very clever. He knows how to whip up anger and hate, and national pride. We've underestimated him for too long."

I went across to the window. The view stretched to the line of hills in the blue distance. Those bright sunbirds were dipping at the edge of the fountain. It all seemed so far away and so unreal. I stood there, trying to digest all that had been said. Bwana had become a danger, possibly a German agent. And we had been housed with Diddy, next door to him. I turned back to face Darcy. "You knew about this before we came, didn't you?"

He nodded.

"And that's why you were sent out here. That jewel theft, that was just a story to keep me from asking more questions."

"Not exactly. There was a jewel theft, and we did have our eyes on Mr. Van Horn."

I took a deep breath. "So you deceived

me. You lied to me."

He came over and put his hands on my shoulders. "Georgie, you have some kind of idea what I do. There will be times when I can't tell you everything, when I'm not at liberty to tell you everything. And yes, my main reason for coming out here was to assess the situation and the danger he posed to our country."

"Will you promise not to lie if I ask you another question?"

"I'll try not to, if it's a question I'm allowed to answer."

I took a deep breath, staring up into his eyes. "Do you know who killed him?"

CHAPTER 28

Some things are beginning to make sense.
I almost wish I didn't know what I've
been told. It would be so much easier if
a jealous husband followed Bwana and
stabbed him. Well, maybe one did. I am
going to stay well out of it and try to
enjoy my time here. I hope Darcy can
stay out of it too.

The question that had first formed in my
mind was so shocking I could not say it out
loud. It was "Did you kill him?" but I knew
that was impossible. Darcy had been in bed
beside me all night. I'd swear to that. So I
repeated the question. "Well, do you know
who killed him?"

"I wish I did," he said. "It's possible that
the Communist Party also has agents work-

ing in the colony, trying to do what Bwana was doing. And it's possible that one of them decided to put a stop to his activities. But the question remains: how did anyone know he was going to be on that stretch of road at that time of night?"

"Someone at that party is an undercover communist agent?" I said. "That seems highly unlikely. Communists aren't supposed to indulge and spend and have millions of servants, are they?"

"I wish I knew, Georgie," he said. He took me into his arms. "But whatever else is going on, this is your honeymoon and I want you to have a wonderful time here. All right?"

"All right," I said hesitantly. Then I looked up at him and he kissed me.

"We should get changed and be sociable, I suppose," I said. "But what about Mr. Van Horn? You told me he dealt in jewels. He claims he is a broker."

"I don't think that's incorrect," he said. "He makes deals. He travels internationally." He moved closer to me. "We also suspect he is working for the German government."

"So his purpose here was not to receive stolen goods but to meet with Lord Cheriton?"

Darcy nodded. "It is possible."

"Then why stay down in Gilgil? He never had a chance to speak with Lord Cheriton alone."

"Not to cause suspicion, I expect. He must know that his movements are followed. But why do you think he worked on Cyril Prendergast to be invited on a safari with him and clearly to stay a night or two next door to Cheriton?"

"So someone didn't want that meeting to take place," I said, putting two and two together. "Fortuitous that Bwana was killed right before the meeting."

Darcy nodded. "Freddie was supposed to be looking into a communist cell working in Nairobi. But then he got posted here — out to the back of beyond, safely away from the capital."

"Freddie? He's actually one of your lot . . . ?"

Darcy smiled. "Whatever my 'lot' means. Let's just say he's in contact with the British government and he's helping."

I swallowed back the word "golly." "You don't think he killed Lord Cheriton?" I asked.

"I think I would have known if that was the plan," Darcy said. "Actually we are not encouraged to go around killing people, willy-nilly. The boys in Whitehall just want to keep tabs on things and know what is going on."

"Atkins," I said suddenly. "He lives and works in Nairobi. He works for the Kenyan government, doesn't he? And got himself invited to the party when it didn't seem like his sort of thing at all. And conveniently left before the police could arrive."

Darcy shook his head. "I don't see how Atkins could possibly have learned that Cheriton was in the pocket of the Germans. And even if he did . . ."

"He's a true-blue Englishman. He is outraged, especially when that person inherits a British title. He determines to put a stop to him before he can do more damage."

"Possible," Darcy said hesitantly. "Although I don't see how anyone is going to prove it. They'll all swear Atkins was in bed with someone all night — or more than one person, as the case may be." He shrugged. "Anyway, let's not go on with this. The murder inquiry is nothing to do with us. Someone has taken care of the government's problem for me. My only concern is to look out for a stolen jewel and if that was going to change hands it has already done so."

"But if Mr. Van Horn has received the

stolen diamond, wouldn't he want to get out of the country as quickly as possible?"

"If the jewel was destined for him," Darcy said. "Maybe it wasn't. Maybe it's nowhere near Kenya at this moment. I can't say." He put his hands on my shoulders. "Anyway. You and I should now attempt to enjoy ourselves and make the most of our time here. What would you like to do?"

"I wouldn't mind going on safari with Cyril," I said. "I'd like to see some animals."

"Then we'll arrange for him to take us too," Darcy said. "Two birds with one stone, wouldn't you say? Keeping tabs on Mr. Van Horn, although now that Bwana is dead, I presume he'll just leave quietly. Unless . . ."

"Unless he is involved with the diamond?"

"I was going to say unless someone else here is his contact. We do understand that Bwana was part of a small cell of Fascist sympathizers. But our first task is to visit Angel and break the news to her. I'm not looking forward to it."

"I don't think she'll be heartbroken, somehow," I replied.

He had to smile. "Maybe you're right. Neither will his children. I think they'll all want to put the property on the market and be out of here as quickly as possible."

We washed and changed into clean clothes

then went to find Diddy. She was sitting at a table on the front lawn with Cyril and Mr. Van Horn, who was now in his shirtsleeves and looking a little more relaxed. A pitcher of what looked like a cloudy sort of lemonade was on the table in front of them. Diddy looked up as we approached. "Here they are, our newlyweds. What a horrible thing to happen on your honeymoon. Of course, you didn't know Bwana, but finding his body like that. What a shock. Come and sit down and have a gin fizz."

I accepted, reluctantly. They certainly started drinking early here. The taste was not unpleasant, but I took only a sip before saying, "Diddy, we should go over to Bwana's. Darcy was asked to break the news to them before it reaches them by other channels. Do you think you should come with us?"

"Oh, darlings." She looked uncomfortable. "Yes, you're right. Maybe I should."

"Maybe you should be the one to break it to her, since you know her and we don't," Darcy suggested.

She made a face. "If you really think so. Gosh, what an awful thing to have to do. You'll have to supply the details, though." She got to her feet and turned to Mr. Van Horn. "We'll be right back, Mr. Van Horn.

Please help yourself to anything you need."

"Most kind." He nodded to her. Now that Darcy had mentioned he might be a German agent I saw that many of his mannerisms reminded me of Max, my mother's ex-beau. Was it possible that he was actually German and not Afrikaans at all?

"Don't worry. I shall keep him entertained," Cyril said. "I was hopping mad this morning when I thought that he had overslept and I'd gone to all this trouble. But now I understand I maligned the poor chap. So I am at your disposal, dear Mr. Van Horn. May I suggest we take a little stroll up into the forest? There is always something to be seen."

"Go carefully, won't you," Diddy said. "The boys saw elephants bathing in the stream just above. One of them had a baby with them."

"Darling, I know all about elephants," Cyril said. "Elephants and I are on the same wavelength, I assure you. We respect each other."

Mr. Van Horn didn't look convinced or eager to move.

We left them and crossed the lawn to the gap in the hedge. I glanced at the little cottage as we passed it. The door was open and it looked completely empty inside now. At least Rupert wouldn't have to worm out of accepting his father's insistence that he live there.

"Who used to live in that cottage?" I asked Diddy.

"It was built for his first servant when he arrived here, years ago," she said. "A woman who took care of him. She left and went back to her people when he . . ."

She broke off. Joseph was coming out of one of the buildings and saw us. "Memsabu Diddy. You are early visitors," he said. "I am not sure if they are ready to receive guests yet. I don't even think that the memsabu is awake."

Awake? I thought. It must be after noon already! What strange lives they led here.

"It's rather important, Joseph," Diddy said. "I'm afraid you'll need to wake Lady Cheriton."

"Oh dear." His face clouded. "Not bad news? We have received no word from Bwana. But then he was not expected home until later today."

"I should speak to Lady Cheriton first," Diddy said. "You'll all find out soon enough."

We were escorted into the big living room. It felt cold and unfriendly at this hour. We waited what seemed like an eternity, then came the light tapping of high heels and Angel came along the hallway. She was dressed in simple slacks and a pale blue open-necked shirt. There were dark circles around her eyes but otherwise she looked in the picture of health.

"Goodness, you are early birds today," she said. "I've only just finished my bath and my maid was trying a new hairstyle on me. Do you like it? I think it may be a little too curly." She gave a twirl for us. "So what brings you here?"

"Bad news, I'm afraid," Diddy said. "You may want to sit down."

"Sit down? What for?" Then the import of this seemed to sink in. "It's Ross, isn't it? Something's happened to him."

"He's dead, Angel," Diddy said.

"Oh my God." The color had drained from her face. "Was it a car accident? I knew it would happen someday. He always drives that damned road too fast."

"It wasn't an accident, Lady Cheriton," Darcy said. "I'm afraid he was murdered."

I thought I heard an intake of breath from Joseph, but well-trained servant that he was, he said nothing.

"Murdered? Someone killed my husband?" She was still standing, her hands gripping the back of a Queen Anne chair.

359

"But he was at Idina's party all night surely. Was there a quarrel? A fight? They do drink an awful amount and I suspect there were drugs available too. And he can be quite antagonistic. . . ." She gave a little hiccup of a sob. "I can't quite believe it. Not Bwana. He was always so strong. So full of life, wasn't he?"

"He was killed on his way home to you," Darcy said. "Someone waylaid him and made him stop."

Nobody was asking the questions I was dying to ask. Maybe Darcy was about to get to them, but just in case I decided to ask them myself. "You seem to be feeling much better now," I ventured.

"Better?"

"You didn't come to the party because you were feeling under the weather."

She shrugged. "I just had one of my migraines. Loud noise and bright lights are the worst things for it so I stayed home. And frankly those parties are not the way I was raised. Bwana loved them. He loved the chase and the conquest." She stared hard at me. "He was after you, you know. Because you played hard to get. He made a bet with Idina that he would bed you last night. I take it he didn't succeed."

"He did not," I said, indignantly. "I made

360

it quite clear that I was not interested. Weren't you worried when he didn't arrive home?"

She looked puzzled. "But it's only just noon. I assumed he would be sleeping off the excesses of last night. He never comes home until midday after a party."

"But you telephoned him last night and asked him to come home because you were feeling worse. He left around midnight."

"I most certainly did not telephone him," Angel said. "When I have a migraine the only thing to do is to shut myself in a dark room, take a sleeping pill and try to sleep it off. As you can see, it worked."

"Somebody telephoned him at midnight, claiming to be you," I said. "He left to drive home."

"How extraordinary. I can't think who that could have been. Certainly not me. I was in bed by nine o'clock. I left the twins playing cards." She turned to Joseph, who was standing in the doorway. "Joseph, you locked up as usual, didn't you?"

"Yes, memsabu," he said. "The children of Bwana were playing a card game. I locked the doors at ten o'clock and went to bed."

"And you heard nothing after that?" Darcy asked. "No sound of a vehicle?"

"No, sir. Besides, Bwana had taken his

361

Buick motorcar. Apart from that there are only estate vehicles — very slow moving, and the keys are in Bwana's office. Who would know that?"

"There was certainly no big farm vehicle on that road last night," I said. "We would have seen the tire tracks."

"I presume Freddie can find out from the telephone exchange where the call came from last night." I turned to Darcy. "Someone must have been able to impersonate Angel realistically enough to make Bwana leave the party."

"I don't understand," Angel said. "This is very different from a drunken brawl at a party. This is cold and calculated murder. Someone lured my husband to his death and waited patiently to kill him."

"It seems that way," Darcy agreed.

Angel crossed the room. "I need a drink," she said. She opened the decanter and poured a tumbler almost full of what looked like gin. Then she splashed about half an inch of tonic on top and downed it as if it was water. I glanced uneasily at Darcy, not sure whether we should now take our leave.

Luckily Diddy went over to Angel. "Look, my dear, if there is anything we can do to help, please let us know. You'll need to plan a funeral, and think about the future."

"The future?" A look of realization came over her face. "Yes, I suppose I'll have to decide what to do. Certainly not stay on here alone. I could go home, or back to Europe. Get out of this bloody place." A hopeful spark had come into her eyes. "And his children . . ." She broke off. "Oh God. They'll have to be told. Are Bwana's children awake yet, Joseph?"

"Yes, memsabu. They are playing tennis."

"Then please ask them to come in immediately." She turned back to us. "I'd rather break the news while you are here. I'm not sure how they will take it."

"They weren't close to their father, were they?" I said, realizing too late I should probably have stayed silent. "I gather they hardly saw him since they were small."

"Bwana walked out on that wife when the twins were four," Angel said. "Their mother married again. So he has never been in their lives as a father."

"Then whose idea was it to bring them out here at this time?" I went on. "Theirs or their father's?"

"Oh, it was my husband's. I don't think they were at all keen but they are both loafers, so one gathers, and they couldn't turn down a free holiday." She gave a bitter laugh. I could see the gin overtaking her caution. "Miserable little brats, both of them, if you want to know." She glanced toward the door in case they were already coming in. "It was when Ross inherited the title and realized that Rupert was his heir. He started thinking about handing over this estate someday. He wanted his son to run it. I can't see that happening, can you? Besides, this place has only become prosperous with my money. I'm not just about to hand it over to . . ." She stopped as the front door opened and the twins came in. They were both red faced and sweaty with exertion and carried tennis racquets.

"Oh God. Not visitors in the morning! How uncivilized, Angel," Rowena exclaimed, then saw me. "What do they want?"

"We were just in the middle of a cracking game," Rupert said. "Can't you entertain without us?"

"This is not a social call," Diddy said. "We come with bad news. I'm afraid that your father has been killed."

I watched their faces. Disbelief? Wariness? And even relief. Certainly no great grieving.

"Was it an accident?" Rowena asked after a long silence.

"No. It appears he was murdered," Darcy

said. "Driving home from the party last night."

"Last night?" Rupert looked puzzled. "We weren't expecting him home until this afternoon. He told us those parties usually got rather . . . wild . . . and nobody left until after breakfast."

"That's true," Darcy said, "but somebody telephoned him, pretending to be Angel, and wanted him home immediately. And he was intercepted on the way home."

"So, a carefully planned murder," Rowena said. "Not just an argument that got out of hand."

"It seems that way," Darcy said.

"How horrid. Someone must have really hated him."

"Or wanted to stop him from doing something," Rupert added. Then a strange look came over his face. "Blimey, you know what this means, don't you? I'm Lord Cheriton." He burst out laughing. "What a ridiculous thing to happen. I inherit the title and all that goes with it. All this is mine. I come out a pauper and go back a rich man."

"I wouldn't expound that theory too loudly," Darcy said. "It does make you into a prime suspect with the best motive for killing him."

Rupert put a hand to his mouth and gave

a nervous little giggle. "Oh God. I see what you mean. Except that I have a deep man's voice and could hardly imitate Angel on the phone. Also that my father had driven off in the one motorcar so we were pretty much all stuck here. What time was he killed?"

"He left the party just after midnight so we'd have to surmise it was a little after that. About halfway between here and Lady Idina's house. Between midnight and one, then."

"Then we were all safely tucked up in our beds," Rupert said. "And our father's servant boy had locked the front door and the gate for the night."

"I saw you in your pajamas about eleven thirty," Rowena said. "We passed on our way to and from the bathroom."

"There you are then. Alibi confirmed," Rupert said. "I presume Dad had a solicitor out here. I'll need to talk to him about the ramifications. Presumably I can sell his holdings in Africa. He wanted me to stay on out here and run this place." He gave another brittle laugh. "Can you imagine me, herding cows?"

"You might have inherited his title," Angel said, "but this place has nothing to do with the Cheriton inheritance. It was my money that built up this estate. If it's sold the proceeds come to me."

"Not if I'm the heir, surely," Rupert said.

"Did he leave a will?" Rowena asked. "That would be rather important, wouldn't it?"

"I tried to get him to write one, when he inherited the title. He didn't like to think about his own mortality — 'Plenty of time for that sort of thing.' I badgered him and in the end he said he'd jot something down. I don't know if he actually got around to it," Angel said. "In any case I'll fight you in court to get back what I invested in this place, and I can afford to retain much better lawyers than you, I assure you."

"Angel. Children." Diddy stepped between them. "Bwana has been killed. This is not the time or the place to fight over what he is leaving. You should be mourning him."

"That's rather hard," Rowena said. "Since we really didn't know him. He walked out of our lives when we were tiny. He sent us occasional presents but we probably only saw him three or four times in our lives. We were absolutely amazed when he came to see us in London and wanted us to come out here. We wouldn't have come except we didn't really have anything better to do so Rupert said, why not?"

"We should be going," Darcy said. "I was

going to say I was sorry for your loss, but in the circumstances . . ."

"It hasn't quite sunk in yet," Angel said. "I shall miss him, of course. But I don't think I'll mourn him."

CHAPTER 29

August 12
At Diddy's estate

I hardly know what to think about all this. My head is swimming with people and motives. I should do as Darcy suggests and leave it all to the police. It's nothing to do with us. So I'm jolly well going to enjoy our honeymoon from now on.

When we returned to Diddy's estate we found Cyril and Mr. Van Horn about to set off into the forest. Cyril waved when they saw us. "We're off to see the big bad beasties," he called. "Why don't you come and join us?"

Darcy turned to me. "Do you want to join them?"

"Yes, please," I said. "I've been dying to see animals."

"Are you wearing stout shoes and thick

trousers?" Cyril asked. "There are snakes, you know. And ants."

"If you can wait a minute we'll change," Darcy said, looking down at the summery shoes I was wearing. Mr. Van Horn looked annoyed at having to wait. We hurried to change into our stoutest shoes and then off we went.

The path ran beside the little stream, which danced over boulders just like a stream in Scotland. The air was fresh and quite cool, again reminding me of my native land. But the creepers hanging from the tall trees, the bright fluttering butterflies and the strange echoing birdcalls reminded me we were far from home. Mr. Van Horn was clearly nervous. "What was that?" he kept asking every time there was a noise near us.

"You really don't have to worry," Cyril said. "Any animal will hear us coming long before we see them and quietly melt away into the foliage."

"Then why are we up here, if you say we shall see nothing?" Van Horn snapped.

"Because one never knows what will turn up." Cyril smiled. He went a few paces then put his finger to his lips. We froze. Then he tiptoed forward and pointed. At first I could see nothing but trees and dappled shade. Then there was the crack of a breaking branch and I saw that an elephant was standing in the shade, not too far from us, blending perfectly into the light and shadow of the forest. It went on browsing from the surrounding bushes, as if completely unaware of our presence.

"I think we've pushed our luck long enough," Mr. Van Horn said and started to walk away.

"Shh!" Cyril put his finger to his lips again.

The elephant looked up, suddenly wary, flapped its ears and started toward us.

"Don't move," Cyril said.

"Don't move? The bloody thing is coming this way," Van Horn said, with panic in his voice.

"He is probably only bluffing," Cyril said in a low murmur. "If you stand perfectly still you'll be all right. If you run he'll definitely come after you and trample you."

The elephant had its trunk raised, its ears extended. We could feel the ground shaking as it charged. There were trees to hide behind, I told myself, and yet I was a good girl and stood still because Cyril had told me to. I sensed Mr. Van Horn backing behind Darcy and me. My heart was racing and the desire to run was overwhelming. But a few feet away the elephant stopped, raised its trunk and gave a loud bellow. The sound was earsplitting. Having done that it retreated again, blending into the forest. Mr. Van Horn took out a handkerchief and wiped his forehead. "I thought I was finished," he said. "You call yourself a safari guide? Ten minutes into our walk and you lead us into danger."

"On the contrary," Cyril replied. He almost looked as if he was enjoying himself. "That was a young bull. I was pretty sure that any charge would be bluff, and it was."

"And if it wasn't?" Van Horn demanded.

"Then one of us would be dead by now," Cyril replied evenly. "Do you wish to continue our little walk? There is a spectacular waterfall on Bwana's property."

"I have had quite enough excitement for one day," Van Horn said. "A murder and now a charging elephant. I can't wait to get back to South Africa and civilization."

We had no choice but to return to the house.

"Sorry it wasn't much of a walk," Cyril complained as Mr. Van Horn went off to his room. "But a little added excitement, wouldn't you say? I think Van Horn must have peed in his pants." He gave a naughty chuckle.

"I wonder why he was keen to go on

safari," I said. "He couldn't wait to go back after one animal encounter."

"I doubt he's ever been on one before," Darcy said. "Did you see his shoes? Highly polished. Perhaps he liked the idea of a safari, but not the reality of close encounters with animals."

"I have to admit that encounter with the elephant was a little frightening," I confessed.

Cyril took my arm and drew me near to him. "My dear, a little secret. I know that bull. I've known him since he was a baby. He always behaves like that. It's a matter of pride for him. When he becomes an adult male, then things might be different, of course. But at this moment he's just a teenager, showing off. And safari guests are not satisfied unless they have one moment of danger." He grinned. Then he added, "I'll be happy to take you for a proper safari, if you like."

"We would really appreciate that," Darcy said. "I think we'd both love to be able to experience the real Kenya before we go home."

"Do you want to come with us tomorrow then?" Cyril asked. "I've already arranged things with Mr. Van Horn, if he still wants to come after the elephant episode. And maybe camp one night?"

"Do you think that will be all right?" I asked.

"Why not?" Cyril was still smiling. "I promise you I will keep you safe."

"No, it's not that at all. I was thinking there has been a murder. The police may want everyone to stay put and to question them again."

"I don't see why they'd want to question any of us," Cyril said. He took out a cigarette packet from his top pocket, offered us one and then lit his own, taking a deep and satisfying draw on it. "We were miles away and in bed at the time. And you didn't even know the man. I say we go, unless instructed otherwise."

We walked on a little across the lawn.

"You don't seem too curious about who might have killed him," I commented.

He shot me a look. "You must know I couldn't stand the man," he said. "I'm actually delighted someone bumped him off."

"Really?" Darcy looked at him with interest. "Why the animosity?"

"My dear boy, haven't you heard? He ruined me. I wrote an article on him for my newspaper column. He called it libel. Took me to court and of course he won. It cost me money I didn't have. And my reputation too." He broke off suddenly. "Oh my God. That does give me a motive, doesn't it? I hope the police don't look into Bwana's background history too closely."

"So who do you think might have killed him?" I asked.

"When I heard the news I assumed it was a cuckolded husband. He has always been very free with other chaps' wives. But since they were all at Idina's, blissfully sleeping . . . with each other . . . one has to assume that it was an outsider. With any luck it will turn out to be a rogue Kikuyu and we can all breathe a sigh of relief."

"Do you think it will turn out to be a native who killed him?" I asked Darcy when we were back in our room, changing out of those stout shoes.

"I think that's highly unlikely," Darcy replied. "It has to be someone who knew Bwana's behavior intimately. Someone knew Angel wasn't feeling well. Someone telephoned him and lured him home and was waiting to ambush him at the right place and the right time. That all points to his intimate circle, doesn't it?"

"I'm afraid it does. I'd say his son has the best motive. He was described by Angel as a loafer and suddenly he inherits a title and a fortune."

"I agree. But again the problem of how he managed to get all that way without a motorcar, and also, why bother to do it so far away? He could have done what Cyril has just done today. Asked his father to take him into the forest and killed him at a convenient moment. Then he'd leave the body to be eaten by hyenas or even by soldier ants and return home as if nothing had happened."

"Yes," I agreed. "You are right. But somehow I can't see Rupert wielding a large knife and plunging it into his father, can you? Bwana is so strong. He'd overpower Rupert."

Darcy nodded. "And the same goes for Cyril. If he was still seething with thoughts of vengeance there would be plenty of opportunities to kill Bwana on his own estate."

I nodded in agreement.

"I hope that inspector has a good brain," Darcy said. "Because he has a pretty puzzle ahead of him."

Just as we were about to leave the room an idea struck me. "You know someone we have completely left out? Jocelyn. Isn't it too coincidental that he arrives on the plane with us — on the same plane as Lord Cheriton's children — purports to be going to

Nairobi but then gets himself adopted by Idina so that he is in the right place for the party? He'd have the opportunity to telephone Bwana, and he does have quite a high-pitched voice, then follow him in one of the motorcars and kill him."

Darcy looked amused by this. "Can you see Jocelyn as an undercover agent of some sort? The poor chap would trip over his own shoelaces on his first assignment."

"Unless it's all a clever act," I said. "How many times have we simply forgotten he was there? He's the sort of chap one does overlook."

Darcy nodded, thoughtfully. "I suppose it is worth mentioning to Freddie. He is in cable contact with London. We can ask them to look into Jocelyn's background. And also see if he has any updates on who might have been part of Bwana's Fascist cell operating here."

I sank down onto the bed. "This is all so horrid and complicated, isn't it? We come on a blissful honeymoon and now suddenly we are mixed up in a jewel theft and a murder and a German plot to take over the colony. Why doesn't life ever go smoothly for us?"

"It will, my love, I promise." Darcy came to sit beside me, taking my hand. "I've told you, I'm going to accept that desk job. Respectable, steady work. No more dashing off to strange places at a moment's notice. I can be home to help change the nappies."

I looked up at him and laughed. "I can just picture you changing nappies. And I jolly well hope we can afford some kind of nursemaid." Then I became serious again. "Darcy, I want you to do what makes you happy. I think you'd be miserable stuck behind a desk, being a cog in the wheel of bureaucracy."

"It could be quite interesting. I'd be involved in foreign policy."

"Yes, but you wouldn't be able to make your own decisions, would you? You'd pass your thoughts to the under-undersecretary who would then pass them to the undersecretary and so on."

"Do you really mean that?" Darcy asked. "That you wouldn't rather see me come home on the 5:45 from Waterloo every evening?"

"I don't want you to regret that you married me."

He put his arm around my shoulder. "You are very sweet," he said. "And I won't ever regret that I married you, I promise."

Chapter 30

Evening, August 12
At Diddy's house

We're going on safari tomorrow. I'm excited about that . . . well, scared and excited at the same time. I find it hard to believe that Cyril really is a great white hunter who can protect us from wild beasts, but I gather we are taking native porters and guards and things so we should be safe enough. I will certainly be glad to get away from this horrid murder.

Darcy and I had an afternoon siesta, much needed after what we had been through. We were sitting on the lawn with our hostess and the other guests, having afternoon tea in a ridiculously civilized British manner, when we heard a vehicle approaching. It was Freddie's old boneshaker. He parked it in the shade of a big magnolia tree and two men got out. As they came into the afternoon sunlight I saw that the man with Freddie was none other than Jocelyn. What's more, he was carrying a small suitcase.

"What-ho!" he called, waving as he spotted us.

Freddie gave an embarrassed grin. "Sorry to disturb, Diddy, my darling," he said. "I'm not sure whether you met Jocelyn yesterday at the polo match."

"Only briefly," Diddy said. "How do you do? I'm Diddy Ruocco. And you're Idina's new chauffeur?"

"Not any longer, I fear," Jocelyn said. "I had to make my escape while the going was good."

"Meaning what?"

"My dreaded father." Jocelyn rolled his eyes. "The murder of Lord Cheriton is bound to make the British newspapers. If he finds out I was actually staying at the house that was involved in this murder, he'll be furious. Livid. Apoplectic. He'll probably send me instantly to the jungles of the Congo or to Antarctica. He has this overexaggerated sense of family pride and duty and frankly I am an absolute disappointment to him. So I try not to do anything more to drive him off the deep end." He

380

chewed on his bottom lip like a schoolboy trying to explain to the headmaster.

"So where will you go now?" Diddy asked.

"We were hoping he could stay with you for the next few days," Freddie said, still looking horribly embarrassed. "At least until this awful business has blown over. If he tries to go back to Nairobi and get a job now nobody will want him."

"And I simply can't go home and face the pater," Jocelyn said. "He'd probably tear me limb from limb even though it's certainly not my fault that some old chap gets himself killed."

"Well, you're certainly welcome to stay," Diddy said. "I rather gather that I'm being deserted tomorrow anyway. Cyril is leading the rest of my guests on a safari."

Jocelyn's eyes lit up. "A safari? How spiffing. Any chance I could tag along? That was one thing I'd set my heart on doing while I was here — going to shoot a few animals. Bag a gorilla or two, you know."

"I regret to inform you there are no gorillas in Kenya," Cyril said dryly, "and I discourage my guests from shooting anything. More likely to get one of the party than an animal. But you can come if you promise to behave yourself."

"Jolly good." Jocelyn beamed. "Frightfully

decent of you, old bean."

He reminded me a little of my brother, Binky, and not just in his use of language. Overly eager to please. But at the same time strange thoughts were buzzing around in my head. Was he really the innocent oaf he claimed to be? Was it possible that he had been sent over to assassinate Lord Cheriton, or, conversely, to be part of the Fascist cell that was going to whip up native insurrection?

At that moment Jocelyn bumped into the tea table, causing tea to slop into saucers.

"Crikey. Awfully sorry," he muttered. "Tend to be a bit clumsy when I'm rattled, which I am right now."

I observed him. Surely both of my suspicions seemed ludicrous. He was the classic bumbling upper-class idiot, not unlike my darling brother. He and Freddie were invited to join us for tea.

"I won't say no to a cuppa," Freddie said, "and some of your delicious scones, Diddy, but I have to get back to Gilgil tonight. There are cables that need to be sent to London." He glanced across at me.

Jocelyn worked his way through the rest of the watercress sandwiches with great speed.

"Are you sure you don't want to spend

the night, Freddie, darling?" Diddy asked.

"You are most kind, but I really have some pressing matters to attend to. I'll be back tomorrow, I'm sure."

"Everyone is going on safari except me," Diddy said. "Come and keep me company. We can work our way through that good claret you brought."

"We'll escort you back to your car," Darcy said and we walked beside Freddie.

"What do you think?" he asked Darcy, glancing back at the group around the tea table. "Any ideas yet on who might have done the dirty deed?"

"Someone needs to establish where that phone call was made from," Darcy said.

"The phone call?" Freddie frowned. "The wife didn't make it?"

"She claims she didn't."

Freddie nodded. "And those cables to London. I thought I might ask the chaps at home to find out a bit more about Jocelyn Prettibone."

"Good idea. We were thinking the same thing," Darcy agreed. "He has arrived on the scene very fortuitously, hasn't he? And surely nobody can be such a hopeless upper-class twit as he is."

"My brother comes pretty close," I had to say.

Freddie grinned. "And about that other matter. I'd like to know if we've any updates on that too."

Darcy nodded. I remained silent. We waved as Freddie drove off.

"Frightfully decent chap," Jocelyn said as we returned to the tea table that he had now pretty much denuded.

Then we went off to change. At dinner a great many ideas were exchanged on who could have committed the murder. I noticed that the subject of Lord Cheriton's political ambitions and far-right leanings did not come up. So either the others didn't think these could have any bearing on his murder or they were also staying wisely away. Cyril and Diddy knew he had been elected to the assembly. They had heard him expound admiration of Herr Hitler at dinner the other night, but the most widely expressed opinion was that the murder had to have been committed by a native outlaw. So much tidier that way and none of the people we know at all implicated. Justice didn't seem to enter into their reasoning.

We had just started to dig into a gooseberry fool (the food in the valley had been excellent so far) when there was a loud knock at the front door.

"Who else can be fleeing to me for sanctuary? I wonder," Diddy asked. "Am I the only person in the valley who is above suspicion and thus a good place to hide out?" She hailed the servant who was standing on duty behind the table. "Hakim, you had better make sure the rest of the bedrooms have beds made up in them. It seems we might be having an invasion."

"An invasion, memsabu?" The servant looked alarmed.

"Not that kind of invasion. Just an awful lot of people wanting to stay here."

"As you say, memsabu."

Another of the servants had opened the front door. I could hear a man's voice and then the servant returned, followed by Detective Inspector Windrush and his sergeant.

"Sorry to trouble you at this late hour, madam," he said, removing his hat as he came in. "Inspector Windrush of police headquarters in Nairobi."

"How do you do, Inspector," Diddy said, holding out her hand to him. "To what do we owe the honor of this visit?"

"You are no doubt aware of the serious crime that has taken place, namely the untimely death of your neighbor, Lord Cheriton."

"I have been apprised of this, but I believe

385

you have already taken statements from Lady Georgiana and Mr. O'Mara, who tell me that they discovered the body."

The inspector focused his gaze on us. "Oh, you are staying here," he said. "I thought you said you were part of the Prince of Wales's party at Lord Delamere's." He said it in a way that hinted he was delighted to have caught me out.

"I think I said that I am the prince's cousin, but we are currently visiting Mrs. Ruocco," I said, trying to keep my voice smooth and even.

"I see." He sucked in through his teeth. An annoying habit, if you ask me. "You are Mrs. Ruocco and this gentleman is Mr. Prendergast, correct? He also lives here?"

"At the moment," Cyril said. "You presumably have seen me in Nairobi from time to time. I go to deliver my newspaper column."

"Ah yes. I thought the face was familiar. The famous Gossip from Gilgil. I've never read it personally. So you did not attend the party last night at Lady Idina's house?"

"We did not," Diddy said. "Mr. Prendergast and I were here on the property all night — since I had lent the young couple my only vehicle."

"Precisely," he said. "Oh, and Mr. Van

Horn is now here, and of course he is in no way connected to this case. But . . ." He stopped, having spotted Jocelyn at the other end of the table, in the process of taking a second helping of dessert. "Mr. Prettibone, isn't it? But I was told you were employed by Lady Idina."

"I was, Inspector," Jocelyn said. "At least, I was helping her out, doing her a good turn, don't you know? But my father would not take kindly to any blemish on the old family escutcheon and all that."

"What?" The inspector looked at him as if he was a trifle barmy.

"You know, blackening the family name, so I'd rather, if possible, that he didn't find out I had been staying in a house where all sorts of things were going on, and one of the guests was murdered. So I high-tailed it out of there *quam celerrime.*

"*Quam* what?"

"Latin, old chap. Means as quickly as possible. Now I just have to pray that when the news gets back to jolly old England my name is not mentioned."

"I see." The inspector sucked in a long breath, his eyes considering Jocelyn. "Well, I must ask you to let us know where you will be staying and not to leave the area without permission until this case is solved."

387

"Surely you don't think I could have anything to do with it?" Jocelyn's voice rose to an alarmed squeak. "I don't even know anyone here yet. I only arrived a few days ago. And you should know that I faint at the sight of blood. And if I was going to kill someone I'd probably want to steal his motorcar, not just leave it."

That, of course, was a very good point. If a bandit, Kikuyu outlaw, or even white criminal, had ambushed Bwana, they would most certainly have made a getaway in his car. Unless they didn't know how to drive, that is. But they would probably have stolen the items on the seat of the car. I was sure this was not a holdup, in the traditional sense. This was a deliberate, planned killing by someone who wanted revenge or had some sort of reason for silencing Bwana.

"I was planning to take our visitors on safari tomorrow," Cyril said. "Is that still permissible?"

"And where would you be going?"

"Only a couple of hours north of the valley. Not as far as the Mara."

The inspector thought then nodded. "I don't see why not. You can't run off anywhere from there. You're not planning on staying away long?"

"Only one overnight," Cyril said. "Just to

give them a taste."

"That's all right, then."

"So what exactly can we do for you, Inspector?" Diddy asked, ever the gracious hostess. "May my servants pour you a drink?"

"I don't drink when I'm on duty, thank you, Mrs. Ruocco," he said.

"A cup of coffee, then? Some lemonade or water?"

"I wouldn't say no to a cup of coffee, thank you kindly," Inspector Windrush said.

"And your sergeant?"

I suspected the sergeant would have not said no to a glass of wine or a beer but he glanced at his chief and murmured that coffee would be lovely. They pulled up two chairs and joined us.

"I just have a couple of questions — things I need straightened out," he said. "We have been speaking with the dead man's widow and children." He paused, waiting for us to react to that, then continued, "I'd be interested to know your feelings about Lady Cheriton, as I'm told she is now. Would you say she loved her husband?"

"What a strange question," Diddy said. "Who could possibly make a judgment about whether somebody loved a person."

"Would you say it was a happy marriage?"

"I wouldn't say Angel was completely happy," Diddy said carefully, glancing at Cyril. "She didn't really take to Africa and this sort of lifestyle."

"From your observation, would you say that her husband treated her well?"

Diddy hesitated, then she said, "I would say he didn't treat her how she would have liked to be treated."

"Meaning what?"

"Bwana Cheriton could not resist other women, Inspector. I think Angel would have preferred a husband who was more devoted to her."

"I see. And I presume now she'll be able to leave Kenya and go back to America if she wants to."

"She could have done that at any time, Inspector," Cyril said. "She is a wealthy woman in her own right. She stayed here. That must be some indication that she was fond enough of Bwana."

The inspector nodded, digesting this. "She might not believe in divorce," he said.

"I don't know why. Bwana was an expert. He had already gone through it several times before. I'm sure he could have made it painless for her had she so wished." Cyril grinned.

I could see what Inspector Windrush was

trying to imply — that Angel had a good motive for wanting her husband dead. And, I thought, the money to pay someone to accomplish this. Interesting theory.

"And these children of the dead man." The inspector accepted the cup of coffee and stirred several spoonfuls of sugar into it before going on. "What do you know about them?"

"Nothing at all. We heard only a few weeks ago that Bwana was bringing his children from his first marriage out to Kenya. We gathered it was because his son would inherit the title and he wanted to encourage the boy to learn to love what he was doing here. Bwana made it clear he had no interest in going back to the property in England that went with the title."

The inspector took a long sip of coffee. I wondered if his mustache got in the way. "You people," he said. "Someone is always giving you property and titles. Must be nice."

"In Bwana's defense," Diddy said, "I have to point out that he came out here with nothing. He lived in a shack. Everything he has now he has built up with his own hands."

"And Angel's money, darling," Cyril added. "Don't forget Angel's lovely money."

The inspector smirked. "And one gathers he has fallen out with quite a few of his fellow settlers. . . . Cheated them? Stolen their wives? Quite a few people with a grudge against him? Makes it quite complicated for me." He took another sip of coffee. "So much simpler if the wife orchestrated the whole thing."

"The only argument against that," Diddy said, "is that she was at home, in bed with a migraine, as her servants and stepchildren can attest."

The smirk broadened. "A woman like that wouldn't do her own dirty work. She'd hire someone to do it for her. And as it happens her husband sacked one of his workers a few weeks ago. The man let one of his cows eat something that made it sick. He dismissed this person on the spot, even though he'd been a good worker for years. Someone with a grievance might well take Lady Cheriton's money and do the deed. And a native would be more likely to have something like a panga to strike with. The wound was too broad for most kitchen knives or even hunting knives."

There was silence. This seemed all too possible. A native after all, not one of the white settlers. I almost heard the sigh of relief all around. They were glad it was not one of them. It seemed jolly unfair. The inspector drained his coffee cup. "Of course we can't overlook his son, who now inherits a tidy fortune. We'll know more when we question the other workers, I suspect. And visit the native villages." He got up, putting his cup down noisily. "Well, I won't keep you any longer, but nobody is to think of leaving the area without notifying me. Oh, and one interesting thing" — again he paused — "Cheriton's daughter said something significant. She said her father had made a pass at you, Lady Georgiana. And that you'd rebuffed him angrily and quite violently."

He was staring hard at me. I'm afraid I found it rather funny and tried not to laugh. "Are you suggesting that gave me a motive to want to kill him? I'm afraid you'll have to do better than that, Inspector. If I went around killing men who had tried to make a pass at me, there would be a trail of dead bodies across Britain." An image of my mother flashed into my mind. There had certainly been enough men who made passes at her. "When he left the party I was actually already asleep in bed beside my husband, and I am certainly not the type who would wield a large knife, even if I knew where to find one."

The inspector actually took a small step back at my onslaught. I suppose the heightened emotion of the day had come pouring out. I was actually surprised at myself. "Oh no," he said. "I wasn't for a moment suggesting that you would have killed him. Of course not." He actually looked rather embarrassed, which pleased me no end. "Well, I should be on my way. I expect this will all sort itself out when we've questioned the natives. I thank you for your time and the coffee, Mrs. Ruocco." He gave a nodding little bow and left, his sergeant in pursuit.

Darcy looked at me. "Well done," he said with a smile. "Most impressive."

"Well, it's been a strange day, hasn't it?" Darcy said when we finally retired to our room. "Not exactly the blissful honeymoon far from the stresses of home."

"Oh my goodness," I said. "I don't know about you, but I'm exhausted." I flopped down onto the bed. "If anything else happened tonight I think I'd scream."

"The inspector likes the scenario of Angel hiring a killer, doesn't he?"

I nodded. "I don't think she's the sort to do that. If she wanted to go home to America, she'd go home, don't you think? And

Bwana wouldn't stop her."

"I don't know. In America they are used to having gangsters fix things for them."

I laughed. It sounded so absurd. "I'm going to try not to think about it anymore," I said. "Let's go to sleep and enjoy our outing tomorrow. With any luck Mr. Van Horn will be chased by a rhinoceros."

"You see, you do have an evil streak." Darcy sat beside me and stroked my hair. "I can see I'll have to make sure I never offend you."

We got into bed and I fell asleep immediately. I woke to pitch-blackness and Darcy doing something strange, bouncing on my feet — an awfully heavy weight. "What are you doing?" I murmured, still half-asleep.

"What are you talking about?" Darcy's voice came from the pillow beside me.

That made me instantly wide awake. "Darcy," I whispered, shaking him. "Wake up. There's someone in the room."

I have to say I was impressed by the way he leaped out of bed. I heard him curse as he hit his foot on something, fumbling for the light switch. There was a click. The room was flooded with electric light and I screamed. A large monkey of some sort was sitting a few feet from me, at the bottom of the bed. The shutters were wide open and cold night air blew into the room.

"Shoo. Scram. Go!" Darcy hurled a pillow at the monkey and came toward it. It bared horrible yellow fangs but then reluctantly retreated. Darcy slammed the shutters behind it.

"How on earth can it have got in?" I asked, my heart still pounding. "The shutters were closed, weren't they?"

"I closed them myself," Darcy said. "You saw me. I opened the window for fresh air then I latched the shutters."

"It's quite windy tonight. Could the wind have blown them open?" I asked.

Darcy tried shaking them. They remained firmly latched.

Then I said, "What's that on the bed?"

He went over, looked at it and then prodded it. "It's a piece of meat," he said.

I stared at Darcy as the truth began to dawn. "Someone wanted a leopard to come in here, not just a monkey."

"That's more than a joke," Darcy said quietly. "Someone wanted to kill one of us."

"Or at the very least to make us so frightened that we left instantly."

CHAPTER 31

Tuesday, August 13
Early morning, about to set off on safari

After last night's encounter with the monkey I'm not sure that I want to go. The thought that somebody in the house wants us dead is very alarming.

We were awoken with a tap on our door. Darcy got up and opened it, cautiously. One of the servants came in bearing a tray.

"Memsabu said I should wake you because Bwana Prendergast wishes to depart early on safari," he said, putting the tea tray on the table beside the bed. He bowed and left us. Darcy handed me a cup of tea, then opened the shutters. The world was blanketed in mist. The air that streamed in was icy cold. I shivered and the events of the night came flooding back. "After that monkey I'm not at all sure I want to go on a safari," I said to Darcy. "Someone wanted to kill us. How do we know that person isn't coming on safari with us?"

"We don't," Darcy said. "But I don't want us to miss the experience of a lifetime. If we don't go we'll regret it. But now we'll be vigilant. I won't let anything bad happen to you." He pushed back his dark curls from his forehead. "I can't believe last night had anything to do with Jocelyn or Mr. Van Horn," he said. "Neither of them would know about the danger of leopards and leaving shutters open. And Cyril? What would he have to gain? He doesn't even know us. He hated Cheriton. He'd be glad he was dead."

"But why would anyone want us dead, or at least terrified?"

"Obviously someone thinks we saw or know more than we do, since we were the ones who found Cheriton's body."

"What could we possibly have overlooked?" I said. "And anyway, nobody from this part of the valley could have been involved in his murder. We saw that no vehicles from this direction had come down the road after Bwana. We saw the tire marks. The only identical motorcars we saw were down at Idina's, weren't they?"

Darcy was frowning. "If Inspector Windrush's theory is correct and Angel paid a disgruntled worker to finish off her husband, then that same native could have come over from their estate and opened our shutters."

"But again it comes down to: why want to harm us?"

"I don't know," Darcy said. "Come on. Drink your tea and get dressed. Don't forget the stout shoes and trousers!" He chuckled.

As we were dressing I stopped and asked, "I suppose this can have nothing to do with you?"

"What do you mean — with me?" Darcy had just come out of the bathroom, carrying his toilet things.

"You finally told me that you had been sent out here because of Lord Cheriton's connection with Hitler. Is it possible that someone else is also part of that plan and wants to make sure we don't poke our noses any deeper?"

Darcy shrugged. "That would be Mr. Van Horn, wouldn't it? But we saw how he reacted to an encounter with a wild animal. He was terrified of that elephant."

"I was pretty terrified myself," I confessed. "It was rather alarming, wasn't it?"

Darcy nodded thoughtfully. "You might have a point. People like him are good at playing the part that is called upon at a particular moment. Yes, I suppose he would want us scared away, or even killed." He hesitated, holding his shaving kit in his hand instead of putting it into the overnight bag. "If you don't want to go, I quite understand. Presumably we can arrange for a safari later."

"But you want to go, don't you?" I said. "You want to keep an eye on Van Horn."

"Ideally yes, since Freddie is not coming along."

"Then we should go. Forewarned is fore-armed, as they say."

He took me into his arms. "You're a cracking girl, Georgie. I made a good choice when I asked you to marry me."

I felt all warm inside and it took me a while to remember that we were going off into the middle of nowhere with an un-known person who might want to kill us. Hardly a comforting thought. Then I rea-soned that Cyril was responsible for us. He'd make sure we were safe.

We finished packing the overnight bag and went to find the others at breakfast. Given the early hour there was toast and cold meat and fruit. Frankly I was still so shaken from the night before that I found it hard to swal-low anything. Mr. Van Horn was wearing a

400

safari bush jacket that looked as if it came straight from the stage set of a play about a great white hunter. It had certainly never been near the dust of a real adventure. I remembered what Darcy had said about playing the part required of him. Cyril looked quite different in his work clothes — no longer the man-about-town but the genuine bushman.

"Have you given Samuel your luggage?" he asked. "Oh good. You are only bringing a small bag. We're tight on space. He'll make sure it's safely stowed."

An elderly Kikuyu was standing by the door and took our bag from us. Diddy came into the room, still in her robe and looking rather washed out and worried. "You're all set, are you? Georgie, I insist that you take my hat. Yours is very nice but it's not nearly big enough. There is no shade on the savanna. I don't want you dying of sunstroke."

"Very well. Thank you," I said, accepting it from her.

"You will take good care of them, Cyril?" she said. "I don't want to have to contact the royal family and inform them that one of their members has been eaten or trampled."

"Diddy, you know they will be perfectly safe," Cyril said in an exasperated voice.

"Now don't worry and let us get started. We've a lot of ground to cover."

We were led around the house to the outbuildings at the back where Cyril's vehicle was parked. It was something resembling a lorry, with a roof but open sides. At the front were three rows of wooden seats and behind them the equipment was piled. Samuel stood patiently beside it, ready to help us on board. At that moment there was a shout. We turned to see Joseph, followed by Rupert and Rowena.

"Hey, wait for us," Rupert called.

I looked at Diddy. "Did you know they were coming?"

Diddy shook her head. "Angel said something to me the other night at dinner about wanting the young people to experience a safari. I suppose she must have asked Cyril."

Joseph reached us first. He was laden with various pieces of equipment, which he carried over to the vehicle. Rowena and Rupert looked ridiculously out of place, both dressed in light linen slacks and cardigans. Rowena was wearing a jaunty little straw hat and Rupert a panama hat.

"Don't you have better hats than that?" Diddy asked. "You'll die of sunstroke."

"All we've got, I'm afraid," Rupert said.

"Joseph, run back quickly and find them a

couple of real hats," Diddy said.

"I try to tell them, memsabu." Joseph shrugged. He ran back and appeared in a short time with two large bush hats.

"These are awful," Rowena said, trying to reject hers. "No thank you."

"You'll need them if you're coming with me." Cyril came to join us. "And on the safari you understand that you do what I say at all times. It can be a matter of life and death." He moved closer to Darcy and me. "I tried to dissuade them from coming but Angel said they were distressed about their father and she wanted them well away from the investigation."

Interesting, I thought. Either Angel wanted them out of the way or one of them was not keen on coming under police scrutiny. How convenient to be out in the middle of nowhere. If it weren't for the transportation problem my money would be on Rupert. Clearly he had little love for a father he had never known and now had inherited quite a large fortune. But then . . . another little thought came to me. If Angel was indeed the person who had planned her husband's demise, she would also have a good reason to get rid of Rupert, who was now the legal heir to an estate she had poured a lot of her money into.

"All right. Load up!" Cyril called. Mr. Van Horn was assisted up onto the front seat beside Cyril. I was given the place next to him. Darcy, Rowena and Rupert sat behind us with Jocelyn, Joseph and Samuel bringing up the rear. I remembered what had been said about guards. Weren't there supposed to be plenty of guards to take care of us? Instead we had one elderly Samuel and one Joseph. I didn't like to ask Cyril about it. He was, after all, giving up his time to entertain us. But the thought that Joseph was coming along reassured me somewhat. He seemed like a competent young man.

We set off, heading out of the valley in a northerly direction. The road deteriorated after a mile or so and the wooded mountains gradually became hills. Then we struck out to our right and bounced along a sort of track. It was really most uncomfortable and we had to hold on to the bar in front of us for some kind of stability.

"Thank God I didn't eat much breakfast," Rowena complained from behind me. "It would all be coming back up by now."

For once I had to agree with her. Mr. Van Horn kept sliding into me and the alarming thought struck me that if he wanted to get rid of me one good push would send me out of the vehicle. I held on extra tightly.

Then we were no longer among cultivated fields and trees. This was scrubland, with occasional flat-topped trees, but mostly low bushes alternating with dry grass. Then suddenly someone gave a shout. Ahead of us stood a herd of buffalo, heads down, still and defiant. Their snorts came out like dragon breath in the cold morning air.

"Nasty creatures, buffalo," Cyril said cheerfully. "They are the one animal that is totally unpredictable. Give me a lion or a leopard any day. If they charge it's never a bluff and what's more they won't give up. They'll keep on until they gore you and stomp you to death."

"And you say we shall be sleeping in small tents tonight?" Mr. Van Horn asked, his voice trembling. "Then what is to stop some animal from stomping us to death?"

"We'll have a big fire going and keep guard all night. You'll be quite safe. You have to understand that all animals won't bother you if you don't annoy them. Like this lot. We'll give them time to move on."

After fifteen minutes it was clear the buffalo had no intention of moving on, so Cyril sounded the horn. They snorted, then, as the lorry came toward them, they took off. "Round one to us," Cyril said.

After that we saw zebras and wildebeests,

a warthog and all sorts of birds. It was quite enchanting and I forgot to be afraid or uncomfortable. Then Cyril slowed. "Look over there," he said. "That's a sight you don't see too often."

We saw a group of small, dainty antelope standing beside a water hole. Then we saw what he was pointing at. I thought it was a leopard, creeping stealthily through the tall grass.

"Cheetah," Cyril said, nodding with satisfaction.

The antelope were alert now. The cheetah suddenly broke from cover and dashed toward them and they took off, springing over the ground at amazing speed. But the cheetah was faster. It ran so fast it was a blur of gold. It sprang onto the back of an antelope and brought it down. We couldn't see what happened next but Cyril told us it would bite the throat until it suffocated the antelope. That part was rather horrid but it had been exciting to see the chase and I had to remind myself that in the animal world it was always a balance of predator and prey. After all, I ate meat every day. I just didn't have to chase an animal to get my diet.

"I hope I managed to get that on film," Darcy said. "It will probably be all a blur."

We drove on. The countryside became open and drier, with hills rising in the distance and above us an enormous arc of blue sky, bigger than any sky I had seen before. Then Cyril stopped again and pointed. Over to our right we saw dust rising and I strained my eyes, expecting to see more animals. Instead a group of men came toward us, running at an even pace. They carried spears and wore cloaks around their shoulders. Having just seen the cheetah, I was now witnessing humans moving with equal grace.

"Maasai," Cyril said. "I wonder what they are doing here. Their nearest settlement is usually to the west of here in the Rift Valley. Do you know, Joseph?"

"I do not," Joseph said. "I do not recognize these men."

They came closer and then were going to pass right ahead of us. But they showed no interest in us at all, not slowing their pace, as if we didn't exist. Joseph shouted words to them in a strange language and a short reply came back without any of the men turning their head to acknowledge us. We could hear their costumes jingling and the pounding of their feet, but then they were gone, leaving only a cloud of dust behind them.

"They go to a ceremony," Joseph said. "The creation of new *moran* — new warriors."

We drove on for about another half hour then came to a halt near a small river. "This is where I usually camp," Cyril said as Samuel sprang down with great agility, considering his years, and started unloading the lorry. We climbed down, all stretching our legs gratefully. Joseph helped and in no time they had three small tents set up and a campfire going.

"You can sleep with us beside the fire," Cyril said to Jocelyn, handing him a blanket.

"Out in the open? Unprotected?" Jocelyn said, a look of alarm on his face. "What if wild animals come in the night?"

"You'll be quite safe. We'll build up the fire and that keeps them away," Cyril said.

"I'd much rather be in a tent, if you don't mind."

"Very well, the boy can share with me," Mr. Van Horn said. "I understand his apprehension. I too would not want to sleep by the fire."

They carried their belongings to one of the tents. The twins took another; Darcy and I, the third. "I don't think this exactly gives us as much protection as Jocelyn hoped," he said with a grin. "A charging rhino or elephant would knock it down in a second."

"Thank you for that encouraging thought," I replied, making him laugh.

"First we need lunch," Cyril said when we had all assembled again. "Who wants to come and shoot meat with me?"

I didn't really want to but Darcy shook his head. "I think we should all stick together," he said. We set off on foot. The day was now baking hot and I was glad of Diddy's large brimmed hat. I glanced across at Rowena and Rupert. They looked red faced and uncomfortable.

"My God, this is hard work," Rupert said as we slogged up a small hill. "I don't think we would have come if we had known. Whose idea was this anyway?"

"Not mine," Rowena replied. "Angel's, I believe. Wanting to cheer us up."

"I was quite cheerful sitting in her living room and drinking champagne," Rupert replied.

I studied the back of their heads as they went in front of me. Why was Angel so keen to get them out of the way? Did she suspect that they knew something incriminating? Had one of them overheard the telephone call summoning Bwana home? I didn't know how we'd ever find out. In fact I thought that Inspector Windrush had little chance of solving Bwana's murder. If Angel had paid a native to do the dirty deed then he was well away hiding in a distant village by now. I fell into step beside Joseph.

"You must be quite upset at the death of Lord Cheriton," I said.

"It is strange," he said. "It is almost like a dream, as if it didn't happen. This morning I expected to hear his voice, yelling for me. I don't know what will become of me now."

"Would you go back to your own people if Lady Cheriton decides to sell the estate?" I asked.

"Maybe, but that is a waste of an education, is it not? I will have to think carefully. At the moment I cannot think clearly."

"You speak the language of the Maasai well," I said. "Did you ever actually live among them?"

He smiled. He had a warm and friendly smile. "My mother spoke the language to me when I was a baby. But yes, I did go back to my people for one year, when I wanted to become a man. It was important to my mother that I learn the skills of the warrior."

"Does your mother live among your people? Do you see her often?"

"She does. I do not see her often now," he

said. "I miss her wisdom." And the smile faded. I thought how lonely it must be, being the only Maasai in a house of spoiled white people. I wondered how old he was. No more than twenty, surely. And he was different from the other house servants — with his English education and of a different race — poised between two worlds. He stopped to help me up a rocky outcropping. We stood as a group, most of us huffing and puffing after the exertion, and surveyed the scene. At first I could see only scrub and occasional trees, but then I picked out a group of zebras, blending in perfectly with the tall grass. In the distance a giraffe was eating at an acacia tree.

"That will do nicely," Cyril said. He indicated a group of large antelope with curved horns. "Kudu. Good eating. All right — anyone who wants to come with me must move silently and know how to shoot."

"I will come," Mr. Van Horn said.

"Oh rather," Rupert agreed. "I'm quite a good shot, actually."

I glanced at Darcy. I knew he had been on plenty of shoots. But he shook his head. "We'll watch, thank you."

"I think I'll come too," Rowena said. "I'm just as good a shot as my brother."

"Very well." Cyril nodded to Samuel, who

411

handed each of them a rifle. "Only understand you do exactly as I tell you. You don't say a word and you stay close to me. I don't intend to rescue anyone who has been gored."

"I think I should probably stay up here," Jocelyn admitted. "Knowing me I'd shoot myself in the foot." He gave an embarrassed grin. "But it will be jolly exciting to watch."

They set off, Samuel and Cyril going ahead, followed by the others. I felt relief as they moved farther away from us. Could it really be one of them who had opened our shutters in the night? But then again Jocelyn was standing right beside us and he had also been sleeping at Diddy's. That was ridiculous, I told myself. If Jocelyn had come into our room to unlatch the shutters he would have tripped over something, knocked over a lamp.

They were crouching down behind some bushes. There was an explosion that echoed across the countryside. All the animals in the vicinity took off, running. One of the animals was down. Samuel and Joseph were left to butcher the meat as the rest returned.

"Well done, Mr. Van Horn," Cyril said. "A clean shot through the heart."

"I must be lucky," Van Horn said.

A clean shot through the heart, I thought

as we walked back to camp. He might well be a trained German agent and want Darcy out of the way. Again I found myself wishing we had stayed safely behind.

CHAPTER 32

August 13
At a safari camp

Is it just me or do I sense an atmosphere of tension? I keep telling myself not to be silly. The others are having a good time. I should too.

The kudu steaks, grilled by Samuel over the fire, were delicious. Diddy had sent salad items and fruit to accompany them, along with fresh bread, and a couple of bottles of good wine to wash them down. After lunch we all slept in our tents. Toward evening Cyril took us out in the safari vehicle — I'm calling it that because I don't know if there is a proper word for it — and we went on a search for lions. We came upon a pride lying in a sandy hollow: a big male with a dark mane, three females and three cubs. We stayed where we were, high up in the lorry, and they didn't seem at all concerned about us. I was really glad that nobody suggested shooting them because they were quite magnificent.

"I am glad I came after all," I said to Darcy as we returned to camp.

"Good," he replied but he didn't smile.

For dinner Samuel had made a stew with the kudu meat, as well as potatoes, onions and peppers. It was really tasty and defense against the cold wind that had sprung up with the onset of darkness. The dishes were washed up in water brought up from the river and every scrap of food was buried. "We don't want animals rooting around us in the dark," Cyril said.

As we sat around the campfire after dinner we heard a sound I had only heard before in the London Zoo. A lion was roaring. It sounded unnaturally loud and it was impossible to tell which direction it was coming from.

"He's probably found the remains of the kudu we killed," Cyril said. "Lions aren't above being scavengers when they choose. He's probably driving off hyenas. But don't worry, Samuel and Joseph and I will take turns on guard all night."

I knew we were safely in a group around a campfire and that both Samuel and Cyril had their rifles handy but I had seen the size of those lions earlier in the day and I felt pretty defenseless. We retired to our tents for the night, leaving Cyril, Samuel and Joseph with their sleeping bags around the campfire. We went to bed in our clothes, and I was glad to have Darcy to snuggle up against. In the middle of the night I awoke. Through the tent flap I could see a sky speckled with a million stars. There was a moon, rising over distant hills. I wondered what had woken me then I heard it again. It sounded like a throaty cough, right outside our tent. Then a shadow moved between us and the campfire. A large shadow, moving softly, making no sound. The lion was in our camp.

I didn't know what to do. If I woke Darcy and he made a noise or a sudden movement would that alert the lion to us? Should I pretend to play dead? But did I want to lie there and feel its breath on me? There is a guard, I told myself. One of them is on guard with a gun. They will scare it off. But it came closer. I could sense it right outside my tent now. An enormous head was look-ing in through the tent flap. I looked around for a potential weapon, anything I could throw at it, defend myself with. All I could come up with was my shoes. I fished around but couldn't put my hands on them. Maybe the lion was just curious. Maybe it would move on. . . .

Suddenly there was a shout, a snarl and then a horrible noise I can't really put into words . . . a terrifying sound, more shouts and a gunshot. Then there was pandemonium outside.

"What the devil?" Darcy sat up, tried to stand up and bumped his head as the tent was only about four feet tall.

I grabbed him. "Darcy, don't go out there. There's a lion."

"I heard a shot." He pulled back the tent flap. Silhouetted against the fire I could make out Cyril and Joseph and Samuel. They were standing over a dark mound.

"Well done," I heard Cyril say. He looked up at Darcy, who now emerged from the tent. "We had a rogue lion come into camp. Joseph speared it. I finished it off."

I tried to locate my shoes. As I crawled forward my hand touched something cold and squishy. I recoiled, crying out in alarm.

"What is it?" Darcy was with me instantly.

"I touched something . . . something dead and cold."

He squatted beside me and reached for what I had indicated. "It's part of that antelope we ate for dinner," he said. "Feels like a bone with meat on it."

"How did it get into our tent?" I asked. Darcy said nothing. Outside we could now hear that everyone was awake. Voices sounded anxious and alarmed.

"Oh my God. It's a lion!" The voice was Jocelyn's, high as a girl's and quite hysterical.

"A lion? You allowed a lion to attack us, Prendergast?" That was Mr. Van Horn. "You claimed to be a professional? And you promised we should be safe? I should never have trusted you."

"We could all have been eaten in our beds," I heard Rowena saying. "Weren't you supposed to post a guard?"

"I was on guard," Cyril said. "I heard a noise and it sounded as if something was trying to get into the lorry. So I left the fire for a second to go and see. I suppose it could have been a second lion, sniffing around where we'd stored food. Thank God that Joseph was awake and alert and had brought his spear."

I had now reached the group. The body of the lion lay there with a spear sticking out of its chest. Joseph retrieved it. "It is lucky that I brought it with me," he said. "I almost didn't but then when I lived among my people I was told that a *moran* never goes

418

anywhere without his spear."

"Your aim was good," Samuel said. "You speared him through the heart."

Samuel made coffee, Cyril put a generous splash of brandy into it and we all went back to bed.

"What did you do with that meat?" I whispered to Darcy.

"I threw it onto the fire," Darcy whispered back. "I didn't want to attract any more predators."

"Somebody put it in our tent deliberately, didn't they?" I asked. "The same person who opened our shutters and put the steak on our bed."

"Someone really doesn't like us," Darcy agreed. "Wants us out of here one way or another."

"Dead or alive," I muttered.

I lay down beside him, feeling the comforting warmth of his arm around me, my head lying against his shoulder. But sleep would no longer come. Which of them could it be? I could rule out Samuel. He had only just met us and could have no grudge against us. Also Joseph. He had been nothing but pleasant. I couldn't see what possible reason Rupert or Rowena could have for wanting to harm us, or how they would know to lure a lion close to the camp with a trail of meat.

Then there was Jocelyn. I had heard his voice, absolutely terrified, when the lion was discovered. No, he'd never have the guts even if he had the expertise. That left just Mr. Van Horn and Cyril. And the latter . . . Well, he had no reason to want us out of the way. So my money was on Van Horn. I had seen the way he shot the antelope. A clean kill from quite a distance. It was quite obvious to me now that he was a trained German spy. We'd have to talk to Freddie and have him out of the country as soon as possible — at least back in Gilgil or Nairobi, safely far away from us. I shivered as I went through the incident again — that enormous head, that grunted growl. If the lion had come into the tent would it just have taken the meat? If I hadn't moved, if Darcy had stayed asleep, would we have been left unharmed?

When we woke in the morning the lion's carcass was gone. We were told that Samuel had skinned it and we were bringing the skin home as a trophy.

"Would you like me to cure it for you so that you can take it back to England?" Cyril asked me. "A belated wedding present?"

I thought of that magnificent lion and wondered if I wanted to be reminded of this night, but Darcy said, "We'd be honored. I think this is a night to remember, don't you?"

"I won't ever forget it," I said, "but if you don't mind, I'm going to stay in camp while you take the others game viewing. I have a terrible headache from last night's excitement."

They were all really nice to me. Samuel made me tea and scrambled eggs and brought me a cold water compress from the river. "I think we'll take the lorry and go farther afield this time," Cyril said. "There are hippos where the river is wider in the valley. And we may see elephants there too."

"Then I will stay with this memsabu." Joseph moved over to stand beside me. "Just in case more lions come."

I hadn't really considered being left behind with no real shelter and gave Joseph a grateful smile.

"And I don't think I feel like bumping around in that vehicle," Rowena said. "I agree with Georgie. I also have a frightful headache. Actually I've had a headache since I got here. Altitude, I believe."

"Well, I better stay and keep an eye on Ro," Rupert said. "I can't leave my sister undefended."

"How about you, Mr. Van Horn?" Cyril asked. "Are you game for a game drive?"

"Game for game? Ha-ha. That is very good." Van Horn nodded appreciation. "But I think, considering what we have experienced, that we should make our way home. It is clear that most members of our party have no more interest in seeing animals at such close quarters."

Nobody disagreed with this. We started to dismantle the tents. That was when I realized that Jocelyn was not among us. I was about to sound the alarm when there was a muffled shout and Jocelyn's tousled head appeared from the collapsing tent. He had apparently slept all the way through breakfast.

I went over to Joseph as we loaded gear onto the lorry. "Thank you for saving our lives last night," I said. "It was about to come into our tent."

He nodded, solemnly. "I don't know what brought it into our camp and then wanting to enter your tent. It must have been a man-eater, although how a lion develops a taste for human flesh so far from the nearest settlement is a mystery. And it did not appear to be old or injured, which is when a big cat will usually take to preying upon humans." He turned away, staring out toward the vastness of the savanna. "I know I had to protect you and I had to do the deed, but I am sorry I had to kill a lion. I killed my one lion during my year of training for manhood. It is not good luck to kill more than one."

"Well, I'm very glad you did, or I wouldn't be here this morning," I said. He gave me a gentle smile.

We drove back slowly, stopping to look at various animals, including a pair of rhinos who trotted right past us, apparently not aware that there were humans in the lorry, stopped for a picnic lunch beside a small lake, where we saw flamingos, storks and even a crocodile, and arrived back at Diddy's in midafternoon. She was surprised to see us so early.

"You should have stayed out longer," she said. "We've had another visit from that awful inspector. He's been badgering Angel and wanted to talk to Lord Cheriton's children. He was most put out to find they were far away on safari. He thinks they are hiding from him."

Perhaps they were, I thought. They had never wanted to visit their father before. They had stayed well away from him, and once he had inherited the title they turn up instantly. An idea struck me. What if Rupert had hidden in the back or the boot of the motorcar? If Rowena had made the telephone call luring him home and Rupert had struck as Bwana drove? The only thing against that was that there was no hint of blood or disarray in the car. Could Rupert have arranged for him to stop and get out for any reason? It was an intriguing thought and I couldn't wait to share it with Darcy.

Diddy also informed us that Freddie had paid a visit. She told us that Lord Cheriton's funeral would be held on Saturday and that Lord Delamere and the Prince of Wales would attend. Apparently Lord Delamere was concerned about me, since we had discovered the body and were staying so close to the Cheriton estate. He was upset that our honeymoon would be spoiled and suggested that we come to stay with him right away.

"Freddie will be stopping by tomorrow, I expect," Diddy said. "Do you want to go and stay with Lord D?"

A debate waged inside my head. Which would be worse: a person who was constantly trying to kill us or a stay with Mrs. Simpson? Reason won out but Darcy answered before I could. "I think that might be a lovely idea, Diddy, if you don't mind our deserting you. That way we could see the countryside down by Lake Elmenteita and we'll be closer to Freddie in Gilgil in case there are more questions to be answered or a coroner's court to attend."

"I'll be sorry to see you go," Diddy said, "but I have to say that I agree. It's not pleasant to have your honeymoon interrupted by murder and the police. So go with my blessing, children. We'll have a farewell dinner tonight."

I felt a huge weight leave my shoulders as Darcy and I walked back to our bedroom.

"Thank you for saying that," I whispered to him. "I really wanted to leave but I didn't know whether you'd think we were being ungrateful to Diddy."

"My darling, this is one time when gratitude has to give way to common sense," Darcy said. "If someone is trying to kill us up here, then I want you to be safe and far away."

"Now we just have to get through tonight," I said and gave him a nervous grin.

CHAPTER 33

Saturday, August 17
At Lord Delamere's estate

> We've just had three blissful days with no
> murders, no police and even Mrs. Simp-
> son being quite pleasant for once. We've
> been out riding, we've been out in a boat
> and saw hippos and flamingos and we've
> had lots of jolly good food and wine.
> Today is Lord Cheriton's funeral. I won-
> der if the police are any closer to solving
> the case.

On Saturday morning we rose early and
dressed for the funeral. Of course I had
brought no black outfits with me (well, one
doesn't expect to attend the occasional
funeral on one's honeymoon, does one?).
Darcy had no black suit, apart from his dinner jacket. Luckily Lady Delamere lent me
a dress and Lord D lent Darcy a jacket so

we were at least presentable, even though Lady D was a little broader in the hips than I. She also managed to find a black pillbox hat with a veil for me, which made me look like a character from *The Merry Widow* and made Darcy laugh.

Everyone was in good form at breakfast except for Mrs. Simpson (who was no longer Mrs. Simpson, one gathered — the divorce had come through; I just prayed she didn't expect to be called Her Royal Highness Princess Wallis anytime soon!).

"I don't know why we have to waste good time attending this man's funeral," she complained to my cousin. "We didn't even know the guy. And we only have two more days before you have to go back to your damned royal duties and I have to fly home like a good little girl."

"I'm sorry, Wallis." David was always apologizing to her. "But that's just the way it is. Royal duties are my job. I have to do what is expected of me, you know that."

"Your father works you too hard. Why isn't he doing this tour?" She served herself half a slice of toast, while the rest of us were working our way through the kedgeree and eggs.

"You know he hasn't been well. And he wants me to get to know my Common-

427

wealth people before I take over the firm, so to speak."

Wallis sniffed and took a bite of her toast. "It won't go on all day, will it?"

"There is a luncheon afterward, but we'll have time in the afternoon," David said.

"But no polo tomorrow because the community is in mourning," she said sweetly. "What a shame. I know you were looking forward to that."

But she wasn't, I thought. I was awfully glad there was not to be a repeat of the polo match. I'm not sure how I managed to survive the first one and didn't want to trust my luck a second time.

We were just getting ready to leave for the church when Freddie arrived.

"I thought I'd drive you two in my old boneshaker," he said. "Lord D can drive the prince."

I pictured my black dress after an exposure to the dirt roads and the boneshaker but Darcy accepted right away. As we walked to the car Freddie drew near to Darcy. "I came to pick you up because there are some developments I wanted to share with you," he said. He had lowered his voice and I suspected I was not supposed to listen, but I listened anyway.

"We intercepted a cable that Van Horn

428

sent to Berlin," Freddie said. "It was coded, but easy to break."

"Well?" Darcy said impatiently.

"It said, '2 unstable. Abandon for now.' "

" 'Too unstable'?"

"The number two, not 'too.' "

"The number two?"

Freddie nodded. "Precisely."

"What do you think that means?"

"I'd like to believe it meant a second-in-command, someone who would be a right-hand man and presumably take over the operation on Cheriton's death," Freddie replied.

"And any thoughts on who that might be?"

"Cyril," I interjected, making them both turn to look at me.

"Cyril? Cyril Prendergast?" Freddie sounded amazed.

They hadn't realized I'd been eavesdropping and I blushed. "It makes a lot of sense, doesn't it? Cyril pretends to loathe Lord Cheriton, but they are secretly working together. That's why he stays with Diddy, next door. He pretends to be the languid man-about-town, the sort of man nobody would suspect, but he goes to Nairobi to write his newspaper column and can stir up things behind the scenes."

When they said nothing I went on. "Why else would he agree to have that long chat with Mr. Van Horn at the polo match and then invite him on safari? He doesn't strike me as the sort of person who does acts of charity. It was so he and Van Horn could have some good strategy sessions with nobody listening."

"Then why invite us on safari with them?" Darcy asked.

I wagged a finger excitedly as everything became clear. "They had just been tipped off as to who you were and why you were here. The safari was a perfect way to get rid of you."

"What's this?" Freddie asked. " 'Get rid of you'?"

Darcy told him about the monkey, the meat and the lion.

"Good God," Freddie said. "Cyril put meat in your bedroom and opened the window? And then in your tent? The chap was taking a big risk luring a lion into camp. It might have gone for any one of you, including him."

"The haunch of meat was in our tent," Darcy said. "Cyril must have known exactly what he was doing. He stood by and watched."

"Who did you tell about this?"

430

"No one. We've told no one," Darcy said. "So what do we do now?"

"Van Horn has already booked to fly out of Kisumu on Monday. We'll have him and his baggage searched, but other than that he's committed no crime."

"And Cyril?" I asked.

"We'll keep a close eye on him in future but from the cable it's clear they've already decided he is not the type to lead their little scheme." Freddie sighed. "I don't expect for a moment that they will give up. I'm sure that Hitler is setting up agents in every country of the empire."

"You really think he is planning for a massive war?" I heard my voice tremble as I said it.

Freddie nodded. "I'm afraid so. We must just try to be one step ahead of him, even in backwaters like Kenya."

There was a long pause during which we all digested this.

"You said there were developments, in the plural?"

Freddie nodded. "I received a second cable."

"And?" Darcy demanded.

Freddie smiled this time. "There is no such person as Jocelyn Prettibone."

"Then who is he and why is he here?"

431

Darcy asked.

Freddie shrugged. "You tell me."

"The jewel thief?" I asked.

"Possible," Freddie replied. "I'll make sure I get his fingerprints today and send them to Scotland Yard to match. And as I say, we'll search Van Horn on his way out. But now it seems apparent that he wasn't here to receive stolen property."

"None of this throws any light onto who killed Lord Cheriton," Darcy said. "Certainly not Van Horn, who was miles away in Gilgil with no transportation. And Prettibone, or whoever he is, was at Idina's house."

"I suppose it is just possible that Jocelyn could have killed Bwana," I said. "He didn't sleep in the main house but in one of the outbuildings. What if he called, pretending to be Angel. He does have a high voice, doesn't he? And as Bwana went out to get into his motorcar Jocelyn was ready and killed him. Then wrapped him in some kind of blanket, bundled him into the car, drove to that spot, tipped him out of the blanket onto the grass and left a shoe print and the motor running."

Freddie was looking at me warily. "You seem to be surprisingly au fait with methods of murder," he said.

432

"Trust me, she is." Darcy flashed me a grin. "You don't ever want to cross her."

"You make a good point," Freddie said, "but how did he get back to Idina's?"

"He'd have to have walked back in the dark. It's at least six miles," Darcy said. "Unless he had an accomplice who followed him in another vehicle."

"But we didn't notice any other tire tracks," I said.

"If there were, we drove over them," Darcy pointed out.

"You're right."

Freddie opened the door of the backseat for me and I climbed in. "So what do we do now?" I asked.

"Not much we can do until we find out more about Prettibone and why he's here. As I say, I plan to get his fingerprints today."

"How will you do that?"

"Hand him a glass. Easy." He grinned. I thought how different real spies looked from the ones you read about in books. With his freckled face and easygoing manner he would have been at home at a village cricket match.

We set off. The road down there by the lake was a bit better than the track through the valley, but not much. I was glad when we pulled up beside a white wooden church.

There were many other cars parked on the grass and a crowd had already assembled at the gravesite. We picked our way past other graves and I glanced at the names of the few Europeans who had come out here then died too early. Aged fifty-one. Aged eleven. Aged forty-three. As I walked I found myself wondering what had killed them. An accident? An animal? A tropical disease? Too much booze? And I thought how sad it must be to die so far from home.

The new grave had been dug near the white picket fence that surrounded the churchyard. It all looked remarkably English and I realized how much we need the comfort of feeling at home in a strange country. The only thing that jolted the illusion was a group of small monkeys who bounded away from the roadside as our motorcar approached. We joined the other mourners beside the open grave. Angel stood there, looking elegant in a sleek black dress, her face completely hidden under a long black veil. Rupert and Rowena were beside her. I looked around for Joseph and spotted him standing off to one side, behind the cluster of Europeans. Everyone was suitably dressed for mourning. Babe Eggerton was dabbing at her eyes. Tusker was either glaring or fighting with emotion. Idina

looked white and shaken. I noticed the Tomlinsons — had they driven all the way from
Nairobi or had they stayed with Idina all
this time? And there, in the background,
was Inspector Windrush, observing everyone's behavior, no doubt. He couldn't have
been more obvious if he'd held a notebook
and pencil in his hands.

The vicar came out of the church and the
service began. I have always found burial
services incredibly unsettling. Dust to dust.
Ashes to ashes. One doesn't like to think
about it. I glanced across at Darcy, hoping
that I never had to stand beside a grave at a
funeral for him. And as I looked around I
saw a movement beyond the fence. Someone was standing outside the churchyard,
almost invisible in the shade of a big tree.
As I looked more closely I saw that she was
a native woman, wearing traditional dress,
with heavy collars around her neck and
many bangles on her arms. An attractive
woman with high cheekbones and a proud
expression, staring out at the mourners,
almost defiantly. Then her gaze seemed to
fasten on a particular person and she nodded almost imperceptibly. I looked across
and saw Joseph giving her a brief smile. I
noticed his expression, and then hers. And
suddenly I understood.

The vicar finished the prayers. The family came forward to throw the first earth onto the coffin. One by one the mourners moved off. Instead of following I slipped behind the other mourners and made my way to Joseph. "That's your mother," I said. It was a statement, not a question, and he nodded.

"She was the one who used to live in the cottage?"

"Bwana built it for her," he said. "When he first came here she helped him. She took care of him. He would not have survived without her. And through her he learned the ways of my people. How to keep cattle in this land. How to thrive here."

I dared to take this one stage further. "And he was your father."

"Yes," he said. He was staring out past me, out across the lake. "He was my father. And he said to my mother, 'Don't worry. I will recognize this boy as my son. I will educate him in the British way. He will have a good life and I will provide for him.'"

"But he didn't treat you like a son."

"When he brought home the first white woman as his wife, my mother continued to live in the cottage and the wife said nothing. She was agreeable with this arrangement or she did not dare to cross my father's wishes. But then the American

436

woman came and she demanded that my mother leave and go back to her people. And he started to treat me more and more like a servant. Then he learned that he was now a lord, and he sent for his children from England. Until then he had never talked about them, never wanted to see them. But when they came, he made it clear that these were the children that mattered."

"And so you killed him." The words just came out. I could hardly believe what I was saying.

He was still staring out past me. "He deserved to die. He banished my mother, who had devoted her life to him. Who loved him. And he was writing a will. I saw it. There was no mention of me. It was as if I didn't exist."

"But how . . ." I stopped.

"How did I manage to kill him?" His expression was still composed. If anything he looked pleased with himself. "I placed the telephone call when they had all gone to bed," he said. "I told him, 'Come home soon. Your wife is not at all well.'"

I was about to ask how he could have placed that telephone call and then been at the spot where Bwana was killed. He anticipated my question. "I put down the receiver and then I ran. I am Maasai. Running is in my blood. I knew I had time, that he would not leave right away, that he would come home grudgingly. I knew I would intercept him somewhere along the road. It did not matter where. But I was lucky. I got as far as the place where the motorcar must slow down to cross the stream. And when his car came through those rocks I was standing there, in the road, with my spear in my hand and my lion skin cape around my shoulders." He looked proudly defiant. "He stopped the car and got out and said, 'Is it bad news, Joe?' and I said, 'Bad news for you.' And I threw the spear into his heart. As he fell I removed the spear and carried him into the bushes. And he spoke to me as he died. He said, 'I'm sorry, son.' "

"Your cape caught on a thorn," I said. "We saw what looked like lion's fur."

He nodded, still quite composed.

"But there were no footprints that we saw."

"My people are used to covering our tracks," he said. "And it is easy when one does not wear white man's shoes."

We stood for a while in silence as the last stragglers of the crowd moved away. I heard Lord Delamere saying, "Luncheon will be served on the lawn outside the hotel. You're all welcome." And then the sound of a motorcar starting.

"Who have you told about this?" he asked me.

It was the first time I realized that I might be in danger. Would he now have to silence me? But I couldn't lie to him. "Nobody. I only realized the truth when I spotted your mother standing outside the fence."

"But you will now go to the police or Lord Delamere?"

"I don't know." I paused, fighting with conflicting emotions. "I suppose I have to. We can't risk someone innocent being arrested for this crime, can we?"

"You have to do what your conscience tells you, just as I followed mine," he said. "But I believe that Lord Delamere has just driven off in his motorcar. You will not be able to tell him for a while. Maybe you will only share your suspicions with him when the luncheon is over so that the atmosphere of the day is not spoiled." Now he looked directly at me. And I saw the look of the European in his expression — the uncertainty, the fear, that is never seen in the face of a Maasai warrior.

"And what will you do?" I asked.

"I will be far away when they come looking for me. I shall have to go far from this place but maybe I shall cross the border to

Tanganyika and then I can live out my life in peace among my people there. Maybe I shall not make it that far; I will be caught and I will be hanged and that will be the end of it. But I hope not."

"I hope not too," I said. "One question, Joseph. You didn't bring that lion into camp to kill us, did you?"

His eyes flashed then. "Why would I do that? I killed the lion, even though it will bring bad luck to me."

"Of course. Thank you," I muttered. "You should go now."

He held out his hand to me. "I wish you God's blessing, memsabu."

And I heard myself saying, "And I you, Joseph."

Then he took off running with easy grace. When I looked under the big tree, the woman had gone.

CHAPTER 34

August 17
At Lord Delamere's estate

I debated long and hard whether to tell anyone or not. Much as I liked Joseph and could appreciate his reasons for killing his father, it was murder. A life had been taken.

Darcy sensed that something was wrong as we sat at the luncheon. As soon as we were alone he asked me about it and I told him exactly what had happened between Joseph and me. When I had finished he frowned. "You have to tell someone. You can't let him get away with murder."

"I realize that. It's just that there hasn't been an opportunity to get Lord D alone and I'm certainly not going to tell Inspector Windrush. He'd be particularly brutal because he hadn't figured it out for himself."

"But Joseph did kill a man, although I won't say he wasn't provoked."

"A life for a life," I said. "Is that always fair?"

"It's not up to us to judge," Darcy said. "And we can't let them try to pin the crime on an innocent man, just to appease the white community."

I sighed. "I'll wait until the inspector leaves and then I'll tell Lord Delamere. At least that will give Joseph a fighting chance."

"You might find yourself in trouble for aiding and abetting," Darcy pointed out.

"I'll say he ran off before I could try to stop him."

Darcy smiled. "You are too soft."

"No, I like justice to be fair." I looked up. "Ah, it seems that people are leaving. I'll go and tell Lord Delamere now."

It was a difficult conversation and I wasn't completely surprised at Lord Delamere's reaction.

"I always suspected that he was Bwana's son," he said. "Well, poor chap. I can't say that I blame him, do you? But a native killing a white man. My God."

We went back to Lord D's estate but

somehow the magic of Africa had been spoiled. The Prince of Wales and Mrs. Simpson left, heading in different directions, he to resume his royal tour in Nigeria and she presumably back to Europe. And Darcy suggested to me that it might be time to go. "Van Horn has gone," he said. "He was searched and nothing incriminating was found on him. And now it seems that Cyril is not deemed fit to lead a coup in Kenya, I suppose we can breathe in peace for a little while. Although I don't doubt that the Nazis will be fomenting trouble anywhere they can in the world."

"So you've given up looking for the jewel thief?" I said. "Now that you've decided Mr. Van Horn wasn't here to obtain the diamond."

"I don't think we'll ever know that," Darcy said. "As he told you, he does broker deals as well as being a Nazi spy. It might have been passed to him, although it didn't turn up when he was searched."

"Pity," I said. "I rather hoped that Rupert or Rowena might have been our jewel thief."

"You really dislike them, don't you?"

"Don't you?" I replied. "They are both horrid. And you should have seen how mean she was to me at school."

Darcy laughed. "If I bore a grudge about

443

all the boys who weren't exactly pleasant when I first went to boarding school I'd be a basket case. I just got even when I became a good rugby player." He paused, thoughtfully, then he said, "So let's forget about those twins and think about us. Are you ready to leave, do you think?"

"Yes, I believe I am. I've seen every animal and bird. We have a lion skin coming to us when it's cured. What more could we want? And frankly I would like to be back home where people behave normally."

"Your mother behaves normally?" He chuckled again.

"Well, except my mother. And Belinda, maybe. But I do have one request."

"What's that?"

"Could we go home by ship instead of by aeroplane? I don't think I'm ready to give up our honeymoon just yet and on a ship I'd have you all to myself with no crimes and no intrigues."

Darcy laughed. "Of course. I'll book us passage on the next steamer from Mombasa."

Lord Delamere gave a farewell dinner for us. Diddy came down to join us. Cyril did not join her and she let it be known that he was moving back to Nairobi. He found life in the country too restricting. "And I tell you who else has gone," she said. "That affable twit Jocelyn. Apparently his father has flown into a rage and demands that Jocelyn return home instantly. Between ourselves he wasn't at all cut out for the life here, was he?"

So it looked as if we might never find out who Jocelyn Prettibone was and why he had come to Kenya. We took the train from Nairobi to Mombasa, where we enjoyed the beach and the sights for a few days until we caught the steamer home, up through the Red Sea, the Suez Canal, and the Mediterranean, arriving home in late September. England was already in the middle of autumn. The skies were heavy and gray and the pavements were piled with dying leaves. After that great arc of blue sky it seemed terribly dull. Zou Zou was over in Ireland so we decided to go straight down to Eynsleigh, where we were greeted by my mother.

"You look frightfully well, my darlings," she said, embracing me as she always did, with a kiss three inches from my cheek. "You see, I was right. All that sex is good for one. Did you have a good and relaxing time?"

"Good but not all relaxing," I said.

"Well, of course not. All that energetic stuff in the bedroom gives one an appetite, doesn't it?"

"I was thinking more about being charged by elephants and nearly eaten by lions," I said.

"Heavens! How frightfully uncivilized. And how was Idina? Is she really naughtier than me?"

"Much," I said. "She made a pass at Darcy. I didn't want to like her, but I did, in spite of everything." I looked around. "Where's Granddad?" I asked nervously. "He's all right, isn't he?"

"He went home, darling. About a week ago. He said he'd left his little house for too long and he wanted to get back to his routine. He said he didn't feel right being waited on. He's promised to come often to visit you, after I've gone."

"You're leaving?" I asked.

She nodded. She had that excited but uncertain look on her face, like a child about to do something risky and maybe naughty. "I've heard from Max," she said. "He misses me terribly. He says he can't live without me. He begs me to be patient. He can't risk upsetting his mother at the moment and he is overwhelmed with work but he suggests I go to our villa on Lake

Lugano and he'll join me whenever he can."

"Goodness," I said. "That's a turnabout."

"No man can resist me for too long," she said with a self-satisfied smile.

"But what about Sir Hubert?" I asked later when we were alone. "I thought the wind might be blowing in that direction again."

"I was tempted," she said. "He's a lovely man and I'll always have a soft spot in my heart for him. But Max — well, he is so frightfully rich and the sex is so divine."

"But living in Germany, Mummy," I said. "Please think this through carefully. Darcy's worried about the way things are going. He thinks they are planning for war again. This Hitler chap wants to take over the world. Do you really want to be part of that?"

She hesitated. "You know I'm not good at seeing into the future. Hubert wants to head off to somewhere remote and dangerous again. Max wants me to go to our villa and I'm sure you'd rather your old mother wasn't breathing down your neck here at Eynsleigh. I'll just have to see how things turn out, won't I? Of course, if you make me a grandmother soon, I shall return to be adoring."

And she smiled.

"It's good to be home, isn't it?" I said to

Darcy as we changed for dinner that evening. "At least one doesn't have to worry about ants or snakes or elephants every time we go out here."

"Back to real life." Darcy gave a sigh and I saw the worried frown. I went over to him and took his hand. "Darcy, I don't want you to take that desk job. I know what you do is dangerous, but you love it. I know I'll be left alone at times and I can't ask you too much about where you are going, but that is you. I don't want you to become old and bored and depressed."

He swept me into his arms. "If you're really sure?"

"I want you to be happy. And I don't think you would be, filing papers at a desk."

He sighed again, this time with relief.

Back to real life. The thought echoed through my head. Starting my new life as Mrs. Darcy O'Mara in a lovely house in the country with an exciting future ahead of us: it was certainly nothing to be sighed about.

We settled back into this new real life with ease. Zou Zou came to stay. I received an invitation from the queen to come to tea and recount our adventures. The invitation was written by her secretary but underneath in her own hand she had written:

The king is not at all well. I am quite concerned. I hope David has learned a thing or two about the obligations of the monarchy on his tour and will come home prepared to step into his father's shoes.

I hoped so too.

Mummy didn't seem in an awful hurry to leave and I wondered if she was reconsidering what I had told her about the current situation in Germany. But at least Lugano was in Switzerland. It might be a good compromise for her — visits from Max but no Nazis present. After a few days Darcy collected our holiday snaps from the chemist's shop in the village. We showed them to Mummy, from the animals on the savanna to the polo match. She was interested to see Idina.

"Doesn't she look old?" was her first comment.

Then she peered at the snap more closely. "I know that face," she said.

She was pointing at Jocelyn Prettibone. "You know him?"

"Yes, that's a fellow called Roderick something. He was in a play produced by a friend of mine. He was rather good, playing a Swedish count. He had the accent down pat and he looked frightfully Scandinavian — and very evil. What was he doing in Kenya?"

"Playing another part," Darcy said.

He went up to London instantly with the snapshot of Jocelyn and my mother's information and at last the truth came out. Jocelyn was no third son of a peer. He was no jewel thief either. He was a drug runner. He supplied cocaine, adopting different personas that no one would suspect, to a community and then giving a plausible reason for leaving again. Mummy was right. He certainly was a good actor.

The last we heard from Freddie was that Joseph still hadn't been caught. It seemed he must have made it across the border into Tanganyika. I was glad.

And a last postscript on this whole story: it turned out that the diamond necklace had never been stolen in the first place. The maharani had set the whole thing up to claim the insurance. She had run up debts she didn't want her husband to know about and needed the money. Her maid cracked under the pressure of questioning and revealed the truth. It's interesting how often the truth finally comes out. Personally I'm glad that I don't have to live a lie. I'd find it horribly tiring, wouldn't you?

HISTORICAL NOTE

You might think that this is a work of wild fiction, but I can assure you that it is firmly based on historical fact.

Lady Idina Sackville was the leading hostess in the Wanjohi Valley, known as the Happy Valley, where a group of English aristocrats led lives of drink, drugs and partner swapping in the 1920s and '30s. My other characters have fictional names but are in part based on the real inhabitants of that time.

The inspiration for the murder of Lord Cheriton is the real-life unsolved murder of Lord Erroll, the charismatic leader of the valley set. He was found slumped over the steering wheel of his car on a lonely road. There were many suspects, including husbands of wives seduced by him, and hints of his Nazi affiliation, but the case was never satisfactorily solved.

And a word of apology to the purists

among you. I have shortened the time of the journey from London to Kenya. In reality it would have taken longer, with overnights in Cairo and in Juba. But in the interests of getting on with the story I have made the ground crew handling more efficient! And as for the accuracy of the flight and the aircraft . . . I have firsthand knowledge. My father-in-law was one of the founders and heads of Imperial Airways and was on the first flight from London to Cape Town. We have his letters home from stops along the route and snaps that he took!

BIBLIOGRAPHY

These books helped me re-create the time and place accurately.

The Bolter: The Story of Idina Sackville. Frances Osborne. Vintage.

The Ghosts of Happy Valley: Searching for the Lost World of Africa's Infamous Aristocrats. Juliet Barnes. Aurum Press.

Lion in the Morning. Henry Seaton. John Murray.

West with the Night. Beryl Markham. North Point.

Out of Africa and *Shadows on the Grass.* Isak Dinesen. Vintage.

White Mischief. James Fox. Vintage.

The Flame Trees of Thika. Elspeth Huxley. Weidenfeld and Nicholson.

Britain's Imperial Air Routes, 1918 to 1939. Robin Higham. Foulis.

Pictorial History of BOAC and Imperial Airways. Kenneth Munson. Ian Allan.

455

The Seven Skies: A Study of B.O.A.C. and Its Forerunners since 1919. John Pudney. Putnam.

And various novels, including M. M. Kaye's *Death in Kenya.*

Plus the study guide to wildlife in East Africa, with extensive notes from his trip by Dr. E. Hook.

And thanks to Google Earth for keeping me accurate!

ABOUT THE AUTHOR

Rhys Bowen, a *New York Times* bestselling author, has been nominated for every major award in mystery writing, including the Edgar®, and has won many, including both the Agatha and Anthony awards. She is the author of the Royal Spyness Mysteries, set in 1930s London, the Molly Murphy Mysteries, set in turn-of-the-century New York, and the Constable Evans Mysteries, set in Wales. She was born in England and now divides her time between Northern California and Arizona.

The employees of Thorndike Press hope you have enjoyed this Large Print book. All our Thorndike, Wheeler, and Kennebec Large Print titles are designed for easy reading, and all our books are made to last. Other Thorndike Press Large Print books are available at your library, through selected bookstores, or directly from us.

For information about titles, please call:
(800) 223-1244

or visit our website at:
gale.com/thorndike

To share your comments, please write:
Publisher
Thorndike Press
10 Water St., Suite 310
Waterville, ME 04901